# WINTER OF
# THE SIOUX

# WINTER OF THE SIOUX

ROBERT STEELMAN

CUTTING EDGE

ISBN-13: 978-1-957868-30-1

Published by
Cutting Edge Books
PO Box 8212
Calabasas, CA 91372
www.cuttingedgebooks.com

# WINTER OF THE SIOUX

**Item 1.** Canvas in oils, 8 × 24 inches, a locomotive and passenger train, ca. 1875, standing in the station at North Platte, Nebraska. Probably Union Pacific "Emigrant." Signed B/M.

At North Platte the snow started. While the engine gulped water, the flakes started to fall, hissing on the hot sheetiron and dancing in the gleam of the oil headlamp. The station was deserted except for a few huddled travelers crowding around a stove. Rubbing his mittened hands, one of them turned to watch the two men standing close together on the station platform. When the fireman of the Emigrant kicked the firebox door open, the orange glow shone like a jewel on the manacles that joined their wrists. The firebox door closed, and the man in the mittens smiled knowingly to his companions and said, "Prisoner. Must be someone pretty important to bring all the way back from Chicago."

No one was interested. It was too cold. Someone said plaintively, "Ain't we supposed to pull out of here at six-fifty?" Another produced a large watch and popped open the lid.

"It's after eight now."

The man in the mittens wrapped his muffler an extra turn around his neck and pushed open the door against the wind. A downdraft sent a billowing ash-laden cloud to envelop him, and he stood pawing at his eyes, cursing. The two men on the platform eyed him.

"Friend," the smaller of the two said, "revile not the Lord."

"Hell," the mittened man said, "I wasn't reviling anyone. I just got a shovelful of ashes in my eye, that's all. If this ain't a fine way to run a railroad!" He blinked at the pair, the small drab man in the fur cap and the tall lean one that reminded him somehow of an elegant A. Lincoln. "Which one of you is The Law?"

The tall man's jaw twitched in hidden amusement.

"You mean you can't tell?"

The mittened man brightened.

"I expect you are, ain't you?"

The tall man howled with laughter, and beat his companion on the back.

"Thee is a fool," the small man said wryly, and led the other one away and up into a coach, while the man with the mittens looked disappointed.

The snow grew thicker, falling in heavy flakes until the outline of the rails ahead grew dim and then was lost in white. An argument developed between the conductor and the station agent over freight manifests, and they spoke strong words to each other. The fireman hacked a steak from a frozen haunch of venison that was piled atop the cordwood in the tender, and slid it into the firebox on the flat of a shovel. The engineer drank coffee moodily.

"Cheyenne at one thirty-five tomorrow," he complained. "Ain't that a laugh!"

"What you need," the fireman said, "is a compass. If you ain't got one, this here train is as apt to end up in Yankton as in Cheyenne."

In the coach, three cars behind the engine, the drab little man in the fur cap wiped frost from a window with his sleeve and peered out. The world was dark and white, wrapped in a cocoon, and the window rattled sudden and sharp in the wind like the tapping of a telegraph instrument. The tall man shifted his position as well as his manacled wrist would allow, and chuckled, white teeth sparkling in a long jaw.

"I know what thee thinks," the small man said. "But joke or no joke, Mr. Mannix, I am the Law, and I will deliver thee to the authorities at San Francisco four days from now. Thee had best compose thyself. It is not a joke to have killed a man."

Beau pulled the collar of the buffalo coat tighter around the long hair on his neck. The coach was getting cold.

"Mr. Shadduck, you're absolutely right. But it's no joke to call a man a liar in a friendly stud game. That's what Jim Duffy did. When I called his attention to it, he came at me with a knife. That was no joke either."

The detective sighed and shook his head, and went to staring out to the blackness. The engine whistled twice, short challenging blasts; the sound came to them softened and muffled in the blanket of snow. The coach lurched, and the oil lamps swung in their brackets, and the Emigrant was on its way again, toward places like Alkali and Ogalalla and Lodge Pole and Antelope, names that meant as much to Beau Mannix as Zambezi and Pekin and Budapesht. For a while he studied the Union Pacific timetable to pass the time; but the conductor came through, turning down the lamps, and Beau wadded the folder into a ball and tossed it into the aisle. Shadduck dozed beside him, fur cap rolling and bobbing as if it were on an oiled bearing. Finally the detective's head fell back on the seat and he slept, snoring in a mild and plaintive tenor.

Across the aisle a small girl wrapped in a blanket stared at Beau with bright curious eyes, but when he smiled at her she turned her head away and stared at the back of the next seat.

Always, for as long as he could remember, he had carried a deck of cards in his pocket. He got them out, and fanned and cut them with one hand, a trick he was proud of. Across the aisle the small bright eyes watched him, and he was grateful for the audience. He always worked better with an audience. That night at the Pacific Club there had been a large and appreciative audience; if there were not, he might not have shot Jimmy Duffy. At any rate, he had done so, and Duffy's brother-in-law had been secretary to the mayor, and Beau Mannix had emigrated quickly to Chicago. Now he was on his way back.

As the chill light of dawn came, he was still handling the cards with long dextrous fingers. When he saw the little girl in the seat opposite open blue eyes, blurred with sleep, he extracted the ace of spades from her ear, but her mother was not amused. Beau put the cards away, looking instead out the window at the white-swathed land. For a moment it stopped snowing, and the sun rising under a low gray bank of cloud sent slanting red shadows across the land, painting half-buried trees in fire and glinting from the ice of frozen ponds and streams. Once, while he watched, a heavy-laden fir dropped its load of snow and sprang suddenly and proudly upright. Then Shadduck stirred beside him and the spell was broken.

"Good morning to thee," the detective said. He blinked, and shot his cuffs, and took off the fur cap and brushed the nap on his sleeve. "Did thee sleep well?"

Beau shook his head.

"I didn't sleep at all."

"Conscience?"

"There isn't any such thing. I just wasn't sleepy, that's all." He spoke sharply, nettled at the way the persistent Quaker was beginning to get under his skin. "Just see me to Frisco, Mr. Shadduck. You don't have to convert me."

"Nevertheless," said Shadduck, "I am bound to try."

At Antelope, the detective shackled Beau to the seat and got off to buy bread and sausage. The San Francisco authorities did not believe in wining and dining criminals, or the men who brought them back from far places. While he was gone, Beau found a stub of a pencil and an envelope in his pocket and on the back of a cardboard box filled with Shadduck's soiled linen, he began to sketch. Occasionally he looked from the corner of his eye at the small girl opposite and was pleased to see that the bait had worked. She was watching his careful strokes with saucer eyes, and he grinned to himself and went back to work on a painstaking portrait of Samuel Shadduck. He outlined the face heavily, and shaded in the lines that gave the detective the appearance of a small and dogged terrier. He topped off the face with the scrofulous fur cap, and the girl giggled loudly.

"Madame," he said to her, "I'm pleased you like my work."

Faced with her mother's disapproval, she put a small hand, wide-spread, over her mouth and was frightened, but Beau handed her the envelope with as much of a flourish as his manacled wrist would permit, and the mother did not object too much. He would not have cared, anyway. He was too delighted to see that the worthless skill was still there. Most things that required skill with the fingers he was good at; he had never tried to crack a safe but felt that he could if the occasion ever arose.

Shadduck squeezed in front of him with a package wrapped in newspaper.

"Snowing again," he said. He handed Beau a piece of bread, and cut off a slice of sausage with the penknife that hung from his watch-chain.

Beau looked at the food with distaste. Shadduck shrugged, looked at his watch, then bent his head for the customary half-hour of silent prayer. Each morning he went through the ceremony. Beau wished he could jeer at the detective's habit, but there was something of the child in the man's sincerity, and Beau liked children. He bowed his own head, feeling somehow he had been taken advantage of.

When the prayer period was ended, he slumped in his seat, staring out the window past the wink of Shadduck's badge. For a while he amused himself by opening his eyes quickly, like the shutter of a photographic camera, and then closing them again to allow the image to glow, remembered, in his brain. He got some very nice effects that way, and examined them with an artist's eye. That frozen meadow, with the high creek-cut bluff to one side, and a bare spider of a tree leaning under a sheathing of ice. A flavor almost Japanese in the scene; spare, tight, graceful. And a group of section-hands, bundled in furs, standing beside the track, warming mittened fingers at a small fire. Breughel, something, mediaeval, in spite of the nineteenth century mechanical marvel that spat steam and sparks as it roared by. His puzzled parents had once paid his way for a year of art-school in Philadelphia. That, and gambling, was all he knew now. He dozed, and then woke to the sound of Shadduck's voice.

"What?"

The detective took out his watch and looked at it.

"I said that was Pine Bluffs we just passed. We are making very good time."

Beau's voice was cool.

"Good time? For who?"

Shadduck shrugged, and put the watch away.

"Not for thee, Mr. Mannix."

The detective's composure was like the ice that covered these western lands; hard and smooth, affording no purchase.

"You seem real sure of yourself."

"I have never lost a prisoner yet."

Many times Beau had pricked at his captor, demanding to know how a Quaker, with violence foresworn, could make a good detective. He knew the answers, from long and patient reply. Shadduck was a better detective than he was a Quaker. That was about all there was to it. He did avoid violence, although once he had been forced to shoot a runaway forger in the leg. And in Beau's case, Shadduck told him, God's law and man's agreed, so there was no real conflict. A murderer was abhorrent to God and to Quakers alike. Beau knew all this, but time passed so slowly on the Union Pacific that he started all over again, remembering the hundred dollars hidden in the sole of his boot.

"I'll bet you ten dollars you never get me to Frisco."

Shadduck smiled.

"Thee knows I do not bet."

"You told me you'd give me a Bible if I'd repent. I'll bet you fifty dollars you can't make me. No, on that one I'll give you odds. Fifty to one. Put up a dollar."

The detective's leathery cheek twitched.

"Hell," Beau said, "you got all the aces on your side. Afraid of a little bet?"

"Thee had better forget this talk of betting and give a thought to thy soul."

Beau chuckled.

"Not me. I don't hold with philosophizing. We're born, we have a good time, we die. As a matter of fact, if I hadn't stopped to think, against my better judgment, you'd never have caught up with me. I was standing on State Street, looking into that pawn-broker's window, thinking about a girl I'd known once, how maybe she'd like to have that pair of green ear-rings to make up for the way I ran out on her. Isn't that right? Isn't that exactly what I was doing when you put the cuff on me?"

Shadduck shrugged, pleasantly.

"So don't give me advice," Beau said. "Five more minutes, and I'd have been on my way to New York, and then Paree."

He hadn't run out on Clara. Clara was no good, and she had stolen money from his pants. But she had had pretty red hair, and a skin like milk, and the baggage had stolen the money he wanted to spend for canvas and paints to do her picture. And she had tipped off the police, probably.

"Life is often a waste of time," he murmured.

He was unprepared for the furious onslaught Shadduck turned on him.

"Does thee think so, Mr. Mannix? Is thee not instead a waste of man?"

Blinking, Beau sat up in his seat.

"What does that mean?"

Shadduck's stained teeth bared in a grimace. "Thee is a sensitive man, a man with a fine body and brain, a man with feeling. Is all this for fleecing fools at cards, for drinking and betting and rousting? Is thee not better employed than killing a man who doubts thee, and riding to San Francisco to hang for it?"

For once in his life, Beau's glibness deserted him.

"Why, I—I—" He floundered. "The bastard yelled out I was cheating! Right out loud, in the Pacific Club, in front of everyone!"

"Was thee?"

Beau swallowed, and his face got red.

"That isn't the point!"

Shadduck made an indignant sniffing sound.

"Examine thyself, Mr. Mannix, with as much care as thee would a fresh deck of cards, at least. I know more of thee than thee does."

From there into Cheyenne they were no longer on speaking terms. Shadduck read his Bible, tracing heavily-underlined passages with a thin stiff forefinger, lips moving without sound. Beau crossed one leg over the other, and made the conductor walk around him every time he passed through the train. A midmorning silence descended, and the passengers dozed again. Ahead of Beau and his captor a whisky-drummer scribbled notes in a ledger, and behind him a fat woman snored over a shoebox of half-eaten lunch. The small private world moved with him across the snowy plain. Egbert, Hillsdale, Atkins—and finally Cheyenne, at four in the late afternoon of a winter's day.

"All right," Beau said to Shadduck. He fidgeted, uncomfortable. "You're right. Right as rain. About me being no good, that is. Guess it's too late to worry about it, though."

"It's never too late," Shadduck said.

He looked as if he intended to say more—a great deal more—but Beau peered out the window past him and grew excited.

"Say, what's all the stir about? What are all those wagons and people and lanterns bobbing around? Looks like a medicine show getting ready to roll."

"I expect," Shadduck said, "it's people for the Black Hills. Gold miners. Custer found gold last year while he was passing through there." He shook his head, watching the scene with misgiving. "They'll find their graves, most of them. That's Sioux territory. This whole country is filling with violence. There will be great bloodshed before long."

"Move over," Beau said. "Give me room."

He was always like this when he saw something that might merit painting—rude, abrupt, even unpleasant. But as he drank in the scene his heart swelled as if it would burst. The muddy street, ankle-deep in cold blue-black mud. The flicker of torch-light on the wet broad backs of mules, and a man standing in the door of a saloon, the light pouring out behind him and freezing him for a moment in a superb careless gesture. Steam from the nostrils of draft-horses harnessed in pairs to freight-wagons, and a torn wagon-canvas flapping. Over it all the sift of snow—whirl-ing flakes that softened the harsh outlines of men in a hurry, and made them seem to move glidingly about beneath a silken veil, so that even their shouts and curses came muffled and distant.

"God," he said. "Isn't that beautiful?"

Shadduck blinked at him, puzzled. Then his face changed, and he said, half-seeming to understand. "Why, I suppose so. It's all in how thee looks at it."

With an almost apologetic air he manacled Beau to the seat and stood in the aisle, buttoning his overcoat and pulling the fur cap down over his ears.

"There's bound to be a grocery somewhere near. I'll get us something to eat. Does thee like sardines and crackers? The money is running low."

Beau waved him away.

"Cheese, crackers—anything."

He didn't notice when Shadduck left.

For a long time after the train left Cheyenne, Beau sat slumped in his seat, half-drunk with sensation. Colors raced in his head, carroming pinwheels of yellow and orange and red, the colors of fire and torch and lamp and lantern, and their reflected images from snow and from ice and from black pools of slushy water. He had never painted much in oils—somehow that seemed too serious a venture. After all, sketching was only a hobby. But black and white couldn't do it. Life was color and color was life, that was all there was to it. Maybe he could get some paint somewhere, and canvas. Maybe—

"Thee does not seem to hear me," Shadduck said. He nudged Beau with his elbow, holding out a paper sack. "More crackers? Cheese? There's a sardine left."

Beau looked at him.

"No," he said. "No. I'm not hungry."

"But thee has scarcely eaten."

"No, that's right," Beau said. But he continued to stare unseeingly at the plush back of the seat ahead of him, wrapped in a private reverie, and Shadduck shrugged and ate the rest of the provisions himself. He had seen many men so, dazed and almost stupid, coming suddenly to the realization of their folly. He would watch Beau Mannix very carefully from here on in.

While Shadduck had analyzed Beau's thoughts moderately well, he was completely mistaken in their motivation. Beau was conscious of no particular folly; he had lived a full and satisfactory life, even if not a moral one. The thing that bothered him was the sudden realization that he wanted to paint that scene at the Cheyenne station, get it down somehow or other, and here he was balked by a set of manacles and an improbable Quaker policeman. On the ride out from Chicago, he had not been impressed by either. There was something comfortingly unreal about the whole situation, all of a piece with his disordered life, and so nothing to worry him. But this sudden want, this quick feeling that he had to catch the Cheyenne moment, catch it on canvas or burlap or the back of an old theater program, if nothing else—this shook him as nothing else did. He wanted to do it, he had to do it—and now he was being pulled away to a court of law and various legal processes and perhaps a noose at the end of it all. While he had these colors fresh in his mind, and his fingers ached with pentup images, he was being kidnaped.

"I've got to go to the toilet," he said to Shadduck, his voice surly.

"All right." The detective got up and sidled ahead of him through the aisle, swaying a little from side to side as the Emigrant rocked on through the blizzard. Faces followed them, upturned pale faces, and one woman whispered to her companion behind the cover of a shawl. At the end of the aisle they paused, and Shadduck knocked discreetly on the door, then cleared his throat. He knocked again, and opened it.

"Now wait a minute," Beau protested. "There's not room in there for both of us. Look—we've both got on overcoats, and that's a damned small room. Anyway, can't a man have a little privacy?"

His voice was loud, and necks craned over the backs of the seats. Shadduck looked unnerved. This had been the arrangement up until now, and although it had been crowded, he had at least managed to keep his prisoner in sight.

"I'm not a damned fool," Beau complained. He pointed to the window. "Thirty miles an hour in a snowstorm! Where in hell do you think I'm going? Up in a balloon?"

"Keep thy voice low," Shadduck said. His face was red. "There is no need to shout so, Mr. Mannix. These arrangements are not a public matter, surely."

"All right, then," Beau said. He pulled open the door. "Wait outside, damn it."

Shadduck caught at his arm with an expert flip of the manacles.

"Thee will hardly begrudge me this," he said, catching the other half of the cuffs on a brass water-pipe within the doorway. "There—that gives thee sufficient slack." He slammed the door, and Beau was standing inside the closetlike room, realizing he had been outsmarted.

He pressed his face close to the small window over the basin. Black—black as the inside of a cow. But then a smear of lights raced across his view for an instant, and in the quick brightness he saw a house—perhaps two or three of them at a crossroads— and falling snow, and then darkness again. Under his feet the wheels kept up their click and chatter. The Emigrant was making time, real time. Every click, every clack, every sway and jolt was taking him closer to San Francisco. Three more days.

In the flicker of the oil lamp he examined the brass water-pipe that dropped from an overhead tank to the toilet below. Hardly more than a tube. One good jerk would pull it loose. He looked again at the window, and tried to pry it up, but it was tight. If he went out that way, he would have to smash it. And when he smashed it, he would have to leave right away. Shadduck would shoot through the door, he knew. In spite of the detective's pleasantness, Beau knew he would not hesitate to shoot. Shadduck had a way about him that Beau recognized. If he broke the window, he was committed.

"Mr. Mannix?" The detective tapped on the door. "Is thee—is thee finished?"

Beau took a deep breath.

"Just be a minute. Washing my hands."

He splashed water in the bowl, and then, in sudden resolve, jerked hard at the supply pipe. It came loose, as he had figured, swaying in the air unsupported like a cobra and gushing water. Feeling his heart pounding like the iron wheels below, he made a fist and looked at the window.

"What is thee doing in there?" Shadduck demanded. "There's water—" His voice broke off in disbelief.

Beau drew back his fist and smashed the window. The central pane disappeared, leaving a ragged border of splinters spattered with his blood. He got his foot up and kicked out the rest of it. Small hole, but it would have to do. Headfirst, that was the only way. Tuck his head in and roll when he hit, and hope there wasn't a telegraph pole in the way. What were the odds? A pole every hundred feet or so—why, the odds were good!

"Mr. Mannix!" Shadduck's voice was shrill. "Come out of there at once or I shoot! Does thee hear me, Mr. Mannix? Don't be a fool!"

"Just a minute," Beau yelled. "Just one minute, that's all." The coach slowed suddenly and he reeled toward the window, aware that Shadduck must have pulled the cord. The pressure of the stopping pushed him against the wall like a giant hand. He clawed his way into the window, feeling the spikes of glass rip and tear at his hands and his clothes. The blast of icy air outside hit him like a solid numbing wall, and for a moment he hung, half-in and half outside of the window. The damned big coat had trapped him! He couldn't get through that window with the coat on. Behind him, muffled in the shriek of the wind and the pound of wheels and the shriek of brakes, he heard a shot, and then another. Something plucked at his coat, between arm and body.

With a final desperate lunge he pushed through the window. For a long time he wondered when he was going to hit, and he tensed his body for the crash and the roll and the tearing and mangling that would follow. *Keep the head tucked in,* he told himself. *Fall all in a bundle.* But he kept falling, and falling, and falling, into a bottomless dark abyss, and the world he knew spun away from him into the distance like a star. And finally he was away from all knowledge and reckoning of time and distance, lost in a rich furry blackness that licked at him like the tongue of a sable cat. That was all.

**Item 2.** Pen and ink drawing on stiff parchment (scraped and cured animal skin). Small Sioux war party in snow, chest-deep to horses. Some water stains, and diagonal cracks as though once folded. Signed B/M.

---

Shouting at the top of his voice, Shadduck jerked at the signal cord. He emptied the magazine of the revolver, and when he had pulled the trigger three times on an empty chamber he chopped at the door panels with the butt, ripping his way through the thin wood as if wielding an axe. Reeling and falling in the rapidly decelerating car, the conductor lumbered up, face crimson and mustaches quivering like a hooked catfish.

"What the hell's going on in here? Who pulled that cord?"

Shadduck got one hand inside the shattered door and found the latch. The severed pipe still spouted water, and as he watched it gave a bubbling gurgle, then subsided. He stood in the doorway, looking at the broken window, feeling the cold air sucking all the warmth out of him. So that was the way Mr. Mannix had done it! Jerked the pipe loose and plunged from the window.

"My prisoner has escaped."

Shadduck stuck the revolver in the waistband of his trousers and pushed by the conductor. Moving like a brown ferret, he glided down the car to a door, and jumped into the deep snow beside the tracks. As he sniffed at the air, the brakeman floundered by, lantern swinging in his hand.

"Give me that," Shadduck said, and reached for the lantern, but the brakeman wrested it away from him, and ran on past the stalled Emigrant, the light winking on the snow. Shadduck followed him, breathing hard as the falling snow beat into his face and eyes. In a storm like this, he'd never find Mannix unless he did it quick. A hole in the snow where the prisoner had hit, perhaps a few footprints if Mannix had managed to get to his feet and stagger away—the snow would blot it away in minutes. He trotted behind the laboring brakeman, reloading the revolver and trying to figure in his mind how far back the Emigrant had been when Beau jumped.

Somewhere ahead, the dim figure of the brakeman stopped, and the light began to swing to and fro in a fuzzy arc. Shadduck looked over his shoulder toward the red lights on the last coach. He wasn't even sure he saw them—perhaps there was a smoky wink back there, but the wind beat at him and flapped his coat around, and he shivered, squinting his eyes in an effort to penetrate the stinging snow. To either side, there was only blackness. Blackness, and silence, except for the howl of the wind and the needle-like prick of the snow on his face. Mr. Mannix might as well be in Egypt.

Stumbling, falling, he ran to the little group that had joined the brakeman.

"How far's the next stop?"

"Don't stop again till Laramie," the brakeman said.

"But can't you let me off someplace where I can start looking for this man?"

The conductor broke in, patience lost.

"Mister, the Union Pacific ain't being run for your benefit! We've got a couple hundred people that's anxious to get on their way."

"But isn't there some stop—"

The official spoke up, in terms of finality.

"We'll let you off at Hazard, up the tracks. There isn't much there, but you can get off if you want. No refund on your ticket, though. You've cost the UP enough already."

Shadduck nodded.

"Thee is justified. I do not want a refund. What I want is my prisoner."

"I know," the brakeman growled. "You never lost one."

Together they plodded back toward the Emigrant, leaning their bodies into the wind. The brakeman, after a consultation with the conductor and much looking at watches in the light of the lantern, ran ahead of them to the locomotive, and they all climbed stiffly up on the platform of the last car and went inside, stamping snow-laden boots and grumbling. Only Shadduck remained on the platform. Oblivious of the cold, he stood with eyes searching the blackness until the Emigrant lurched again into motion. Only then did he go inside and search for his valise and the rest of his effects. For a moment he thought the Christian thing to do was to say a small prayer for the soul of Beau Mannix, but the devil was strong in him right then. He pulled so hard at the strap of his valise that he broke it. He knew he would stop looking for Mannix only when he had found the man, or his body.

Beau did not know for how long he had lain in the soft bank of snow he had fallen into. From some unknown black land he wavered back into consciousness, lying perfectly still, not knowing where he was or what had happened. He seemed buried in an icy tomb, and his hands and face were wet and chilled. The fall had knocked the wind out of him, and he realized with sudden painful clarity that he was sobbing for breath, and that the thick rasping sobs came from his own laboring chest. Floundering to his feet, he stood wide-legged in the snow, staring about him, still gasping for breath.

The shriek of the wind and the heavy sifting down of snow were what saved him from immediate detection. Although the Emigrant had been doing a good thirty miles an hour, the engineer had managed to sand the tracks so that the train had stopped only a few hundred feet beyond where he had fallen.

Now a brakeman passed him a few yards away, red lantern swinging smokily in his hand, and lumbered on into the driving snow where the wink of the lantern was almost immediately lost. Beau shrank back into the depression his falling body had made, and whispered "Snow, damn it, snow!" between his teeth. If this spring blizzard covered his tracks quickly enough, they would never find him. At least, he would never be taken alive. He would burrow in the snow like an animal, and lie there till he froze. But they'd never find him—not till the snow melted, anyway. By then, what was left wouldn't be much good to Shadduck, or anyone.

More men passed, running down the tracks, and he could hear their breath coming hard and sharp and whistling as they ran. They swam into vision only when immediately opposite him, and then they were gone, swallowed into the storm. Lying in his burrow, he wrapped his arms tighter about his knees, swathed in the indispensable buffalo coat. He had paid three hundred dollars for it in Frisco, and the money was better spent than he had thought at the time. If the storm kept up, and if Shadduck figured him for dead, and if he managed to find food and shelter someplace, and if—. He grinned wryly. It would take a better gambler than Beau Mannix to figure all the odds. But he was still alive, and they hadn't found him. He heard the engine of the Emigrant give two lonesome toots. They must be getting ready to pull out; even though Shadduck had managed to stop the UP to search for his prisoner, the Emigrant was not about to spend all night stalled on the main line, waiting for a Frisco detective.

All he had to do now was sit tight and play 'em close to his belly. It was not bad, after all. Wound up tight in the bulk of the buffalo coat, making as small a ball as he could, he began to feel almost comfortable. He even closed his eyes, once, and liked the drowsy sensation. He was well into it, floating on a fleecy white cloud, when he remembered that this way was the way you died of the cold.

Panic-stricken, he struggled to get to his feet. His hands and feet were like lumps of wood, senseless and clumsy. He threw the snow about him like a wounded animal, trying desperately to shake off the lassitude he had fallen into. Shadduck or no, let them find him or not, he refused to freeze to death. Thrashing and stumbling, he finally got to his feet and tottered erect, rubbing frost-bitten hands together and stamping on numbed feet. His hands and his cheeks burned like fire, a million needles pricked at his outraged feet, but he managed to stand up, breathing hard. From somewhere, more distant now, he heard another toot, a thin frail sound. The Emigrant must have pulled out. Turning his face against the storm, Beau floundered across the tracks, feeling them hard and slippery under his boots. Now he would leave those tracks, get as far away from them as he could, and the farther he got by daybreak, the better his chances to stay a free man, and to do what he wanted to. Whatever he did, he had to get away from the damned UP tracks. Slipping, falling, feeling his twisted and bruised body unwillingly doing his bidding, he fought his way northward, so far as he could tell.

Sometime during the night the snow stopped. A ghostly moon came out, ringed with luminous circles, and in the new and windless quiet he could see black clumps of stunted trees that grew in gullies like scars raked across the land. Now that the snow and wind were gone, the land lay silent and dead under the moon, but the cold grew worse, like a nail driven into his body, and when he came to the trees he heard them crack and groan as the temperature dropped. Under their branches was a thick dry carpet of pine-needles, and he burrowed gratefully into them like a rooting animal, pulling the buffalo coat around his body. He was so tired and sleepy that he did not care, this time, if he were dying or not. The only thing he knew was that here he was comfortable as a man could be in a blizzard, and after a while he dozed off and slept. The last thing he remembered was the faint luminous moonlight that filtered down through the gnarled branches.

When he awoke it was broad daylight. He blinked his eyes in the white glare that came from morning sun on snow, and tried to remember where he was. A small brown bird cheeped from a bough over his head, watching him with curious bright eyes, and some kind of an animal bounced away into the undergrowth, leaving a blurred hasty track in the snow.

With infinite and painful effort he sat up, and it was only when he saw the manacles dangling from one wrist that it came back to him. He had felt worse on certain mornings, but it was not easy to remember them. At least he had had the memory of women or liquor or money to sustain him along with the headache; this morning he had nothing but a pair of handcuffs and a raging thirst. He crawled to the edge of the trees and scooped up a handful of snow, and then fell down again in sheer exhaustion, letting the snow melt in his mouth and run down his throat. At that moment Samuel Shadduck could have had him without protest. Every muscle in his body ached with a separate and characteristic intensity.

So far as he could see in all directions, the world was white and still. Only in the gullies and protected places were there the dark outcroppings of bushes and dwarfed trees. He closed his eyes against the glare, thinking that perhaps he might hear a UP whistle, to judge his distance from the tracks. But there was no sound. The world was wrapped in silence. So far, so good. The Emigrant was gone, Samuel Shadduck was gone. He had better start traveling.

By noon he had floundered no more than a mile in the knee-deep snow, dragging the buffalo coat behind him like a dead furry animal. A fresh warm breeze had started to blow from the south, and the land seemed to remember that it was now spring. The heavy fall of snow turned crusted and brittle, and started to melt. His boots were soaking where they plunged through the crust, and rivulets of icy water ran down his legs. He was no longer in danger of freezing to death; in this perverse land it appeared that he might now eventually drown.

He reached an outcropping of rocks, and lay for a long time in a sun-warmed saucer-like bowl, content to let the heat bake into him, loosening the knots of pain in his body. Looking ruefully at his torn and scratched hands, he wondered if he would ever again deal a hand of cards. Cursing himself, he thought also of the greasy sandwich Shadduck had offered him the night before, and wished he had had the foresight to stuff it into his pocket. But foresight had never been one of his strong points. *Duffy,* he thought angrily, *why did you have to pull that damned knife?*

The cards were still in his pocket, and he drew them out, not remembering until he heard the clink of steel on rock that the manacles still dangled from one wrist. He worked ineffectually at the lock for a few moments, breaking a thumbnail back into the quick, and then gave up. As a kind of consolation, he held up the cards in the harsh flat light of the sun, and spread them out into an awkward fan, pleased to see that his fingers still worked, after a fashion.

He did not know when he was first aware he was being watched. The presence of other eyes was a light probing pressure on his body. For a long time, he did not even care, gripped in a curious lassitude. He lay propped against the rock, fanning the cards, palming one and then another, flicking one high into the air, hopefully, and then catching it with an awkward lunge when it soared down again. He jerked his body around until his other hand was free, and shuffled the pack with a quick roll of his thumbs. It was then that he saw them—the Sioux.

Three of them ringed him, peering over the rocks, and a fourth was at the edge of his vision, so that he could see only a blur of color. The shock of their coming suddenly, being all around him, snatched him back from the daze that had enveloped him. He felt himself hardening into a kind of frozen attention where the sound of his breathing was loud and insistent, and the riffle of an eagle-feather in the wind scraped in his ears. For only a moment his hands stopped their maneuvering of the cards, and then he knew that his only chance lay in keeping on with the sleight-of-hand, pretending not to notice them, or not to care. Deliberately, forcing himself to be casual and unworried, he took the ace of hearts between thumb and forefinger and waved it. Then he snapped his fingers, and it disappeared. He held up his palm, flat out, carrying it around the circle of his eyes, and then he snapped his fingers and the card reappeared. Perhaps he caught a quick intake of breath from somewhere behind him; he was not sure.

He flicked another card into the air, and it soared like a paper bird up and up, and he was aware of the dark eyes following it, and a wondering hand clapped over a mouth. Then it darted down and he caught it and flicked it back into the pack. Feeling the sweat break out on him wet and cold, he worked at the cards, fanning and palming and cutting and snapping. Holding the corner of the deck between thumb and forefinger, he opened them out into a neat circle, and then collapsed them with a quick rushing sound. After a while, he rose unsteadily to his feet and faced them. Staring into the hard black eyes, he dropped the pack into his pocket. Reaching out quickly, he pulled the ace of hearts from a brave's ear, and the man howled as if burned and drew back his lance. But the rest of them shouted with laughter and crowded close, grinning and jabbering in delight. Beau took a deep breath. He had always worked best with an audience.

They were a war-party of some sort, he supposed; four men straight of back and bowed of leg. Two of them carried lances and two had rifles slung over their backs. They wore leggings of a dark woolen material, ornamented with bands of colored beads, and flannel geestrings of bright cloth—red and yellow and green. In spite of the weather, only one of them wore a shirt—a buck-skin garment with the hair outside. The rest were bare-chested, and their chests were painted with red and yellow stripes in a zig-zag pattern, interspersed with suns and moons. One of them was apparently some kind of leader among them; he was a younger man, with a roach of porcupine quills on his shaven skull, but was deferred to.

Another was a pockmarked man who wore a folded blanket around his hips like a kilt, held in place by a cartridge belt. He reached out an imperious hand and took the deck from Beau. Cautious, he sniffed at it, and touched one of the cards to his tongue. He threw one into the air and the wind caught it and sent it scurrying high and far, until it was lost to view. Angry, the man thrust the pack back at Beau and jabbered at him while the others giggled.

"It's easy," Beau said. "See?"

He pulled another card out of the pockmarked man's ear, and for good measure took three more from his kilt. The pock-marked man stared at him for an instant, and then slapped him across the face. But the rest of them broke in with some kind of entreaty, and their fingers flew in signs, and the pockmarked man shrugged and turned away.

"You son of a bitch," Beau murmured.

Now that he was on his feet, he could see their ponies and a couple of pack-mules nuzzling at the snow in an effort to find the grass beneath. They had ridden up on him like that, and he had been so far gone he did not know they were there. But now that the show was over—

"*Hopo!*" one of them said, or something that sounded like that. He prodded Beau with his lance, nodded toward the pack mules. "*Hopo!*"

Beau picked up his buffalo coat, but the man snatched it away from him, and motioned again to the pack mules. Did they want him to ride the mule? Were they taking him with them? Or were they going to stand him out in the open and amuse themselves by taking potshots at him as he ran? He stumbled toward the mules, and stood by one, wondering. He'd never run, he told himself. He doubted if he could run, anyway. If they wanted to shoot him, they'd have to do it right here, and the pack mule would flinch at the sound of the shot, and perhaps Beau Mannix would hear it but it would make no difference. There would be a deep red stain in the snow, and the state of California would be revenged for Jimmy Duffy's death, whether they knew it or not.

"Go to hell!" he cried. He waved his arms. "Go to hell, all of you!"

For one frozen moment they stood that way, the sun beating down and the sound of water loud from the melting snow. The pockmarked brave pulled a skinning knife from his belt and advanced on Beau Mannix, eyes fixed on the manacles that hung from Beau's wrist. The steel bracelets glittered in the sunlight, and the pockmarked man's mouth was slightly open and his lips wet as he came forward, crouching. He wanted those manacles—they would make a good necklace, or a wrist ornament that no Sioux ever had possessed, probably. There was only one way to get them off, without a key, and the man's brown fingers tightened around the bone haft of the knife. *This land is filling with violence,* Shadduck had said. Here it was, some of it.

As the man sprang, Beau lashed out with the manacles, swinging them murderously through the air. They caught the pockmarked man across the nose, and left a wide-lipped gash that showed, too, a white splinter of bone.

"Want some more?" Beau demanded.

Standing spraddle-legged over the fallen brave, he twisted the knife out of the man's hand and stuck it triumphantly in his own belt. He was not, however, prepared for the reaction of the rest of the war-party. For a moment they stared, wide-eyed; then they broke into loud and derisive laughter, pointing their fingers at the pockmarked man, and guffawing. Beau's victim tried to get up, but Beau pushed him down again into the snow and put his knee on the men's chest, swinging the manacles and threatening to strike him again.

Still giggling, Roach-Head slipped down from his pony and pulled Beau away by the arm. By signs, he indicated that Beau was to mount one of the packmules, and he even made a kind of a step with his hands and helped Beau on. Then he got his lean arms under the fallen brave's shoulders and dragged the man to his feet, and with a handful of snow wiped the blood away from the man's face.

They all rode away like that, Beau's packmule following the Indian ponies docilely. The pockmarked man was still behind, treating his shattered nose with handfuls of snow, but none of them looked back. They seemed to think it had all been a good joke, but it was over now.

**Item 3.** Watercolor on cheap paper (apparently wrapping paper) thin and brittle with age. Shows several Sioux warriors bathing in stream. Ponies grazing on banks, war impedimenta, etc. piled at edge of water. Signed B/M.

---

Beau had no idea where the Sioux were taking him, or why. They seemed to go generally northward, away from the UP tracks, and that fitted in with his plans. They were not unkind to him; even Pock-Mark, his nose healing awry, treated him with a sullen deference. He ate the same food they did, and rode one of the packmules most of each day where the country permitted. They did not seem concerned with the probability of his escape. Until they reached the vicinity of some settlement, or came on a wagon-train bound for the diggings, there was no place for him to go. So they bore northward, and each night around their small campfire they demanded entertainment, and he supplied it. He even began to develop a kind of pride in his skill, and when Pock-Mark or Low-Legs or Droop-Eye or Roach-Head failed to find the ace of spades in the deck where they had just seen Beau place it, he laughed uproariously and poked fun at them, not caring that he was a captive. He was, he began to suspect, only a kind of queer bird which amused them; a white jester who might be ransomed or traded for something valuable on a day to come.

Roach-Head was Beau's principal admirer. The rest of them merely tolerated him as a curiosity they had picked up, one which might conceivably be traded or bartered to advantage, although his present value was doubtful. But young Roach-Head became almost a friend to Beau. He smiled often, and sang on the march.

In the evenings, around the fire, he watched Beau's tricks with gaping mouth, perpetually astonished, and acclaimed each new variation of the card-from-the-ear performance. When the rest of them were discomfited or angry at being made the butt of one of Beau's tricks, Roach-Head laughed hard, holding his sides, and the others were apparently too conscious of his preferred status to make an issue of it. Once, as a reward for a particularly hilarious trick played at Pock-Mark's expense, the young man took from around his neck a gorget of lustrous shells and put it on Beau, patting his arm and chuckling. The rest of them were angry at this, particularly the broken-nosed Pock-Mark, but the young man silenced them all with an imperious shout, and that was the end of it. Beau wore the necklace as a kind of talisman from his protector.

They were careless with the guns they carried, and more than once Beau saw the opportunity to snatch one of the breech-loading Springfields. But the odds were long, and so he kept both his tongue and his head, content for the time being to travel with them. The wad of greenbacks was still in his boot, too. Beau had the gambler's confidence in money. If the worst came to worst, he might buy them off—money would buy them the whisky he had heard they craved—and get on to Custer City or Deadwood or one of the boom towns he had seen on the UP map on the Emigrant. That was as far as his plans went. He had never been much of a planner, but when the right time came he would know what to do. That was all the plan he had ever needed, or wanted.

In the meantime, he amused himself by picking up a few words of Sioux. The Indians had a meager supply of white men's food with them, probably raided from some emigrant wagon. *Pazutasapa* meant coffee, and it was precious to the Sioux, hoarded in a rawhide bag and doled out into a battered iron pot to boil fragrantly every night. Beau never got any. Sugar was likewise dear to them; *chahumpiaska,* or something close to it, and they would wet an index finger and dip it into the tin can, sucking it like a child does a lollipop. In grassy dells they found a wild mushroom they called *yamanuminnigawpa,* and boiled them with dried corn and beans to make a stew.

He did better with signs. His fingers had always been nimble, and he found himself catching on to their finger-play, the quick decisive gestures that meant so much in the flash of a knuckle, the sweep of a palm. *Eat* was simple; the tips of the fingers of one hand brought close to the lips, the hand nearly compressed, and the fingers rolled as one plays scales on the piano. *Cards* was a popular sign. When they wanted the cards, all that was necessary was for Roach-Head or Droop-Eye to hold the left hand near the chest and make dealing motions with the right. Tobacco was a little more complex. The left hand was held out, palm up, and the edge of the right palm scraped across it, back and forth. It might have had something to do with their way of mixing bark with the little tobacco they had, to make it last longer. The way to make a query out of any of these signs was simply to point the extended index finger of the right hand, and then crook it into what looked like a question mark. Absorbed in these gestures, Beau forgot he was a white man in peril of his life, living on a precarious basis with a war party of hostile Sioux.

According to his own rough calculations, they must by now be over a hundred miles north of the UP tracks. One day they forded a wide shallow stream he thought was the Platte, although he was not sure. One thing he could be sure about, though; this rough life, the clean sharp air, the wrestling with the packs on the mule and the constant forging northward, through tangled ravines and rock-strewn gullies, had sharpened and whetted him. Never much for physical effort, preferring instead to lie late in bed and have his breakfast brought up to him when he was in the chips, he was now surprised to find he could take up a notch in his belt. His wind was much improved, and he was develop-ing muscles in arms that had for a long time known no more effort than the support of a draw-poker hand. He sniffed the air with new enjoyment, astounded to find that he could smell rich and varied odors. Even his companions, he found, had a delicate scent that identified them. Taken as a whole, they had a musky bouquet of sweet grass and wood-smoke and sweat, but among them there were individual differences. Pock-Mark, for instance, carried a medicine-bag slung by a thong around his neck, and something dead was in it, Beau judged. Bow-Legs constantly chewed handfuls of a red berry he found along the trail that smelled like cinnamon. And Droop-Eye was subject to attacks of gas that made it prudent to ride upwind of him. There was all this, and the smell of pines and of horseflesh and of black powder carried in a buffalo-horn and of wet meadows in the night and of wild-sage, trampled by the hoofs of their mounts.

They made camp on the south bank of the Platte. Midway in a sunny afternoon, they turned the stock loose to graze on the thick grass that grew near the muddy banks. Slanting rays of the sun filtered through the trees and lay in an ever-changing lacework on the bosom of the broad Platte. Beau strolled to the edge of the stream and looked up and down. Nothing. Nothing but the whisper of the water and the rustling of leaves.

The thought struck them all at the same time, as similar thoughts run through a group of school boys. This was the time for a swim. Beau shucked his threadbare shirt, took off the jeans with more care because they were almost transparent in the seat, and pulled off his boots, the stoutest item of raiment he had left. Pock-Mark and Bow-Legs and Droop-Eye were ahead of him, having only a geestring and moccasins and blanket to shed, but Beau's legs were longer. He lead them by a jump as they plunged together into a shallow pool of water and came sputtering up, to blow and puff and grin at each other. Roach-Head ducked under, bubbles marking his disappearance, and a moment later Beau felt an iron grip on his ankle. He fell over backwards, to the immense amusement of Pock-Mark, and wrestled his tormentor underwater till they were both forced to come up for air, panting and grinning. Roach-Head flopped down on his belly and began a mad churn toward the far bank, and then by way of showing off, turned on his back and returned, feet going like windmills and both hands clasped behind his head.

Beau looked around him; the grassy banks, overhanging willow and cottonwood and box-elder, the patches of sun, ponies grazing peacefully. It took a vivid imagination to think that these skylarking men were his enemies—that they would kill and torture him on a whim when they tired of him and his bag of tricks.

Droop-Eye came up to him in the water and held his arms, pulling him to the bank. The Sioux took the roots from a stocky green bush and crushed them in his hands, nodding to Beau to do the same. Dipping them in water and rubbing them over his hard brown body, Droop-Eye worked up a froth that served as soap. Beau pulled off a handful of the leaves and tried it. They smelled like tar, but they did foam and bubble. He scrubbed himself industriously, and Pock-Mark and Bow-Legs came quietly up and examined his naked body with clinical interest, marveling at the whiteness of his skin and the resemblance of his body parts to theirs. After a while he began to feel uneasy, and plunged back into the shallow pool and washed the froth off, feeling clean for the first time in many days, and wishing he had some of the clean linen that was waiting unclaimed in the hotel in Chicago.

Afterwards they all stretched naked on the grassy bank, in the golden hour of twilight. Pock-Mark dozed, and Bow-Legs whittled at a willow-shoot with his skinning knife, trying to make a whistle. Roach-Head got out a clay pipe and a bladder-like pouch of tobacco, and puffed on it, gazing through half-shut eyes at the placid current. For this brief moment, suspended in the sunny golden haze, they might all have been friends.

"Smoke," said Beau, and reached out for the pipe, grinning. The young man hesitated, and he regarded Beau for a long time, a curl of smoke hanging undisturbed around his lips. Then he removed the pipe, spat, and handed it to Beau, face impassive.

Beau took a deep draft of the smoke, anticipating the pleasure. But Roach-Head, short of tobacco, had been supplementing it with red willow bark. Beau had watched him strip the saplings along the small streams they came to, and slice the inner bark into fine bits that he laid to dry on a leaf in the sun. One good drag on the clay pipe was enough. Beau's eyes watered, and he coughed. Blinking, he handed the pipe back and said *"Hie, hie,"* the words for thanks. Thinking it over later, it came to him that Roach-Head's action had meant much more than Beau had realized; to smoke a pipe with a man meant he was your friend.

They came one night to a gorge bordered by high bluffs of colored sandstone. The higher reaches were covered with scrub pine and juniper, but in the protected valley below was a thick stand of cottonwoods, and somewhere in the bottoms must be water. The sheer high walls of the canyon burned for one last moment in the rays of the setting sun as they started down the trail that led into the deep cleft.

Beau saw the party of surveyors almost as soon as the Sioux did. In a grassy meadow below them winked a small fire, and shadowy figures moved around it, passing from wagon to fire and back again. Supper was on; even from that distance he got the quick rich tang of coffee, bubbling in a pot over the fire. There were no more than three or four of them, moving about the homely tasks without knowledge of the Sioux on the ledge above them. Beau opened his mouth—whether to shout a warning or not, he never knew—because the pockmarked man got him around the throat with a forearm that was like a wagon-tongue, and choked off his breath. Moving quickly, they tied and trussed him like a pig on the way to market, and stuffed a handful of grass into his mouth, tying his jaws shut with a scrap of rawhide. Then they rolled him into the brush and drifted down the slope, flitting like ghosts in the dying light. Only he and the ponies and the mules were left on the brim of the gulley, and though he rolled and twisted and tried to wriggle out of his bonds, he could not.

How long he lay there he did not know. A cup of a moon came up, hovered for a moment on the canyon wall with the trees like black lace across it, and then climbed into the sky. One of the ponies nuzzled at him, and then went back to jerking at the grass with big yellow teeth. It seemed he could hear the sounds of voices from the surveyors' camp below—a man laughed, or maybe it was some trick of the blood pounding in his ears. Bats flew overhead in the dusk, darting this way and that in the dusk, searching for insects. Then there was the sharp flat slap of a shot, and the echoes carromed up and down the canyon. Another shot, and then another, and a heavier answering boom of a big rifle. A scream shivered in the night air, or perhaps it was a Sioux war cry. That was all—a sound like a nail scratched on slate, and silence.

In a short time they were back, loaded with loot, but Roach-Head walked bent over, hand clutching at his stomach. When they reached the top of the trail, he toppled over and lay flat on his back, staring up at the moon and biting his lip with pain. They dragged him into a sitting position beneath a twisted dark juniper and Pock-Mark released Beau, with a curt sign to start a fire. Droop-Eye searched in the brush, and came back with a handful of dry gray leaves, which he ground to a powder in his hands. Moistening it with spittle, he made a sort of paste and plastered it over the small deadly wound in the young man's middle. In the firelight, Beau could see Roach-Head's face, curiously gray, and a thin dark trickle came from his lips where the teeth had clenched on the skin. Below them in the canyon the wagon of the surveyors, and all the paraphernalia the Sioux had not wanted, burned brightly.

They had taken scalps, several of them. As Beau squatted by the fire, warming his hands, he watched them at the business of scraping bits of skin from the trophies, rubbing the inner side with ashes and earth. Finally they hung them on sticks poked into the ground near the fire, where the heat and smoke would cure them. Pock-Mark watched Beau as he scraped. With a grin he picked something out of the grass and flung it at Beau. It hit him full in the face, and he snatched at it with his hand and held it up in the flickering light. It was a scalp—one apparently of little value. It had belonged to a man almost entirely bald, and as he stared at the limp cap of flesh, dotted with freckles and dripping blood from a fringe of grayish hair, he became suddenly sick. He doubled up and fell on his side into the grass, and vomited. For a long time he lay there, dizzy and weak and Pock-Mark and the rest of the brigands grinned and giggled at his weakness. Finally he managed to get to his feet and stand, swaying, with a fine bead of sweat breaking out over his whole body, so that he shivered and shook. Ignoring their stares and nudges at each other, he dug a hole in the ground with a pointed stick and buried the scalp. After that he lay down out of the circle of firelight, wrapped in his buffalo coat, and lay sleepless throughout the night, listening to the whistling breath of the wounded Roach-Head, still propped against the tree.

During the night, the rest of them snored quietly near the fire, but from time to time one would awaken, almost as if on signal, and pad silently around the camp, staring down into the canyon at the still-smoldering wagon, or slipping into the brush for a reconnaissance. No one seemed to concern himself with the wounded Roach-Head, beyond that first handful of moist leaf-dust. Beau carried a gourd cup of water to the wounded man, and tried by signs to ask what he could do to help. When he came near to Roach-Head, he could smell the leaf-dust, faintly aromatic, like sage. But the wounded man, eyes closed, only pushed his hand away and groaned. During the early dawn, he sang a kind of death-song, an eerie wailing sound. When the sun came up, he died.

When they found out he was dead, the three Sioux streaked their faces and bodies with wet ashes and dirt. Wrapping their fallen comrade in his blanket, they piled a cairn of rocks over him to keep the wolves away. Atop the pile of rocks they placed the dead man's meager possessions, keeping his rifle and ammunition and pair of field glasses. Then Pock-Mark grabbed the dead man's buckskin pony by the nose-rope and pulled him, wide-eyed and frightened, up to the pile of rocks. One quick slash with the skinning knife, and the pony quivered and dropped to its knees, blood pumping from the severed blood-vessels of the throat. For a long time it lay there, watching with piteous eyes while the Sioux shuffled around the monument in a slow and deliberate dance, howling a nasal chant. Finally the animal was dead, and they piled stones over it, too, high-backed saddle and all. The three of them lit a pipe, and blew puffs of smoke to the four quarters. Pock-Mark propped the still-glowing pipe atop the rocky cairn, and the obsequies were complete. The dead man had his pony and his lance and his pipe in the other world, and this spot and what had happened here had no hold on them any longer. It was up to *Wakan Tanka,* the deity they prayed to every night and every morning. Pock-Mark gave Beau an angry shove and pointed toward the pack-mule, and they left the canyon and the still-smoking surveyors' wagon behind, to push northward again.

From this point on, there was a subtle change in his relationships with his captors. Now Pock-Mark watched Beau with a baleful and glittering eye, as if coming to the conclusion that their prisoner was a nuisance. Beau Mannix had been stalked by experts in the back-alleys off Kearny Street in Frisco. Unarmed, he was at Pock-Mark's mercy, but he made a point of keeping out of the sullen brave's path, and saw to it that if Pock-Mark suddenly decided to take a potshot at him, he stood a good chance of winging one of the other Sioux. It was the best he could do under the circumstances, and it gave him a few percentage points.

As the days wore on, Beau lost all track of where they were, even approximately, or where they were going, except that they were somewhere north of the Platte and forging steadily north-ward, by the stars and the sun. Their scanty store of dried meat and corn was gone, and the empty leather bags flapped loosely on the pack-mules. Once there was speculation as to whether they should slaughter a mule, and sharp debate among them, but Pock-Mark, who was riding a few hundred yards ahead, sud-denly paused on an open ridge, holding up his hand. As they rode up, he made two fists and held them to his temples, the index fingers curved in a gesture that could have meant only one thing—buffalo. To Beau's eyes, the grassy plain was empty, with a few outcroppings of scattered rocks. The wind riffled the grass in waves, like the ocean, and that was the only sound—the whisper of the grass beneath high-piled clouds marching into a sunny distance. But Pock-Mark and Droop-Eye and Bow-Legs clapped heels to their ponies and pounded away, waving their rifles and bows overhead and yelling.

On the mule, he could not keep up with them. He followed, slowly, watching them dwindle dot-like in the distance. They were becoming increasingly careless of him. By the time he reached the next ridge, they had dropped a lone cow with their lances. The rest of the small herd had fled a few hundred yards away where they circled uncertainly, tossing their big heads and bawling. The cow, unable to get to her feet because of the prop-ping of the lances in her side, lay quietly, nostrils dilated, watch-ing the Sioux with fear-bright eyes.

They slaughtered the cow with flashing knives, after a pre-liminary small ceremony of thanks. With much gesture and sign-talk that Beau had learned to associate with something otherworldly, Droop-Eye squatted beside the dying cow and whispered into her ear, as if to reassure her. Then, with a shout, he sank the keen knife into the hide between the shoulders and made a long cut along the backbone to the tail. With another yell, he cut forward, over the head and between the horns, to the lip. Pock-Mark signed to Beau for help, and with two of them on each side, they peeled the hide off, laying half on either side.

The cow had been heavy with calf, and Bow-Legs cut the belly open and drained the fluid from the sack, pouring it into a tin cup and a leather bucket and whatever other containers they could find on short notice. Droop-Eye drank some, plunging cupped hands into the bucket and smacking his lips. They laid the foetus carefully aside and went on with their butchering, moving with the skill and precision of professionals. Their skinning knives flashed in the sun and dripped red. They pried open the jaws and cut out the tongue, laying it carefully on a blanket of hide. The outer slabs of flesh were cut free, and fell in fat-marbled chunks. Bow-Legs hacked loose the hump and the rest of them cut off the front and hind-quarters. Droop-Eye hacked off a hind leg, and using the hoof as a hatchet, broke the ribs from the backbone. The kidneys, the liver, fat and brains were dumped into a pocket-shaped piece of gut torn from the intestines, and finally the work was done, the meat wrapped in the hide to make two neat packages. Beau started a fire, and the Sioux sat cross-legged around it, licking bloody fingers and sniffing at the smell of unborn buffalo calf simmering in an iron pot.

To a city man like Beau Mannix, accustomed to seeing his meat delivered to him on a platter, well-done and ornamented with a sprig of parsley, the scene should have revolted and sickened. But he had changed a lot in these past weeks. There was something in this wild performance of blood and flashing steel and mystic ceremony that excited him. He was too stirred even to roast a chuck of the humpribs that Droop-Eye tossed him. The meat didn't look much different from what he had seen in a butcher-shop, and he could have skewered it with a stick and held it over the blaze, but he was not hungry. While the Sioux devoured half-cooked chunks of the calf, ripping into it with their strong white teeth and wiping hands on their bellies till they shone with grease, he paced back and forth, hands clasped behind him. This was something he would have loved to paint, if he had had the tools. The huge head of the cow still lay in the blood-smeared grass, horns glittering darkly in the late sun.

The Sioux were too busy in their meat-orgy to pay attention to him. They went to sleep, full and contented, while he watched the ponies and the mules. They belched loudly in the sleep that overcame them after the surfeit of meat, and lay slumbering, faces masked with congealed grease and meat drippings. Once, on a quick impulse, he moved for the breech-loading Springfield that lay beside Pock-Mark, but the man started suddenly in his sleep, and rolled over, and Beau shrank back and squatted on his heels. There would be other opportunities, though. With the growing friction between him and Pock-Mark, he would have to seize the time when it came.

The opportunity came sooner than he had expected. The next day, shambling into the endless distance with the heavily-loaded mules, the war-party came across wagon-tracks in the grass. There was only one wagon, and a team, and the tracks were fresh. This was a target made to order for them, a wandering white man, perhaps lost. Atop the next ridge they saw it, trundling whitely along in the deep grass. A wagon, a wagon pulled by a smart span of mules, the canvas shining like alabaster in the sun.

It was going away from them on a quartering course, and a long way off. Almost as if triggered by an unseen spring, the Sioux clapped heels to their ponies and pounded away, waving their bows and rifles and lances, shouting with excitement and anticipation. They left him with the pack-mules.

He knew what he wanted, and he went after it with desperate haste. Roach-Head's rifle and fieldglasses were packed in one of the leather bags that hung from the pack-mules. He ripped and pulled at them, and finally with combined aid of teeth and fingernails, got the bag open. The gun was a fine one—an eight-shot Spencer carbine, well-oiled with stinking buffalo-fat, and carrying seven copper-cased cartridges in a tubular magazine in the stock. He found a handful of the odd-sized cartridges in a small leather bag, and loaded the piece, hands trembling as he heard the shouts and rifle-fire in the distance. There was a heavier boom interspersed with the lighter crack of the Sioux rifles, and he knew that someone in the wagon must have a big Sharps. When the surveyors had been slaughtered in the canyon that night, he had been helpless. Now he pulled the leather saddle-bags from the lead mule and climbed on, the carbine in one fist and a handful of mule-mane in the other. He was free, and it was up to him and the carbine to keep it that way.

When he topped the ridge, he saw that the wagon was still going, the mules at a gallop. But the Sioux were stopped short of it by an obstruction that lay between them and the vanishing wagon. As Beau watched, he saw a puff of smoke from a narrow spine-like ridge of rocks that bisected the plain, and seconds later heard the flat heavy boom of the big gun. Someone had dropped off the wagon to delay the charge of the Sioux, and he was holed up in those rocks, banging at them with the big gun.

Beau dug his heels into the mule's ribs and bucketed away down the slope, hanging on with tightly-clamped knees. The frightened mule laid its ears back and galloped. Reined up for a quick conference, the Sioux did not see him until he was almost on them in a clatter of hoofs and a shout that burst from his throat almost unbidden. He rocketed through them, abandoning his grasp of the mane to level the carbine and fire quickly. Like the shutter of a photographic apparatus blinking, he saw one of them—in his speed he did not know which—clap his hands to his face and fall backward into the grass. Then he was past them, going like a loosed arrow toward the rocks, holding the carbine over his head and shouting defiance. After all these months of bondage, he was free again, and he was filled with a crazy exultation.

Suddenly the mule stumbled and went to its knees, grunting. He shot over its head and slid through the grass, spinning and turning until the sky reeled above him. The mule lay on its side, legs threshing.

He was no more than a hundred yards from the rocks, and he ran toward them, long legs pumping, his boots slipping and grinding in the shale that lay on the lower reaches of the rocks.

"Don't shoot!" he yelled. He stopped and waved his arms. "I'm a white man. I'm not a damned Indian!"

In the slipping and sliding of his ascent, he was unaware that two of the Sioux were behind him, pounding toward the rocks on their ponies, bending low over the roached manes of their ponies and yelling in a high-pitched yammering. The Sharps went off and at that close range the sound made his ears ring.

"Here!" a voice called down. "Up here! Behind you! Come up here. I'll cover you!"

On a pinnacle of rock above him stood a man, a big man with a rifle to his shoulder. At almost the same instant Beau saw him, the big gun boomed again. The shot spangled in the shale just beyond him, and he yelled in exasperation just as the Sioux rode him down and charged up the slope.

The action was immediately confused, so close had the fighting become. Beau felt a numbing blow on his neck, and one of the ponies must have swerved in the rush and struck him a glancing blow with its shoulder. He rolled head over heels in the loose shale. Lying there for a moment, ears ringing with the blasting of gunfire, he was stunned. Only when he saw a quick shadow pass between him and the sky did he realize that he was in danger. Droop-Eye loomed over him, arm upraised, and the pale light shone on the tip of his feathered lance. Beau struck out violently with his feet and rolled aside just as the blade drove its length into the ground and snapped off with a tinkling sound. Droop-Eye threw his full weight on him, fumbling in his belt for a knife, but Beau caught his wrist and pulled it away, reaching for the broken lancepoint that was stuck in the earth beside his head. He wrenched it free, and wrapped his long legs around Droop-Eye in a rib-crushing lock, hearing the Sioux grunt with pain.

They rolled through the loose shale like fighting dogs, snarling and grunting. Somewhere above them the big gun boomed again, and then once again. After that it was silent. In one final roll they brought up against a projecting ledge, and Beau's luck—the Mannix luck people talked about in Frisco—came to his help when he needed it. Droop-Eye was on the bottom, head and neck wedged for a moment into a cleft that restricted his movements.

Beau drove his knee into the man's chest, and heard the breath leave the Sioux in a gasp. Half-blinded by blood that welled into his eyes from a cut on his forehead, he raised the splintered lance-blade and drove it into the man's middle, feeling the skin give and pop, and the blade slide smoothly in and then suck as he pulled it free. Droop-Eye struggled violently for a moment; he kicked out and tried to squirm away. But the deadly sliver of steel bit at him again and again, and finally his struggles subsided. His breath bubbled in one long last wheeze, and he lay still.

Beau swayed to his feet, putting out a hand for support. Blinking, wiping at his eyes, he located the carbine a dozen yards away, wondering at the strange new silence. The grassy plain was still in the dying sun. Droop-Eye lay flat and dead in the shale. Squinting, Beau could see another crumpled body out in the grass, where he had ridden through them, and a paint pony grazed nearby. He looked in the other direction, beyond the ridge. Pock-Mark had fled. He had had enough. The red and white pony dwindled in the distance.

"Up here," a voice called again. It was a weaker voice this time, one that was suddenly thin and lost.

He could see no sign of life in the rocky ridge, but he started to climb, uncertainly, his whole insides feeling like broken rubbish and his own gasping sounding strange and foreign. A spatter of rain hit him in the face, and he looked up in wonder at the dark clouds that seemed to suddenly cover the sky. Another drop hit him, and then another. Big, cold drops. He threw the splintered lance from him, shuddering, and held his hands out in the rain, trying to wash them clean.

"I'm coming," he said.

On the highest point of the ridge, a man lay propped against a rock, a burly man with a red beard, wearing a straw hat like the farmers wore in the rich black-dirt country around Chicago. A big Sharps lay at his side, and one freckled fist still clenched it. A red stain still grew across his broad chest, and Beau could hear a tiny gurgling sound as the blood leaked from him. As he watched, the last spark of life fled. The life gushed out of the man and he fell sidewise, red beard poking stiffly into the sky, his face white and wet.

"Thanks," Beau said. "Whatever your name was, thanks."

Somewhere in the dim recesses of his outraged brain, he could hear a faint keening sound. It puzzled him, and he frowned, listening intently. After a while it came to him that it was a woman's scream, repeated with a scraping monotony. The screaming went on and on, scraping in his ears. Then he saw through rain-blurred eyes that the wagon had come back for him. He laughed foolishly, holding his side, thinking of how he had fooled the Sioux, fooled Samuel Shadduck, fooled all of them.

**Item 4.** Portrait miniature in oils, app. 2½ × 4 in., done on thin wooden oval, with gilt border apparently hand-carved. Head and shoulders of young blonde woman. Condition of miniature poor; much handled, paint has flaked off right cheek and forehead. Signed B/M.

---

Now he saw, with photographic clarity, that the painted wagon of his late nightmare was actually an ancient and shabby Army ambulance, with the four wheels so loose on the worn shafts that they leaned at separate and crazy angles. The canvas sides, at least, were white and new, and on them were painted various legends in theatrical red and yellow letters; "GAMMILL THE SIGN MAN", "ALL WORK FIRST RATE", "THE EMPEROR OF PAINTERS, AVAILABLE FOR SIGNS, PORTRAITS, LANDSCAPES." Around the wooden bed writhed an intricate series of scrolls and loops and unlikely blossoms and leaves, done in pink and red and green. The unreal vehicle shimmered in the rain like a creature of the imagination. But the mules were real enough. Good stout Missouri mules, standing patiently, little vapors rising from their wet backs.

"Ma'am," Beau said crossly, "that's about enough of that yelling."

The lady on the seat put a hand over her mouth, as though this physical pressure were the only thing that would help. In her lap she clutched a black valise, and she swayed a little in the seat, eyeing him fearfully.

"Those Indians—" She took the hand away from her mouth. "I didn't mean to scream."

He put a hand inside his torn shirt and felt around. Drawing it out smeared with blood, he looked wonderingly down at it. The fine drizzle of the rain faded the blood and made it blot and run until his hand was clean again.

"You came back," he said. "That took some nerve."

For a long moment she stared at him, and he was conscious of his beard, of his torn clothing and battered appearance, and especially of the manacle that hung as always from his wrist. It had been a part of his clothing, almost, for a long time. It had never bothered him; he had carried it these last weeks as a convenient weapon, ready to hand, but her eyes fastened on it, and he was somehow angry with her.

"Indians," he said. "There was a party of three or four of them. They made me go with them. I didn't have any choice. But they're gone now. One got killed in a fight and I—I—"

It was ridiculous the way her face seemed to blur and change before his eyes. The pink oval of her countenance grew and expanded like an unfolding bud, shot with streaks of darker red, almost a crimson. He took one step forward, hanging on to the wagon for support, frowning and perplexed. A dark smoke seemed to envelop the wagon, and the lady on the seat also.

"Ma'am," he said, screwing his eyes up tight and then opening them again, "that's no way to do. That's—that's—"

His own voice sounded loud and empty in his ears, as if he were in some sort of echoing cavern. He hung on tightly to the wagon for support, feeling that as long as he clutched the wooden ledge, he had a purchase on reality. But even that failed him. The smoke came gently up around him, loosening his grip, and he slipped as gently down to the wet grass.

He was a long time coming back, it seemed, and he did not know where he had been. The rain pattered on a kind of a roof over his head, but after a while the soft splatting sound came to an end. The light grew and swelled until he knew the sun was shining. Painfully, he rolled over and got up on his elbows, and the India-rubber poncho that had been rigged over him collapsed, so that he fought blindly in its folds. Then its smothering weight was pulled away from him, and he was sitting dazed and foolish in the grass, the blonde woman standing over him.

"You're all right," she said. "I knew you'd come around."

With the aid of her arm he got to his feet, wincing. There was a curious tightness around his ribs, and he felt there, and then pulled aside the ragged fringe of his shirt. He was wound tightly in strips of clean white cambric, with whorls and arabesques of embroidery on it.

"It was my best petticoat," she said. "You can pay me for it when you're able. But I thought to myself, maybe there's a rib broken in there someplace, and it ought to be bandaged tightly, and besides you were bleeding awful bad from those cuts around your middle."

He looked at the small fire, the cracked saucepan in which coffee boiled, the thousand glints from new sun on the small lenses of rain in the grass. Unhitched, the mules grazed in pastoral quiet, and a bird in a sodden tree overhead cleared its throat and tried a few tentative trills.

"I'm all right," he said.

He staggered to the fire, and sat down heavily while she poured him coffee in a tin cup. Over the rim of it he stared at her, sitting composed on an upended box across the fire. She no longer screamed. She was dignified and competent, and a little ashamed.

"He's dead," Beau said. He nodded toward the rocks. "Up there. One of the Sioux got him dead center in the chest."

"I'm sorry."

He frowned at her casualness, perplexed.

"You Mrs. Gammill?"

"No."

That was all she said, and he felt uncomfortable, and shrugged. But he poured himself more coffee, and went on studying her over the rim of the cup. She was a strikingly handsome woman, in a soiled muslin waist that looked expensive, and a balmoral skirt. Brassy light hair was piled high on her head, and held in place by a remarkable structure of tortoise combs. Her lips were full and red against the whiteness of her cheeks, and her eyes, so well as he could see under the downcast lids, were large and blue, rimmed with long dark lashes that gave them an emphasis and authority unusual in a woman. To him she seemed a lady, a remarkable woman who was keeping herself under control in a very unpleasant situation.

"What have you got in that satchel?" he asked, in a heavy attempt at humor. He jerked his head at the black valise between her high-buttoned shoes. "You handle it like a baby, only more careful."

Lips parted in unconscious deliberation, she thought for a moment, and then said, "Money. Nothing but money. I've robbed a bank, you know. Does that satisfy your curiosity?"

He swirled the coffee in his cup, looking down at the grounds.

"If you say so, ma'am. I didn't intend to be nosey."

"There's tools in the back of the wagon," she said. "Maybe you could find a hammer and a chisel there. He had a lot of tools. We could put that handcuff on a rock and I could hold the chisel while you hammer."

Wincing with the pain from his ribs, he looked down at the manacle, dangling rustily from his thin brown wrist.

"Not till I bury him." He nodded toward the rocks, and threw the rest of the coffee away. "You don't seem to take his dying very hard."

Her white cheeks flushed, and she put her hands flat on the skirt and stared down at them.

"Gammill?" She spoke in a low voice, not meeting his eye. "No, he wasn't anything to me. I'm—I'm grateful to him, but he wasn't anything to me." Her voice was a curious mixture of defiance and pity, and Beau Mannix thought that the better part of it was a kind of self-pity that sat strangely on so handsome a young woman. He got to his feet and went to rummage through the wagon for a shovel.

He found the shovel. A shovel, and at least one each of everything else a man might imagine a need for. Paints and brushes, of course; the interior of the wagon was filled with crudely carpentered lockers jammed with pots and pans and bottles of paint. Rose, blue, pink, brown, a sickening yellow, a blue like the color of a jay's wing. Dozens and tens of dozens of brushes; wide, narrow, housepainters' brushes and delicately wispy things that did not encompass a dozen slender China bristles. There was also an old harmonium in disrepair, a broken shotgun, several ornate clocks which still ticked, a feather mattress, a leather-bound set of The Mechanic's Encyclopedia, a rusty birdcage, and a patent corn-sheller. Gammill had not been a man to throw anything away.

When he came back with the shovel, she rose unsteadily from the box, holding on to the valise.

"I—I'm afraid I'm going to be sick."

He had been irked at her steady composure, and now he was secretly glad. But in the face of this feminine derangement, he was also suddenly helpless. The best he could think of was to get her a cup of water, remembering from somewhere that this was an accepted remedy. She pushed his hand away, face pale and set.

"I can take care of myself. You—you take care of Mr. Gammill."

"Are you sure?"

She nodded, holding on to the wagon for support. There was something so fierce and decisive in the gesture that he was glad to leave her.

After he had dug the hole as deep as he could manage, he pulled back the blanket. Gammill, the Emperor of Sign-Painters, lay on his back, rusty beard pointed toward the sky. In the sun, the raindrops in Gammill's beard glinted for a moment like diamonds. It was not a bad place for a man to lie, with the wet grass and the new-washed smell of everything.

Tugging and straining at the heavy body, he got it to the edge of the hole. His side hurt abominably and his chest heaved against the restraint of the tightly-wrapped bandage. Furry dark spots danced before his eyes. Pausing to catch his breath, he went gingerly through the pockets and found a worn wallet and a handful of coins, along with a religious medal of some sort. He put the medal in the dead man's hand, closing the stiff freckled fingers around it.

He had the body half-buried in a few minutes, and then stopped, leaning on the shovel. After a while, he went and got the wide straw hat and laid it over the defenseless face. Then he threw dirt in until the entire body was covered, and piled rocks over the raw brown earth.

"It's over with," he said, coming down the slope.

She sighed, a quaver in her voice.

"I—I'm grateful to you. I wanted you to know that. I—I act queer sometimes. A lot of people don't like me, I can tell you that. But I guess I owe you more of an explanation. I'm not used to explaining to people, but Mr. Gammill offered to take me to Custer City. I had to get there somehow. I paid him fifty dollars. That was all there was to it. Business."

He held out the wallet to her.

"I expect the money's in there."

He half-expected her to shrink away from it in distaste, but she took it coolly from him, and slipped it into her bosom.

"I'll pay you the same, if you get me there. What do you say, Mr. —Mr. —"

He scratched his unshaven chin, and blinked.

"I guess it's a bargain. First of all, though, you'll have to help me get this bracelet off my wrist."

She followed him to the wagon, and he said, rummaging through the junk for a hammer and a chisel, "I suppose you're wondering how I got this keepsake."

She shook her head, firmly.

"No."

He paused for a moment in his search, staring at her.

"It doesn't mean anything to me," she said. "You've got your private business, and I've got mine. That's all we have to remember."

"All right," he said, and went on looking for the chisel, feeling he had been somehow taken advantage of.

Her name was Lael. She sat on the seat beside him, combing her long yellow hair and talking rapidly and intricately, like a child.

"That was my father's doing. He was a scholar, that taught in a school in Columbus, Ohio. It's short for Laelia, and that's a Roman name. There was once a very famous Roman lady by that name, but I don't remember what she was noted for. Myself, I never went to school much. Papa taught me and my sister, but she's dead. She had the consumption. That's one reason I came west. I hear it's very good for the lungs." She took a deep breath, and looked out across the grassy plain. "Isn't this exciting?"

During the past days they had borne westerly, hoping to intercept the road between Fort Fetterman and the Black Hills. Beau found an old and inaccurate map in Gammill's things, and they steered by that, and the stars. Once they fell into the considerable traffic of the Black Hills road, they would be safe. Companies of infantry guarded it against the Sioux. But here, in this rich meadow, the thought of violence seemed almost profane. They drove for miles along a cold sweet stream bordered with thick groves of willow and box-elder and cottonwood. The grass was thick and juicy, and there were dense thickets of wild plums and grapevines and bullberries. The hand of winter was gone, and now the land lay lush and fertile under the spring sun.

"Do you think," Lael asked, "we'll have any more trouble with the Indians before we get there? To Custer City, I mean."

"I don't know," he said.

Once, although he had not told her, he had seen a thin string-like smoke on a distant hill behind them, but nothing had come of it. The Sioux used mirrors to signal—he had seen Droop-Eye work with one—and he was ever alert for a quick flash from a mountain-top. But he had seen none. Nothing but that thin wavering smoke, and that might have been only another party headed for the gold diggings. It had been miles away.

"That was a small war-party I was with," he explained. "They were 'way south, out of their territory, looking for whatever they could plunder. Maybe they were the only ones around. There's no need to worry."

Tying the reins to the whip-socket, he swung down from the seat to examine the off front wheel. For three-quarters of the circumference the iron tire was loose, and it clattered and banged and protested at every turn. The old ambulance had traveled a rough road.

"How come you and Gammill to be so far off the road this way?" he asked.

Weighing her answer, she looked down at him with compressed lips. Now that the jolting of the wagon had ceased, she was busy expertly braiding her hair.

"Doesn't do any harm to tell you, I guess. He was just a better sign-painter than he was a wagonman. He came out here from someplace in Illinois. Wanted to set up in Custer City or Deadwood or someplace. He figured they'd need a lot of signs there, the way the mines were booming. He offered to take me to Custer City for fifty dollars, and it was a better bargain than the stage." She frowned. "It wasn't, though." She jammed the last comb into her hair indignantly.

There was a kind of small-girl bravado in her voice, and when he grinned, she flounced her skirts and he saw a glimpse of smooth white knee.

"Men are all just about alike, I should think. A lot of talk and bluster, without much behind it."

Gravely he climbed back up on the seat.

"You know much about men, Miss Lael?"

"I know aplenty."

He slapped the reins across the broad backs of the mules and asked, "Now me, for instance. What kind of a man do you take me to be?"

She looked at him from the corner of her eye and laughed a small knowing laugh.

"You're not hard to figure, Mr. —"

"Beau."

"Haven't you got a last name?"

"I suppose so. But it's not of interest to anyone except the man that's chasing me. And he certainly doesn't expect me to go by that name any more. So just call me Beau."

"All right," Lael said. "Beau, then. And you may call me Lael. Not Miss Lael. Just Lael." She touched her lips with the tip of a pink tongue, staring out over the sun-warmed land, and took a deep breath. "Well, then. Let's begin. You're tall, and kind of lanky. Your hands are big, and your feet, too. That argues a kindly disposition."

Taken aback, he looked down at his sturdy boots, but she chattered on, ticking off the points on her fingers.

"You have a long jaw, and that commonly means a thinker, but on the other hand, you've got black eyes with a kind of a sparkle to 'em. I'd say that kind of overbalances, so that you're more the kind to have a good time and let the devil take the hindmost. Is that right so far?"

He swallowed, feeling his Adam's apple slide uncomfortably up and down his throat.

"Maybe it does and maybe it doesn't." Suddenly gruff, he demanded, "What about that handcuff you helped me spring loose? Don't that tell you anything?" He swiveled toward her on the seat, glowering. "You sit there and prattle on like it was all a big joke! Well, then, let me tell *you* something! If I was you, I'd be scared of me. Here you are, out in the middle of Dakota Territory riding around in a condemned Army wagon with a man that's wanted for murder—"

"Murder?"

"Yes, that's right. Murder. Now do you want to read my palm? Is it so damned funny now, Miss Lael, or Lael, or whatever your name is?"

Her face flushed, and she bit at her lip with tiny white teeth.

"I never said it was funny."

"Well, you—you—." Not understanding his own emotions, he floundered. "Ah, the hell with it!" Half-rising to his feet, he whipped the mules into a run, and they jolted away up a steep rise, swaying and banging, while Lael held tight to the seat and did not speak. Finally, when the sullen mules came to a halt, and would not move, he set the brake and got down to examine the loose tire again.

"You're impulsive," Lael said. "That's the way you get into trouble. You do things without thinking them through. Just like whipping the mules that way." She climbed down, and stood beside him as he whittled a wedge to secure the loose tire. "Do you want to tell me about it, Beau? Would that help?"

When he was silent, she said, "My—my husband always liked to talk things out with me. At the end of the day, we used to sit on the veranda and talk. There were locusts there—I think they were locusts. Anyway, they made this kind of screeching sawing sound. Sometimes they made so much noise it was hard to talk. I—I'd like to hear them again, though. I guess they don't have them out here. Locusts, I mean."

"Well," he said, touched by a loneliness in her voice, "I guess we all have our troubles. I—I didn't know you were married. Not that it's a trouble to be married—I didn't mean that. But I reckon maybe you're a widow?"

"I am." She stood firmly against the sky, and the late sun caught her blonde hair and made a glowing nimbus of light all around her high-piled braids. "But I never asked anything from anyone because of it. I can get along all right."

He stared at her, working the knife against the wedge.

The gold was a luminous molten shine and he wondered what colors a man could mix to get that shine, the way the light seemed to come out of the braids, instead of just shining on them.

"There isn't much to tell. I was in the war. They gave me a gun and I shot at a man once and missed him, and I shot again once and didn't miss. I never got any medals. After I got out, I was still only a kid. Didn't know what I wanted to do. Drifted here, drifted there. Went to art school, learned about the old masters, tried clerking in a store, shoed horses, worked as a newspaper reporter for a while."

"You do better with your *hands*," Lael said abruptly.

He grinned wryly.

"That's the way I got in trouble with the law. I was adjusting a deck of cards so I'd get three aces in a stud game. A man caught me at it. When he came at me with a knife, I shot him. That was in San Francisco last year. That's the why of the handcuffs." Reaching in his pocket, he took out the dog-eared deck and fanned them out with a flip of his thumb. "See?"

She shook her head impatiently.

"There are other ways of using your hands beside gambling."

He shrugged, and put the cards back in his pocket.

"Not and make the kind of living I like."

For a moment he thought bitterly of Shadduck. Though he had been too much for the detective, though he had tricked him and outwitted him, here were Shadduck's thoughts come back to haunt him. *A waste of a man,* the shabby terrier in the fur cap had said. Now Lael was telling him the same thing. He pushed the wedge between the tire and the rim and drove it home savagely. "There," he said, "that ought to hold for a couple of miles." Not looking at her, he climbed on the seat again. After a moment, she climbed up beside him, and they rode a long way, neither looking at the other, conscious of a tension between them.

The land, however, drove them together again. There was so much of it, and it pressed in on them and made them lonely and anxious for companionship. For a week or more they quartered across the rolling hills, the mules almost belly-deep in thick grama grass. The knolls and dells were carpeted with flowers; harebells, wild flax, forget-me-nots. Sometimes it rained, heavy drops that stung, or smaller pellets that drizzled through the canvas wagon-sheet and soaked everything, chilling the blood and making them huddle together for warmth. Again there would be hail, great globes that ripped holes in the canvas and whitened the ground. Then thunder was incessant, and louder than anything Beau had ever heard before. Lightning darted all round the sky, from zenith to horizon, and in its glare every least rock and pebble and clump of brush stood out in wet clarity. Frightened, Lael clung to him, hiding her face from the great sheets of flame, and he wished she were less of a lady. It was hard on him.

"It's nothing," he said. "It won't hurt us."

At dusk the sun peeped out, wan and pale under the mantle of dark clouds, and the whole earth was washed in a sea of color. Scarlet and pink, gold, yellow, coppery greens and a last fragment of blue—all were scattered prodigally from the distant hills to the zenith. The broken contour of the ground, with its rank on advancing rank of ridges and rocky spines, looked like a stormy sea that had been stilled at the climax—frozen into a fairyland of color.

"It'll be a nice day tomorrow," Beau said. He had lost track of time.

The morning was dry and clear, with the sky like a dazzling blue bowl over their heads, and a strong warm wind blowing steadily into their faces. They had exhausted most of the salt beef and flour and coffee that Gammill had provisioned the wagon with, but Beau shot an antelope and butchered it while Lael averted her face.

"It's such a gentle animal," she said, but she ate the ribs he broiled over a bed of coals, gnawing hungrily at them and licking her fingers. Her muslin waist with its ruching and embroidery was torn and dirty, and the balmoral skirt hung dustily from her hips. Noticing his gaze, she flushed, and said, "I—I want to take a bath tonight, and wash out my clothes. Is there water near?"

That night they stopped in a copse of pine trees bordering a small lake. The sky was so thickly dusted with stars that the darkness had a luminous quality, and the air was heavy with the scent of pine. A small wind soughed through the tips of the trees. Beau lit the lantern and handed it to her, nodding toward the lake.

"There's your bathtub, ma'am."

She took a heavy brown bar of soap and a towel, along with a comb and a handful of Gammill's clothes. "For while mine are drying," she explained.

"You be careful," he warned, standing the Sharps against a tree. "That water's maybe deeper than you think. And keep the lantern shaded as best you can. Never know when it'll catch someone's eye. You holler if you get scared."

He jackknifed his long legs at the base of a tree and settled back, puffing Gammill's tobacco in one of Gammill's pipes, feeling lordly. It was like being the master of a household. A traveling household, to be sure, but with a warm kinfolk atmosphere to it he had long missed. Well-fed, puffing his pipe, the day's work done, his woman—well, not really his, but a woman—doing her wash and getting spruced up. He sucked contentedly at the pipe, wondering how it would be to have a lady for his own.

After a while, annoyed at the way the damp tobacco refused to burn steady, he climbed into the wagon and rummaged in the dark for matches. Without the lantern, the interior of the old ambulance was like a coal mine, and he barked his shins and stuck a packet of pins into his searching fingers and overturned a can of paint. Something was barring his way, a vague lumpy thing jammed into a box where he had last seen the matches. He pulled and hauled at it, and suddenly it gave, showering its contents in a soft rustle throughout the wagon. He picked up a handful of the stuff, small paper-like tickets. He was still on his knees, puzzled, when the shaft of lantern-light flooded the bed of the wagon. The tickets were greenbacks—dozens and tens of dozens and perhaps hundreds of them. They littered the floor, and floated stickily in the spilled paint, and cascaded out of the worn valise.

"I knew I shouldn't trust you," Lael said.

He blinked in the light. As his eyes became accustomed to it, he could see she was holding the lantern with one hand and Gammill's Sharps in the other, resting the barrel on the tail-gate. Her hair was done up in a bun on top of her head, tied with a piece of ribbon, and she wore Gammill's patched blue shirt and a pair of jeans that stayed up only because of the way Gammill's belt cinched her slender waist. She looked fresh and delicate and clean.

"Now wait a minute!" he protested. He got hurriedly to his feet, bumping his head on one of the cross-bows, and then sagged down as she jabbed the Sharps muzzle at him. "I didn't—I mean—well, I was just looking for some matches, that's all! My pipe went out."

Her face was accusing in the rays of the lantern.

"You tried to take my money."

"Don't be a damned fool!" he snorted. Wildly he reached forward to grab the muzzle of the gun, but he knew he was too late. In one last quick blink of his eyes, he could see her face held close to the sight. He knew, also, that she had pulled the trigger.

**Item 5.**   Canvas in oils, about 10 × 15 inches. Drunken man in buckskins sitting beneath tree, holding bottle in left hand. A small camp of Indians is in the distance, beneath a stand of cottonwood trees. Condition fair. Signed B/M.

---

Samuel Shadduck took the flimsy from the telegrapher and scanned it, lips moving soundlessly. Then he read it again, and once again. Finally he pushed the fur cap back on his brow and stared at it, as though completely without comprehension.

"Bad news?" the Deadwood telegrapher asked.

Shadduck raised his eyes and looked at the man.

"There is a time," he said, "when thee must go forward with only the Lord. This is a time like that. They want me to forget about Mr. Mannix and come back. Does thee know what this means?"

The clerk plucked at his velveteen sleeve guard.

"Don't reckon I do. I ain't paid to have ideas about what comes over the wires. It's just so many words to me, and I collect so many cents a word."

Shadduck folded the message into a square and tucked it into his hatband.

"I never lost a prisoner," he said. "The Lord frowns on vanity, you understand, but this is not rightly called vanity. I look on it as the Lord's work—apprehending desperate men and returning them to custody. Even when they deny me funds to support myself, it's still the Lord's work. Is this not so?"

The telegrapher's mouth came half-open.

"Well, is it not so?" Shadduck demanded.

The man swallowed hard, his Adam's apple sliding up and down, and he said, "Yes, I s'pose so," in a shocked small voice.

"It is, indeed," Shadduck growled, and stamped away into the dusty street outside.

There were many towns in the Dakota Territory that were better situated and better built, but Deadwood had struck it richer, and Deadwood was where the population of the Dakota Territory had taken root. For the ten miles between Crook City and Deadwood, the road was lined on both sides with sluice-boxes and deep ditches, and men toiled and sweated and cursed in the spring sun, scrabbling and digging, sifting the rich gravel that lay along the gulch. The town itself had already been laid off in building lots, and there was a lively speculation in land. Samuel Shadduck, riding by on his bay mare, knew a Gehenna when he saw one. He also knew that a Gehenna was a likely place to find Beau Mannix.

The town itself was situated where the Whitewood and Deadwood creeks joined, and up and down each gulch was a series of blockhouses to repel the Sioux and the Cheyennes. The whole fantastic settlement, so strange to his eyes, was like a rich plum on the end of a scrawny twig. Food, powder and ball, the picks and shovels and hammers and saws, the liquors and women and gambling paraphernalia; all had to be hauled from the railroad two hundred and fifty miles away, through roving bands of savages. Shadduck, standing ankle-deep in dust outside the telegraph office, shook his head and murmured a brief prayer for the inhabitants.

The main street surged and boiled with the tightly packed bodies of hundreds of men, sweating and cursing, lashing packs on mules, trying to clear a way for a wagon loaded with mining tools and supplies, or simply clustered together in the middle of the street, arguing and gesticulating. The dust rose in stifling clouds, and the hot sun slanted down into the moil and press and confusion so that it might have been a scene of souls in hell.

Windows of the upper stories of the saloons and eating-houses and hotels were occupied by women of bad reputation, clapping hands and waving handkerchiefs. The whistle from a nearby planing mill added to the din, and Shadduck winced at the shrill blast.

Against the wall of "The Only First Class Hotel in Deadwood City, F. T." lounged several men, and Shadduck's roving eye stopped on them. There was a subtle difference in their demeanor that pricked at him—they wore clean linen, most of them, and several sucked on cigars. None of them was Beau Mannix, even allowing for a freshly grown crop of burnsides, or a full beard. But they were the Mannix type, certainly. Shadduck walked by them, giving them eye for eye, and went into the Grand Central Hotel, hands clasped behind him in thought.

The lower floor of the Grand Central was office, dining room, saloon, and kitchen, with little separation of the activities. Shadduck elbowed his way to the bar and rapped his knuckles on the dark wood. Heads craned, and the hurly-burly was for a moment suspended.

"Beer," Shadduck said.

The man at the bar frowned, and shrugged, and then sent a schooner sliding down the wood, to slop over and run into a pool at the detective's elbow. Shadduck did not look at the beer, and the buzz of voices began again.

"Fifty cents," the bartender said.

Shadduck opened a small leather purse and handed a coin to the man. It was one of the few he had left.

"I'm looking for a man named Mannix," he said. "A very dangerous man. Can thee help me, friend?"

The burly man at Shadduck's elbow wiped foam from his lips and turned to look at his neighbor.

"Hell," he said, "that ain't no distinction in Deadwood, mister. I figger I'm dangerous myself sometimes."

Shadduck looked him over coolly.

"Perhaps thee is," he said. "This man is a murderer, also."

The bearded man bellowed with laughter, slapping a huge hand on the bar.

A small man in a tattered felt hat crowded in beside Shadduck and stared at him.

"You sure got a funny way of talkin'," he said. There was no offense in his voice. "You some kind of a missionary or somethin'?"

A little knot gathered around the detective, some curious, some puzzled, most of them anxious for a diversion. "Thee could call me that," he said.

The small man nudged a friend with his elbow. "By God," he snickered, "you come to the right place! I guess there ain't any location in the Territory needs missionaryin' as bad as Deadwood does. Ain't that right, fellers?"

They roared with laughter, but Shadduck shook his head. When he put up his hand for silence, they stopped laughing.

"I am not an ordained minister of any faith," he said. "I am only searching for a fugitive named Mannix. Beau Mannix."

Sly glances and whispers went around the circle. A slender man in derby hat and flowered vest spoke up, words slow and thoughtful around the stogie he chewed.

"Mister, there's one sure way to find out if your friend's in the Territory. This is my hotel, and I can say for sure he's not registered here. But I'd advise you to walk down the street a block or so and talk to Mrs. Cool. There's a lady that knows everything that goes on in Deadwood." He turned to the crowd. "Ain't that right, boys?"

There was a roar of approval.

"That's right!" The bearded man grinned, slapping Shadduck heavily across the shoulder. "Mrs. Cool knows everything that goes on and what comes off, too!" He bent over the bar, overcome with laughter, and spilled his beer into a quick shallow puddle that ran the length of the polished wood. Shadduck took his hand off the bar and straightened the fur cap on his head.

"I thank thee, friends," he said. He walked out, deliberate and purposeful, and the door swung shut behind him. They were having their fun with him, he knew, and it was not right for him to have this anger choking up in his throat. Searching in his mind for one of the psalms that covered the situation, he went looking for a Mrs. Cool.

In the confusion and activity that was Deadwood, Shadduck had a hard time finding her. By the law of the community, a gold placer or ledge could be followed anywhere, regardless of property rights. As a consequence, miners were at work everywhere, even in the streets of the town, following the occasional streaks of color with a hound-like persistence, even to the extent of undermining the business establishments that lined the main street. The offices of *The Pioneer*, Deadwood's only newspaper, were on stilts while a placer operation went on under the building. Next door to *The Pioneer* a Chinese laundry was in the same predicament, the miners having worked even farther back under the building, and the laundry seemed to be supported almost in midair, hanging desperately on to the neighboring *Pioneer* establishment, while the almond-eyed Celestial laundryman rubbed shirts on a board with one hand and hung to a doorframe for balance with the other.

He finally found Mrs. Cool's establishment, a raw boxlike structure of green lumber, already sagging against the bulk of the Deadwood Theatre and Academy of Music, where a performance was promised of Miller's Grand Combination Troupe, with a Dazzling Array of Stars. Peering through the lace curtains that veiled the windows, he could see nothing within but darkness, but the sign on the door said, "Madame Gabriella Cool" in large and staggering black letters, and below it in a finer script was the legend, "Voice Instruction in the Latest European Method according to the Method of Signor Viceli." Shadduck knocked firmly at the door. When no sound came from within, he knocked again.

"Who's there?"

Over his head, a remarkable-looking woman with a fringe of orange bangs leaned from a window. She had in her hand a large chamberpot, and seemed prepared to drop the contents on the detective's head.

"Madame," Shadduck said, "I'm looking for Mrs. Cool."

The lady set her lips in a grim line, and balanced the chamberpot precariously on the sill.

"The girls is all in bed."

Shadduck paled a little, but he was persistent.

"I'm not interested in any girls," he said. "I want Mrs. Cool."

The lady withdrew the chamberpot, and brushed the orange bangs into position with her fingers.

"I'm Mrs. Cool, dearie. You just stay right there, and I'll come down and open the door." Her head disappeared, and Shadduck waited impatiently, ignoring the stares and comments of the passersby. Shadduck was reconsidering his interest in Mrs. Cool, wondering if there was another lady of the same name in Deadwood, when the door swung open and she stood before him, swathed in a violet wrapper and peering roguishly over a fan. Her small black eyes bore on him with an intensity that rooted him in place.

"This is out of hours, so to speak," she said, "but I always say I have a civic duty that goes beyond mere business. Won't you come in, Mr. —Mr. —"

"Shadduck," he said. "Samuel Shadduck."

Holding the fur cap in his hands, he moved past Mrs. Cool into the dark recesses of the voice studio. At least, that was what the sign had professed it to be. But as he stood in the gloom within, Mrs. Cool shut the door smartly, and he knew where he was. If the other signs had not told him, the odor did. A musty smell of cheap perfume and face-powder and liquor and long-dead cigars. And if that were not enough, a smell of human bodies.

"Madame," Shadduck said furiously, "I am afraid someone has been having their fun at my expense. This is a sporting-house, that's what it is. A—a sporting house!"

Mrs. Cool looked at him, orange-dyed head cocked to one side like a tropical bird.

"Why, so it is!" she said. She gave him a playful poke with the fan. "My goodness, you're a queer one!"

Shadduck had once dragged a San Francisco embezzler out of a similar place on Davis Street, but the experience had not prepared him to deal with Cyprians in such close quarters. He moved away from Mrs. Cool, sweating profusely, and found himself in the midst of a bevy of giggling and scantily-clad girls who had materialized from the farther reaches of Mrs. Cool's establishment. He was almost grateful for her sharp and sure handling of the situation.

"Girls, girls!" she shrieked, making little sallies at them and poking viciously with the fan. "Now that will be about a goddam enough! You hear me?" She slashed with the fan at an exposed bottom, wielding it like a saber. "Get back to your rooms, all of you! You need your rest, you hear me?"

Shadduck tried to breathe lightly, hoping he did not inhale too much of the fragrance of bare flesh and French scent. When they were gone, he took out a handkerchief and wiped his face.

"*So* high-spirited," Mrs. Cool said fondly. "But that's the way the men like them. I'm a woman of spirit, myself. Our sex don't bar us from it." She waved Shadduck to a divan, and threw herself languidly onto an ottoman.

"I—I was in a saloon down the street," Shadduck said. "A man there told me thee might be able to help me." He show her his badge. "I'm a detective, from San Francisco."

Mrs. Cool blanched slightly, but in her pale birdlike face the effect was slight.

"A detective?

"I was taking a prisoner from Chicago to San Francisco. He jumped off the train outside of Cheyenne and escaped. I know he got away because I stopped at the next station and searched the line back. There was no body. I've been all over the Dakota Territory in the last few weeks. He's a dangerous man—tall, dark hair worn long, a gambler. He killed a man on Pacific Street in Frisco."

"Tall?" Mrs. Cool asked. "Handsome, maybe?"

"His name was Mannix," Shadduck said. "I don't know what name he might go by now. He was an expert with the cards. He could do all kinds of tricks with them—magic, and sleight of hand."

Mrs. Cool shook her head, and the orange bangs bobbed.

"No, dearie, I don't recollect anyone of that description." She pulled the ottoman closer to him, and crossed her skinny white ankles demurely under the hem of the wrapper. "I always took a liking to *small* men, myself. Are you in town for long?"

Shadduck worked at the ear-flaps of his fur cap, held tightly between his knees.

"No, ma'am. I—I plan to look around a little more, and then I'm going to ride toward Custer City and see can I flush him around there someplace. He's a very ingenious and a resourceful man. For all I know, he might even be staying out of the towns till he's sure I've left the Territory. He knows I'd be looking for him in all the saloons and—excuse me, ma'am—sporting houses. Maybe he's skulking out along the Belle Fourche or the Platte. A man with a gun can get along out there."

"If'n the red vermin don't lift his hair," Mrs. Cool said. "I had a client in here the other night—a man named Gunderson, that freighted for the Army up to Fort Fetterman." She waved the fan dreamily. "Got caught by the Sioux once and scalped—left for dead. That's why I remember him so well. The top of his head looked like a beef roast. But he was a very nice man, and wellspoken. A small man, he was—built a lot like you."

The detective shuddered. Mrs. Cool had touched on a tender spot. Samuel Shadduck was a brave man, but he did not consider it was fair to require his bravery to be exercised among Red Indians. Crimps, con-men, footpads, drunks—these constituted the atmosphere he moved in, and was familiar with. It had been an effort of will to make the journey from Cheyenne to Deadwood, even though he rode with a train of freight wagons and a company of cavalry that had been detached to guard them. But he had never lost a prisoner. That was a fact that sparkled ahead of him always in the search, like a guiding star. And he was prepared to do whatever he had to do to maintain that record.

"Can thee help me find a man to guide me in the wilderness?" Shadduck asked. "I am not a woodsman. Perhaps there are friendly Indians who may know of Mannix. Someone who speaks their language, someone to guide me among the wild beasts of the forest—"

Mrs. Cool chuckled, and rapped him on the knuckles with the fan.

"You got such a cute way of expressing yourself, Mr. Shadduck." She wrinkled her brow, and the fold rapidly disappeared in the other convolutions of her face. "Let me see, now—"

"I have money, although not a great deal," Shadduck said. "Enough to outfit us, perhaps. We could split the reward, later."

Mrs. Cool pursed her lips. Her small eyes sparkled with sudden inspiration.

"I've got just the man for you!"

She sprang to her feet in a flurry of purple gauze.

"Now you just sit there and be comfortable. I'll be right back!"

A moment later Shadduck heard her screaming somewhere above his head and the clatter of feet. "Is that Smoke still in here?

Is that drunken loafer in my place of business? Where is he now? Girls, rout him out for me!"

There were sounds of confusion, shrieks of laughter, and heavy thumps. After a while Mrs. Cool reappeared in the parlor, driving before her a large bewildered man in a grease-shiny buckskin coat. "Where's my hat?" the man demanded. "Damn it, Mattie, stop poking me! Where in hell's my hat?"

In the doorway at the rear of the parlor, Mrs. Cool's voice students giggled, and then fled as she rushed at them, waving the fan. Locking the door with a key she took from the recesses of the robe, she stalked back to her guests.

"I'll Mattie you, you big lout," she shrilled.

The man in buckskin retreated grinning.

"Don't pay any attention to his drunken ravings," Mrs. Cool advised Shadduck. "Anyway, Mr. Shadduck, this here is the man for you. He's dirty as a henhouse floor, and the lice can't get a good holt on him any more, for he's so soaked in licker that the fumes dizzies 'em. But you'll do me and you both a favor if you get him out of here. He makes himself a poke full of dust, and then he comes in here and starts trouble. I try to run a decent house, but it's almighty hard with Smoke annoying my young ladies."

Smoke licked his lips, and grimaced at the taste. He scratched his frowsy head, and yawned.

"Thinks a pinch of dust entitles him to a lady's favors for a week," Mrs. Cool sniffed. "When are you going to pay me for that window you broke?" Disdaining an answer, she turned to Shadduck. "But I'll say this for him. When's he's sober, there ain't anyone knows the Territory any better than Smoke does. He can take you into places the whole damned Seventh Cavalry would be scared to go, and bring you out safe again. I daresay he's got more bush-brats than could be counted, and most of 'em are Sioux or Cheyenne. Ain't that right, Smoke?"

"Well," said Smoke, "I got a few." He squinted at Shadduck. "You hirin' me for some kind of a job, mister?"

Shadduck nodded.

"I'm looking for an escaped prisoner." He showed Smoke his badge. "I figure he might be down on the Belle Fourche or the Cheyenne or someplace, holed up. I want a man with some experience to go with me down there; talk to the Indians, see can I get a line on Mannix."

"Who?"

"His name is Mannix. Beau Mannix."

Smoke rubbed an unshaven chin.

"Dunno the name. Out here nobody goes by their right name anyway."

"We'll need an outfit," Shadduck said. "I've got money for that, but no more. There's a thousand dollars reward for Mannix, though; if we catch him, thee and me split the reward."

"You and who?" Smoke asked, blinking.

"Thee and him," Mrs. Cool said. "That's just his way of talking. He's a Baptist or one of them kind."

Shadduck looked at her and blew out his breath as if to relieve his feelings.

"The Friends, madame," he said. "The Society of Friends."

"Well, I ain't got no objection," Smoke said.

"Before we go," Shadduck told Mrs. Cool, "there something I'd like to do."

Mrs. Cool sniffed.

"Take him away from here and you can have your pick of my girls, Mr. Shadduck."

The detective flushed.

"Thank you, no, ma'am. It's something different. Quite different. I—if you don't mind, ma'am—I'd like to say a few words to your girls."

Mrs. Cool leaned back, hands folded over her stomach, and looked down her angular nose. "Now I don't know—" Mrs. Cool stared at Shadduck, then at Smoke, then back at the detective again. "We ain't sinners, exactly. We're just in business, sellin' a commodity, that's all."

"We are all sinners," Shadduck said. "Will you call them, madame?"

Mrs. Cool's mouth opened, and a gold tooth glittered.

"Well," she said, "if that's what you want, I guess there ain't no real harm in it."

For fifteen minutes Samuel Shadduck spoke to the young ladies of Madame Gabriella Cool's singing school, and some of them wept, and others asked him to put his hand on their heads and bless them. Even the most hardbitten, standing defiantly in the corner with arms folded resolutely over their breasts, came at last to kneel, and one of them crossed herself unashamedly. Finally he was done, and he thanked Mrs. Cool and went to the door with Smoke shambling after him.

"That beats anything I ever seen," Mrs. Cool said admiringly. "I tell you, I've heard some pretty good shouters in my time, but you really set the bush afire! Ain't that right, girls?"

Outside, she still clung to his sleeve.

"You come again, won't you, Mr. Shadduck? Smoke, you take good care of him. Hear me?"

He pulled away from her grasp and walked down the street beside Smoke, wondering if his gift were acceptable to the Lord. He had brought the word of the Lord to whores and sinners, and that was good; in the back of his mind, however, he had a rising discomfort. He had never lost a prisoner, but he suspected that it was vanity—the consuming sin of vanity—that was driving him on in the search for Beau Mannix.

A week later, struggling through the rough country where the Inyah Kara flowed into the Belle Fourche, Shadduck slapped at deer flies, and remained stolid and persistent where a lesser man would have cursed. Ahead of him, the man called Smoke rode a wall-eyed pinto and sang endless verses of a ballad concerning a hapless maiden named Charlotte. After many vicissitudes, Charlotte and a young man named Charles slumbered in one tomb. The mood of the song struck a responsive chord in the detective's breast.

"How much farther?" he asked.

"Now I reckon that's the dozenth time you asked me that today," Smoke said. "And I got to tell you agin, I dunno! I *told* you the cavalry's out after the Sioux and the Cheyennes. You don't expect us to find 'em camped on a mountaintop, sending up smokes to signal us, do you?" He slid down from the paint, and untied the lead rope of the pack-mule from Shadduck's saddle. "We got to sneak up on 'em, careful-like, 'cause they're just as likely to cut our throats as not. Once they see we're friendly, then we can git a line on your friend."

Shadduck got stiffly down and stood spraddle-legged, rubbing at his rump.

"What's to eat?"

Smoke searched in his saddlebags. He drew out a draggled and blood-caked bird, and tossed it to the detective.

"Got two or three of them potridge left. That one's the best of the lot. The rest are beginnin' to smell pretty rich."

Shadduck sat gloomily on a rock and started to pick feathers from the limp body. Smoke had never accounted satisfactorily to him for the supplies he had bought with the detective's money. The horses and the pack-mule could be accounted for, but Shadduck supposed that Smoke would also have purchased things like powder and ball and rope and a canteen and blankets. Instead, they slept fully-clothed with a saddle for a pillow. They had eaten only the small game that Smoke had shot—partridge, rabbits, once a small antelope—and that had been half-raw and without salt. For drink Shadduck had been forced to the occasional creeks they crossed, although Smoke did not approve of creek-water. Instead, he refreshed himself periodically from some hidden source that kept him smelling like a saloon.

"I wish thee had brought along a loaf of bread," Shadduck complained. "Or even flour—we could have mixed up some flap-jacks or something." Angry, he threw the bloody bird from him, and slapped his neck where a gnat had stung. "What has thee got on that pack-mule, anyway?"

Smoke held up an admonishing finger.

"Emergency rations, Mr. Shadduck. We dassen't bust into them till we're in bad trouble. Now you jush—you jush let me handle this outfit. When we ketch up with old Turkey-Leg and his Sans-Arcs, everything's gonna be all right. Turkey-Leg's kind of my brother-in-law." Smoke picked up the dead partridge and waved it at the detective, using it as a pointer to emphasize his logic. "Hell, I got brother-in-laws in the Brules, the Two Kettles, the Oglala, the Sans-Arcs—every damn tribe in the Territory. You don't need to worry about nothin'. We'll find your damned prishoner."

*Turkey-Leg,* the detective thought bitterly. So far they had not come up with a single wandering Sioux band. And now they were searching for an improbable Sans-Arc chief named Turkey-Leg. He had spent his official money, and now his own, and all he had gotten out of it was a fiasco.

"All right," he said. "But we had better find this Turkey-Leg quickly, Smoke. I think thee has taken advantage of me, that is what I think."

They found the Sans-Arcs the next day, their *tipis* pitched in a grassy draw at the foot of a chain of rocky bluffs. It would be more accurate to say that Shadduck found them, because Smoke was roaring drunk and his lament for poor Charlotte caused even the persistent jays to squawk away into flight, protesting. When they rode into the Sans-Arc camp, prodded by the guns and lances of the small party that discovered them floundering through the brush, Smoke fell off his horse and Shadduck had to help him to his feet. But there was no doubt that Smoke was somebody's brother-in-law. The women ran up to him, giggling and fondling him. Turkey-Leg himself, a dignified figure in four-point blanket and a bonnet of crow-feathers, embraced Smoke and led him into the lodge. No one paid any attention to Shadduck.

That night the detective found what was on the pack-mule. Smoke and Turkey-Leg undid the lashings, and carefully placed on the ground the two small kegs of whisky that had sloshed all the way from Deadwood under the cover of the lashed hides. One of them was almost empty.

Shadduck was too angry to speak.

"There ain't nothin' like whisky to make friends with an Indian." Smoke muttered uneasily. He and his red brother each took a keg, and rolled them into the *tipi*. That was the last Shadduck saw of them.

About midnight, driven almost to distraction by the dancing and caterwauling of the Sans-Arcs, Shadduck made up his mind. Outside Turkey-Leg's lodge was a rack of peeled saplings on which long strips of meat were drying. No one bothered him when he stuffed his saddlebags with the meat, and tossed in on top a kind of bladder filled with a compound of mashed berries and fat. He took a hide bag from a pile near the *tipi* and filled it with water from the creek. Then he rode away, and no one stopped him. They were all too busy.

**Item 6.** Watercolor on back of poster advertising "Scenes from the Italian Operas" at Deadwood Theatre and Academy of Music, to be given December 23rd, 1876. Approx. 17" × 34"; shows miner spreadeagled on grass, surrounded by Sioux squaws with knives. Not appropriate for gallery display. Signed B/M.

Lael pulled again at the trigger, panting, and saying under her breath what sounded like curses. Beau climbed shakily out of the wagon and took the gun away from her.

"Not loaded," he said. He felt in his pocket and showed her a handful of metallic cartridges. "See?" He wiped a forearm across his perspiring face. "You would have killed me, though, if you could have." Roughly he took her by the arm, and as his chill passed, he shook her. "Wouldn't you?"

She stared at him sulkily.

"I told you men were all alike! Mealymouth and sweet when they're after something they want. You would have stolen it, all of it, and left me here if you could."

With sudden and surprising strength, she twisted away from him and ran to where a greenback danced in the grass, borne by a little finger of wind. Half-amused, half-angry, he watched her pick up the bills in the wagon, wiping the paint from them with the tail of Gammill's shirt, stacking them into a neat wad, talking all the time under her breath. Finally he joined her, mockingly contrite, and helped with the harvest, aware of her watchful eye.

"There." He handed her the last bill, and she stuffed it into the valise and strapped it shut with a strong tug at the strap. "Now you've got it all again. But I want you to tell me something.

I think I've got a right to ask. Where did that money come from? There must be ten thousand dollars."

They were kneeling side by side in the bed of the ambulance, and he was aware of the soft pressure of her shoulder in the confined space. She tried to pull away from him, but he moved relentlessly against her, and she was trapped.

"Where did it come from?" he insisted.

In the flicker of the lantern he could see the throbbing of a small blue vein in her temple, outlined by the shadow.

"It—it was my husband's money. It's mine, now. It belongs to me. He left it to me."

"A lone woman, on her way to Custer City with a satchel full of cash? That won't wash."

"Anyway, it's true. I haven't done anything wrong. I don't have to lie to you about anything." Her voice was sullen. "I married Mr. Corotis in Denver. He was a Greek gentleman, very nice. He was a friend of my father, and he'd loaned papa money once. I—I—well, he wanted to marry me, and everyone thought it was such a good match, even if he was a lot older than I was." For the first time Beau noticed the gold ring hanging from a cord around her neck. It hung in the deep hollow at her neck, and it shone dully when she took it in her fingers and worked at it as she talked. "He died all of a sudden, and he had a lot of relatives. There was no will, and they tried to take everything away from me in court. They sent a man to give me a summons, but I ran out the back door and went to where I knew the money was hidden. I took it all with me, and I ran away. That's all there is to tell."

She lay against him, her deep breath catching a little as a child's does after a crying spell. In the shirt and trousers, she seemed different, more female than she had been in the high-necked muslin waist and the boiler-plate balmoral skirt. He trembled a little, and she turned her face to him and asked, "Are you cold?"

"No." He shook his head. "I'm not cold."

"The sheriff never actually *served* me the summons," she said. "That's why it wasn't wrong for me to leave Denver the way I did. Isn't that right?"

When he did not speak, she turned her face to him, and asked again, "Isn't that right?"

There was a clean, fresh smell to her, laced with a finer fragrance that must have been her hair. He was aware also, with an artist's eye, that the slant of the lantern-light across her face did peculiar things. Her lower lip, for instance, was full and ripe, like a rich fruit, and her nose was straight and high-bridged. She hurt his cracked ribs, leaning against him, but he did not mind.

"Yes," he said absently. "That's right."

He slipped his arm around her and pulled her to him, feeling the soft crushing of her breasts against him, the warmth of her body through the rough shirt and the jeans. For a moment she lay against him, not moving, and his blood tingled as it rushed through his veins, and his face grew hot and his senses seemed to leave him.

"Lael," he said, "that's absolutely right."

Bemused by her, caught up in a joyous cloud, he was unprepared again for the sudden violence that was a part of Lael Corotis. Her relaxed body stiffened, with a whiplike strength that caught him ludicrously off balance. He fell back, pawing the air, and she caught him on the cheek with a full-armed swing of her flattened palm. The sound echoed in the quietness of the camp like a rifle-shot. By the time he got up on his hands and knees in the littered wagonbed, she was out of the wagon, poking up the fire under the coffeepot, her back to him.

"I wish I *had* shot you," she said over her shoulder.

They did not speak to each other again until they reached Custer City, which they stumbled across the next morning. They came into it from a direction no one ever thought possible, because of the Indian menace.

After putting up the mules and the wagon at the livery stable, he saw that she was registered at the hotel across the street. He carried her bags upstairs to her room, but she preferred to carry the shabby black valise herself.

"You're the only woman registered here," he said.

She looked out at the dusty street below, milling with teams and wagons, loud with the stamp of hooves and the clink of harness. A volley of curses drifted up to them, and someone fired a gun, not too far away, but the sound seemed to pass unnoticed in the hubbub and confusion.

"I'm not afraid," she said.

"What do you propose to do here?"

She sat on the edge of a rocker and regarded the tips of her shoes. The sole of one, Beau noticed, had come unstitched all the way round. Her torn skirt and soiled blouse had occasioned lifted eyebrows at the desk below, but the large bill she thrust at the clerk had soothed him remarkably.

"There's always some sort of a business to get in. My husband was a very good business man. He used to give me all sorts of advice. A laundry might be a good thing for this town. Everyone looks dirty enough to need one. Or a restaurant, perhaps. I'm a good cook. But there's money to be made here, and I intend to profit."

In spite of her weathered appearance, there was authority to her words. Whenever she talked about money, she knew her business. And while he was thinking about money, she peeled a bill from a roll in her purse and handed it to him.

"I promised you fifty dollars if you'd take me to Custer City."

He shook his head.

"Keep it. I've got a stake of my own put away in my boot."

She tried to put it in his pocket, saying, "I always pay for what I get," but he pushed her hand away, smiling.

"I'm a gambler. I told you that. All I need is a little stake, and in the time it takes to wink, I'll run it up till I can match dollars with even you, maybe. I've got that stake, and these local sports are ready for a killing."

She frowned, two tiny unaccustomed lines furrowing her forehead.

"You'd better watch out. I heard this was a pretty tough town. Someone might hurt you."

Rummaging in his pocket, he brought out a tiny oval of soft wood, painstakingly carved around the edge to suggest a gilded frame. On it was painted the face of Lael Corotis, the sharp dark-lashed eyes, the firm mouth, the high-piled golden hair and the tortoise combs. She caught her breath in an unbelieving gasp, and took the miniature in a hand that was not quite steady.

"It's—it's me! You painted *me!*"

Pleased, he nodded.

"But—I didn't know you were such an artist!"

"A sort of jackleg artist," he shrugged. "I just dabble around." He wanted to tell her how hard he had worked on it, how he had worn blisters on his fingers at the carving, and the way he had painted by lantern-light, long after she had gone to bed in the wagon, and he had worked red-eyed and squinting, somehow driven on by the soft regular sound of her breathing. But he did not. He was afraid she might insist on paying him for it.

She touched it gently with her finger, feeling the texture of the paint, and then kissed it with a quick fierce motion, pressing it to her lips and staring at him with her dark-lashed eyes.

"I'll keep it always, and I'll think of you."

Usually glib, he was now tongue-tied, and he stood awkwardly in the doorway, first on one foot and then the other. Finally, with relief, he thought of the wagon, and said, "I put up the mules and the wagon across the street. You can sell them for a good figure."

She dropped the wooden oval into her bosom, and patted it with a satisfied gesture.

"They're not mine. They belonged to Gammill."

"Gammill's dead."

"Don't you want them?"

He chuckled.

"Lady, they got me here, and that's all I wanted. Mules and wagons don't interest me. What I need is a good solid stud game, and that's what I'm going to look for, right now." He looked down at his shabby jeans and the buffalo coat hanging over his arm. "Maybe I'll get spruced up a bit first, though." He winked at her, a solemn and prodigious wink, and pulled the door shut after him. He was on the landing below when she threw the door open, and called down to him, "You be careful, Beau. Please." He looked up, surprised, but she had closed the door and the hallway was dark and still.

At the barber's, he found fifty dollars in his pocket, where she had somehow slipped it. On the strength of that, he had a singe and a liberal application of pomade, and after a bath in a tin tub, and fresh linen, he felt revived and confident. Pushing his way through the crowded streets, ankle-deep in dust, he drank in the sights with the hunger of the city man long absent from civilization. This was not exactly San Francisco, of course; it was a raw new town, aching with growing pains, expanding in all directions in a rash of green-lumber buildings, supplemented by tents and lean-tos. Patrick and Saulsbury's Black Hills Stage Line almost ran him down as he hurried across the street, and when he dodged for shelter under the overhang of the Miner's Provision and Supply Company, he was immediately driven forth by the violence of a fracas between two teamsters that had broken out over a place at the hitching post. A lugubrious man in a plug hat droned the advantages of Eell's Electric Elixir to an open-mouthed crowd, and on another corner a small man with a face like a ferret exhibited the mummified remains of what he claimed to be a former Egyptian princess. Custer City teemed with a raw vigor that excited Beau Mannix, and started him thinking about oils and canvas, wanting to catch this color and clamor at its height.

The Dakota House took his eye as several cuts above the run of the mill gambling establishments, and better entitled to his class of game. With thirty dollars in silver clanking in his pockets, and the emergency hundred in the sole of his boot, he figured to cut himself a small niche in the economy of Custer City, a niche that could be judiciously broadened and enlarged by the play of the cards. He pushed open the swinging doors and looked in.

This was a class establishment, that much was apparent. No raucous shouts, or noisy drunks; the best of order prevailed, with only the hum of conversation and the click of chips. The place was dim (that was an advantage) lit at midday only by the smoky rays of a few hanging lamps. Faro, roulette, *chusas*, blackjack, draw, stud; there was a game and a place at a table for everybody. The calls of the banker were polite and well-modulated. "Make your little bets, gents. Make your little bets. The game's made, the ball's arollin'."

When his eyes became accustomed to the dim light, he could see the shoulder-tabs of army officers, and an occasional stiff collar, along with the wink of a diamond stickpin. Good cigars, too, and whenever the pace of the gambling seemed too slow for a moment, the bartender tapped the bell hanging over his polished counter and "drinks all round" were on the house.

Knowing the Army to be inveterate gamblers, not too businesslike in their approach, Beau slid into a vacant chair with a group of them, murmuring politely and sliding twenty-five dollars across the green baize.

"Name's Gammill," he said, taking the first name that came to him. He took the small pile of blue chips the dealer slid to him, and smiled deprecatingly. "I like a good stud game, gentlemen. This looked to me like a good one. I've been watching you play, and I must say you're real card players, all of you."

A fat lieutenant, with a wen on his neck that propped his head at a stiff unnatural angle, gazed at him with interest.

"You from around here?"

"Chicago," Beau said. "I'm in the sign business."

Nodding thoughtfully, the lieutenant rolled a dead cigar around his mouth, and then went back to his cards. "This king is the best card out," he said. "I'll bet a dollar on a king, everytime."

In half an hour, Beau had won forty-six dollars. There had been no need to cheat; the soldiers, bored with long frontier duty and anxious to spend the dollars the paymaster had accumulated for them while they were chasing Indians, were easy prey. They bet into pat hands, they took desperate chances to fill impossible straights, and they bet sometimes out of sheer gregariousness, not wanting to sit out a hand simply because they drew bad cards.

"That was poor luck," Beau said insincerely to a long-faced captain with the bugle of the infantry on his collar, and a number four within the bugle. "You played it real well, though, captain. I hate to take money from the Fourth Infantry. When I came through with my wagon, I was mighty glad to see the Fourth Infantry outposts all along the road. Might have had my hair lifted if it wasn't for them."

The captain wiped beer from his mustaches, watching Beau's long fingers as they flicked cards around the table.

"Red bastards," he said. "I'm glad they finally decided to let us smash 'em for once and for all."

"Oh? I hadn't heard."

" 'Tain't no secret," the lieutenant with the wen said. "What in hell you think Custer was doing, snooping around the Black Hills?"

"I don't know. Wasn't it a geological expedition of some kind?"

They all laughed knowingly, slapping their thighs and poking each other. "A geological expedition! Ain't that a good word for it now? A geological expedition!"

Beau turned his attention to his hole card, which was providentially an ace.

"Is there going to be trouble?"

The lieutenant snorted.

"The Black Hills Commission is sending Louie Richaud out to palaver with Crazy Horse and Sitting Bull. If they come in to Red Cloud nice and peaceable to talk, why, there won't be no trouble. But they won't come. So we go out and get 'em. So it's a war, and about time, too!"

It had not taken spectacles for a man to see that Custer City swarmed with the Fourth Infantry. There was more infantry in Custer City than were needed to police the roads.

"I'll bet fifty cents," Beau said. He smiled winningly around the table. "Just to be sociable."

In another half-hour, he had won a total of a hundred and eighty-six dollars. There was a tendency toward sullenness on the part of some of the players, and a piercing scrutiny of Beau's manner of handling the cards. Sensitive always to these signs, he signalled the bartender.

"Drinks all round for my friends! Doubles all the way round, and brandy for me."

The bartender, a small round man with a gold-mounted grizzly tooth hanging from his watch-chain, shuffled through the sawdust with a tray of glasses. He and the army were old friends.

"For thee, cap," he chuckled, setting down a slopping beer. "And for thee, Lieutenant Potter." He emptied the tray, and then set a big snifter of brandy before Beau Mannix. "And for thee, sir. The best French brandy in the house. Come all the way from Paris, France, around the Horn and up to Frisco and back out to Dakota, just for thee's pleasure."

Beau had stiffened. He took a bill from the pile before him and stretched it between his fingers.

"Thee is a Quaker?" he asked.

They roared at this sally, digging each other in the ribs and guffawing.

"Hell, he's a Bush Baptist!" someone snickered. "Ain't you, Henry? Ain't you a Bush Baptist?"

"Chaplain of the Bush Baptists," the bartender said with mock gravity. "I solve all your problems, gents. No, sir, I ain't no Quaker. It's just a little joke between the boys and me. There was this queer gent in the fur cap come to town yesterday. Real polite, he was. Looking for a friend named Mannix. It just got to be a joke with me and the boys to sort of josh him. We just give him a thee back for every one he give us." He turned to the mournful captain. "You ain't seen him lately, have you, cap?"

The captain took a long pull of his beer, and wiped a hand across his mustaches.

"No," he said, "I ain't. And I hope I never do. Handbills! Him and his damned handbills! One posted in every tent in the damned encampment. A thousand dollars reward! He even went to Colonel Harkins and got permission to post one on the adjutant's bulletin board at Headquarters! I guess there ain't a man in the Fourth Infantry but what's lookin' for that damned Manning, or Stanwix, or whatever in hell his name was!"

Beau handed the bill to the bartender, aware his hand was trembling. But no one noticed.

"Buy yourself a cigar with what's left," he said. Leaving his brandy untouched, he started to stack his chips into neat piles.

"Hey, now!" the lieutenant said in alarm. "You ain't going to leave? There's a good feller—" He patted Beau's arm. "You just sit tight and give us a chance to win back a little of that."

Beau shook his head.

"I've got to attend to some business in town. Something important."

There was general silence. The mournful captain stroked his mustache, and the lieutenant blew his nose and looked stern. Finally he asked, "What's the matter with the army, mister? You got something against the army? After all, here we are out on this goddam lonesome frontier, stayin' between you civilians and the murderin' red heathen. Ain't we done enough for you? You should be a little more sociable." He turned to the others. "Ain't that right, fellers?"

It was fast becoming an issue. Beau could not gracefully leave. Any moment one of them might remember the description on a handbill, and to leave now would surely excite suspicion. No, he had to play out his string.

"All right," he said grudgingly. "I am to be in town quite a while, anyway. Guess my business can wait a while longer."

There was a chorus of approbation.

"I knew you was the right sort."

"There's a man appreciates the Army, I say."

"That's a dead game sport, mister!"

He dealt the cards, and looked in the hole. Another ace. This would never do. He drank the brandy at one gulp, and only called the bet when the lieutenant with the wen shoved five dollars across the table, beaming cheerfully.

"It's just a king, gents," the lieutenant said modestly. "Stay with me for the ride. You can't win without you stick along."

During the next hour, Beau tried to lose money by every stratagem he could think of, but the chips piled higher and higher.

He bought drinks all round half a dozen times, hoping he could get the Army under the table but they stayed doggedly with him, betting into impossible situations, losing their money with dreary persistence. If he had a pair of kings against a pair of aces, the third king would invariably join his other two, leaving the Army crestfallen but game for "one more hand." If he palmed an embarrassing ace, the drunken dealer would give him two more, and he would win that pot also. Finally, in desperation, he stood up.

"Gents, I got to go take care of that business in town. But I'll tell you what I'm going to do." He held up a hand to still the protests. "Now the Army must have some kind of a welfare fund, isn't that right? Some kind of a pot for widows and orphans, or for extra rations, or maybe a little party once a month? Why, of course. I thought so." He shoved his chips across the table to the dealer. "Well, then—here's my contribution. I guess I appreciate the Army as much as the next man."

There was much drunken sentiment expressed. The mournful captain broke down and cried, pillowing his head on his arms. The lieutenant with the wen got unsteadily to his feet and proposed a toast to the Army's benefactor.

"Whash the name? Whash your name, mister?"

Beau bowed.

"Just say 'from an unknown Friend.' "

He left to the accompaniment of three rousing cheers and a tiger. Someone was trying to get the Fourth Infantry captain to his feet, but he kept bending in the middle and collapsing again.

Outside, Beau paused in the shade of the overhanging roof of the Dakota House, feeling sweat break out over his body in stinging small prickles. Who would ever have thought it! That damned Shadduck! That shabby persistent little man! Anyone else would have been satisfied to let Beau Mannix perish in a blizzard and call it quits. But not Shadduck.

He was not frightened, although that had been a close call in the Dakota House. Even the Army, the Army that covered this land like a plague of locusts, was looking for him. Shadduck had turned every man's hand against him. Still he was not frightened; he was rather annoyed, and irritated at the unreasonableness of it all. A gray neutral-looking dog crossed his vexed path, and he kicked at it. This was a thing he did not normally do, and it was a measure of his exasperation.

Rounding a corner, he came suddenly on a poster stuck wetly to a board fence. "WANTED", it said, in staggering black heads. There was a badly drawn likeness of his face, and much detailed data as to his height, weight, and the fact that he was dangerous, and that all persons should communicate with the nearest outpost of law and order if they should see him. Swearing under his breath, he looked around him. When he was not observed, he tore it down and wadded it into a damp ball, tossing it into the street. Shadduck might at least have troubled to get a decent likeness!

"I've never lost a man yet," he muttered under his breath, remembering Shadduck's words. It had not been a boast; it was simply a statement of fact, made quietly and without vanity. He had underestimated Samuel Shadduck.

"Hey?" someone said in his ear. A teamster pulled him by the elbow and grinned. "You talkin' to me, mister?"

Hardly aware he had spoken the words aloud, Beau shook his head and hurried away. In his haste, he almost ran headlong into Sam Shadduck.

The detective stood before a telegraph pole in the main street. Unhurried and methodical, he plastered a fresh poster to the pole, and stepped back, looking at it. Absorbed in his work, a limp pile of freshly-printed sheets over one arm, he moved forward again, smoothing out a wrinkle in the sheet, and wiping paste from his fingers on the seat of his trousers. A crowd of spectators stood at a respectful distance, and as he moved up the street, they followed him, laughing and joking.

Beau shrank into a narrow alleyway between two buildings, his heart beating heavily, like a bell tolling. A kind of sour taste rose into his throat and seemed to throttle him. He swallowed hard, and put out a hand against the wall to steady himself. Here, in Custer City! Reaching unsteadily into his pocket, he took out the dog-eared deck of cards that was always there, looking at it with a kind of horror. This was his way of earning a living, and now it was denied him. What would he do? Where would he go? He had to get out of Custer City, that much was certain. Not only Custer City, but other cities. Shadduck would be looking for Beau Mannix in whatever place called itself a city, or a town, or a settlement. Where would he go? Where was left to go? He tried to calm down, to think of a solution. Muttering to himself and grimacing, he peeked around the corner of the building, relieved to see the little parade was now far up the street. He had to *plan,* that was it! But he had always disliked being forced to plan.

There was only one solution. He had thought of it, he now realized, in a fleeting way without really knowing he was thinking of it. It was too fantastic to bear examination. But it was still the only solution. Shadduck would seek him in the towns and settlements and cities. Well, then, he would avoid those places. He would avoid them all! Gammill's old wagon would be his deliverance. The shabby ambulance was equipped with everything—everything for him to avoid civilization and live off the country. It was dangerous, of course, with the Indian trouble brewing and the Army spoiling for a pitched battle with Gall and Crazy Horse and the rest of the high-handed Sioux. But it was not as dangerous as staying here in Custer City with Sam Shadduck on the prowl.

He would live off the country. Trading, perhaps, with the Indians. He knew a little Sioux talk, much more of the sign language. He would get along somehow. And the paints that were in the wagon; his panic vanished in excitement at the colors that were out there. The sky and the land, the clouds, pools of water after a rain. The breathtaking blue flick of a jay's wing, the red flood of sunset, the deep patient browns and reds and greens in the earth and the rocks. He thought, too, of the shine of rain on a wet red face, the way the sun glinted on a string of ochre beads, the slant of an eagle-feather in black braids. In his pocket was the shell gorget that Roach-Head had given him once, so long ago. He carried it still as a kind of lucky-piece. Thinking back, he found himself recalling the Sioux almost as friends, although he had fought with them and killed one with a broken lance-blade. It was foolish, he knew it, but something out there drew him, beckoning with a weird fascination. He could not pause to examine it; there was not time. The only thing he knew was that Gammill's wagon, the chariot of Emperor Gammill, monarch of all sign-painters, made his whole life come suddenly into sharp focus and take on a direction and meaning it had never known. He went toward the livery-stable at almost a run.

Lael Corotis, however, was not cooperative. She sat demurely in the rocker, listening to his pleading.

"Why, of course you can't have it," she said. "I'm glad that livery-stable man knew his business and didn't let you take it. You said you didn't want it—remember? Now I've already made a very good profit on it. A miner wanted it, a man named Albright. He said it was just the thing. He's given me fifty dollars on account for the wagon and the mules, and he's coming back this evening with another hundred."

"Listen to me," he said. "I need that wagon. I'll give you two hundred."

She rocked a little faster.

"No. I can't. This is business. I can't go back on my word the very first thing I do in this town."

"Two hundred and fifty," he said. Then he bit his lip. "No, I can't. I haven't got that much. But I'll give you every cent I've got."

She looked at him with troubled eyes.

"Are— I mean, is someone after you?"

He took a deep breath. "Yes."

"Then we must get out of here." Taking a scrap of paper from the bureau, she scribbled rapidly with a pen. "Here. Sign this."

He looked at it, not understanding.

"Sign what?"

In sudden impatience, she almost hissed at him.

"Here! Where I drew this line. It's just a note, payable to me. You'll need all your money. I'll take a note for the wagon."

He put his hands to his head in a gesture of hopelessness, and began to laugh.

"What's so funny?"

"You. You and your note. If you really want me to sign it, I will. But it's so damned comical." He took the pen from her fingers and slashed his scrawl across the paper. "All right. You've got your pound of flesh."

She stamped her foot.

"It's not a pound of flesh. It's a very good bargain, and you know it. Just—just because we know each other—"

Smiling, he advanced on her, and she drew back in alarm.

"You remember that night I tried to kiss you?" he asked. "The night your money got loose and blew all over the camp? Well, I know why you slapped me. You had to. It was something you had to do. But now I'm going to do it again. I'm going to kiss you, Lael Corotis or whatever your name is, with your notes payable and a valise full of greenbacks. You've got the wrong ideas in your head but I like you well enough to try to educate you." He took another step forward, seeing the color leave her face and then flood back in a tide of pink. "Only this time you won't slap me. There's no need for you to, now. You've got all the chips, and I'm a busted gambler on the run."

Trembling, she stood her ground.

"Stop! Don't Beau. It's—it's not right."

"A hell of a lot I care what's right," he said. "Where I'm going, there isn't any right and any wrong."

He pulled her to him, and pressed his lips tightly against hers. For a moment she struggled but finally she did not fight him any longer. Instead, she lay in his arms, and her fingers groped along his cheek and into his uncut dark hair.

"Will you come back?" she asked, her voice muffled against his cheek. "You'll—you'll let me know where you are?"

He released her, but she stood close to him, looking up with those incredibly dark-lashed eyes. They were half-closed, as if she were in a kind of daze.

"Will you send me word where you are, Beau?"

In sudden passion, he pushed her away from him and flung the door open. This was a hell of a time for something like this to happen to him! In two long strides he was on the landing below, but she screamed after him, "Beau!" and he stopped, looking back.

"All right," he said. "You'll hear from me."

That night he left Custer City in Gammill's old wagon. The road went straight and true to Deadwood, sixty miles north, but as soon as he was clear of the town, he would turn the mules off the road and point their ears west. That was where he was going. West! His pulse quickened.

Item 7.  Canvas in oils, 12 × 18 inches, condition fair with exception of small diagonal tear in lower left-hand corner. Shows mounted patrol of Seventh Cavalry fording shallow stream. Particularly good in dappling of light through trees, and feeling of tension though no enemy is shown. No signature, but it is certain this is Mannix's work, and one of his best.

Once clear of Custer City, Beau pulled up the mules under a grove of cottonwoods and rummaged through the wagon by the light of the lantern. He had left too hurriedly to do little but throw a sack of grain and another of flour in the wagon, fill the water-butt that hung on the side, and buy a box of cartridges for the Sharps. The moon was rising—low and yellow in the east—and he was grateful for the concealment of the cottonwoods. Sixty miles north, all the way to Deadwood, the road wound in the moonlight. Even at this time of night provision trains for the Army passed, and men on horseback, bound for the better diggings up north, and an occasional herd of cattle, beef for the tables of the newer metropolis. The Fourth Infantry patrolled the entire length of the road, keeping an eye on the traffic from rock and timber dugouts, and mounted cavalrymen trotted in pairs, occasionally galloping off the road to a high point, the better to scan the country for Sioux or Cheyennes. Even now, Beau thought, Samuel Shadduck might be within a mile or two of him, riding in one of the wagons or cantering nearer on a rented horse, eyes searching the night for the prisoner he had never lost. Quickening his inventory of the wagon's contents, Beau nodded with satisfaction. Everything was in its place and well-stowed. No one had bothered Gammill's wagon in the livery-stable.

Putting a boot over the tailgate and searching for the earth, he almost stepped on a small warm body that whimpered, panted, and then dashed back and forth in excited rallies. It was the gray nondescript dog that had followed him in the streets of Custer City, and it was still following him. He had kicked at it then, savagely, but it was a wise small dog and he had missed. Now here it was again, standing uncertainly in the moonlight, a small shadowy lump of hope.

"Here," he called. He snapped his fingers. "Come here, boy!"

The dog sidled closer, pleased but suspicious.

"Come on," Beau urged. "Here, boy!"

There was a homelessness about them both that was a bond. The dog came closer, and nuzzled his hand.

"Sam!" Beau said. "That's it!" He could see Samuel Shadduck in the small indomitable dog, shabby and persistent. There could be no better name for such a dog. "Sam!" he said, delightedly. "Boy, that's your name. Do you hear me?"

Sharing his delight, the dog leaped up on him and painted his face with a wet pink tongue. Laughing, Beau put the dog under his arm and carried him to the wagon-seat, where he put him down and explained the rules.

"No barking," he said. "You eat once a day, when I do. All members of the company share and share alike. Is it a go?"

When he turned the wagon off the road to the west, and heard the sounds of wagons and hoofs and teamsters' shouts fade behind him, he did not feel particularly lonely. He had a friend on the seat beside him, a small friend sitting bolt upright, nose sniffing the night wind and tail wagging furiously whenever Beau's voice sounded.

"You and me," Beau said, "we're on our way, Sam."

By morning, they were in another world. There might as well never have been cities, and horsecars, and newspapers and gas lights. The immensity of the country rolled around them as they went, flowing smoothly and silently into place after them like a gigantic grassy ocean, obliterating the past, hiding the future, making of the wagon a tiny island in a sea of light, a fresh pure light that made every feature of the scene stand out with lambent clarity. There was no light like this in San Francisco, certainly none in Chicago. As a matter of fact, it was suddenly hard for Beau even to remember San Francisco. The name was odd and foreign on his tongue, and he said it several times, looking puzzled at Sam, and then laughed, his whole lean body racked with mirth. The country made him drunk. There was never a land like this before. A painter could go crazy, he decided, trying to catch this land on his canvas. There were not the colors to paint it on any man's palette.

And yet it might have been laid out by a landscape artist, Beau thought. There were peaks of granite, flanks dark with fir and pines. The foothills were velvet with pasturage, and the mules grazed hungrily, wrenching at the juicy grass with their stained yellow teeth. Narrow valleys cut into the low hills, and along the bottoms coursed cold clear creeks, almost hidden in the thickets of live oak, willow, wild rose and plum. On the higher elevations were heavy stands of juniper and hemlock, birch and whitewood, and in their cover flitted deer and smaller animals, watching him with what seemed not fear, but merely curiosity. In this simple and grandly composed scene, Beau felt the elements of what the Indians called *Wakan*. A mystery—a kind of brooding majesty; the old Sioux gods were still there, watching and waiting in the high-piled towering clouds, in the sweep of the wind, in the dry hot sunlight. *Wakan Tanka,* he thought; the Great Mystery. Perhaps a Sioux was not at heart so different from a Presbyterian, or an Episcopalian. The difference was mostly in detail. He shook his head, amused at this odd tendency to rationalize the Indian, to see him perversely as a man and a creature of God when everyone else in the Dakota Territory knew Indians

as murdering, thieving lice. Even the children must be extermi-
nated, people in Deadwood explained, because "nits made lice."
And yet, Beau Mannix sought these people. He did not quite
know why. Perhaps they simply peopled the only space left to
him with Samuel Shadduck in pursuit.

The big Sharps brought down a deer for their dinner, a fat
and trusting doe that ventured too near the wagon. It was not
until Beau had pulled the trigger, and the heavy slap-like report
echoed around like diminishing drums, that he realized he had
unknowingly slipped into a Sioux mannerism himself. For weeks
on the trail with Pock-Mark and his captors, he had observed the
little ceremony which preceded the killing of meat; the mumbled
litany that seemed to be at once a kind of a prayer, and an apol-
ogy to the animal for the necessity to be eaten. Along with it went
an odd gesture; the first two fingers held near the forehead and
suddenly thrust up and out in a spiral. That, he knew, had something to do with *Wakan Tanka,* although he did not quite know
what. Now, aware that his fingers had described the same motion
before he pulled the trigger, he looked down at his hand as if it
were suddenly strange to him. He got the doe over his shoulders
and staggered back to the wagon with it, feeling a bewilderment.

Some of the meat he cut in thin strips to dry on the canvas
top of the ambulance, and he and Sam gorged on ribs and liver
and fat steaks, sliced from the haunch. Sam ate his share raw, but
Beau's was hardly better, barely scorched over the small fire he
kindled from buffalo chips. He was too hungry to wait for it to
be properly done.

While he waited for coffee to boil in Gammill's old tin
pot, he dragged the broken harmonium out of the wagon and
experimented with it. Like most men who are adept with their
hands, he could play a little on the piano and a few other instru-
ments. But the small harmonium gave out no sound but a tone-
less wheeze, no matter how hard he pumped the pedals. Taking
off the scarred and splintered back, he found a rent in a bellows

within, and patched it with a piece of leather and some glue from the many pots within the wagon. He did not quite know why a repaired harmonium should be of more value to a man fleeing for his life than one which only wheezed, but the work with his hands made him forget Shadduck for the moment. When he wrestled the harmonium back into the wagon, he was whistling.

For days the wagon bore west. They met no one, they saw no sign of life or habitation, but there was always the feeling of an accompanying presence, of eyes that watched from cover. It was foolish, of course; it was nerves, mostly. Or so he thought until he came to the ring of buffalo skulls.

The business of the buffalo skulls was something he remembered from his months of captivity. The Sioux were a curious mixture of superstition and practicality. Many times he had seen them seek out the sunbleached eyeless skulls in the vicinity of their night camp, and arrange them into a ceremonial ring. Before meat, before drink, before sleep, the Sioux searched out the skulls left from old hunts and brought them to the camp by armloads. Carefully, reverently, they placed them on the ground, each facing the direction of the morning sun. Only then, after muttered prayers, did they squat around the small fire and eat and drink. And here, where Beau now camped for this night, was such a ring of skulls, near a place where the grass was beaten down as if by many animals.

He picked up one of the skulls and held it in his hand. The grass under it was still fresh and green, and sprang up when he lifted the skull. Sam growled deep in his throat, and sniffed at the nearest skull. Holding the wide-horned head in his hand, Beau walked a few paces away, searching in the grass. The afternoon sun slanted low in his face and he held a hand before his eyes, shading them. It did not take long to find what he was looking for. Many small whitish patches were in the deep grass, places where the skulls had lain, bleaching. It had not been long since someone had picked up those skulls and arranged them in the ceremonial circle.

He found several places, too, where fires had been, but the ashes were cold and told him little. A large party, certainly, moving westerly, ahead of him, not more than a few days ago. He tossed the skull away and wiped his hands on his thighs, feeling a prickle of fear. He was looking for them, but the way he approached was important. It would not do to stumble on them, nor could he afford to be ambuscaded or bushwacked.

"Sam!" he called, grateful for the presence of another living thing. "Come here, boy."

The dog came unwillingly, preoccupied with the scent of danger. For a moment he allowed his grizzled coat to be scratched; then he pulled away from Beau's hand and stalked around the wagon, looking always outward, away, toward the direction of danger. That night they made no fire. Instead, Beau pulled the wagon into a copse of trees and made his bed on a high rock overlooking the grove. All night long the white wagon-sheet glimmered faintly in the moon.

In the morning, stiff, sore, and drowsy, he climbed down, ate a fried flour biscuit from a sack he had prepared the day before, and turned the wagon west again. He had not solved the dilemma of approaching the Sioux, but he knew also that he had not much time to plan. He was deep and ever deeper into Sioux land, and it was a miracle he had not yet been attacked. He could, of course, turn south toward Fort Fetterman, but that was no solution. News traveled fast in the Army. If Shadduck made inquiries of them, it would not take him long to find out that a man answering Beau's description had come into Fetterman with an outlandish painted wagon. No, he was committed now. This was the only way out for him.

On the banks of the Belle Fourche, over a hundred miles from Custer City, his dilemma was solved. He had, it was true, an active part in the solving of it, but the opportunity was thrust into his hands by the luck he always believed in. Fording the sluggish stream, the heavily-laden ambulance slipped into a mud hole. Try as they would, the mules could not pull the wagon free of the hole. Beau urged them at first, hauling on the harness himself till he was waist-deep in the sucking mud and in danger of going under. Then he tried the whip, and the spattered mules, panting and blowing, did no better. Finally, almost in desperation, he let them stand, blowing and heaving, and went along the banks of the river to search for a fallen log to serve as a sort of pry.

Finding a dead cottonwood that might serve the purpose, he was dragging it after him toward the stranded wagon when he saw a sight that made his heart stop for a moment, lurch, and then resume its beat quickly and furiously. Only yards away from him, examining the trapped wagon with a kind of indolent interest, was a Sioux. The Indian was a gangling man in a gray flannel shirt and breech-clout, and on his head was an old black Army hat with the top cut out and the sides bound around with feathers, fur, bits of scarlet cloth, and verdigris-green brass buttons. In one big knotted hand he held a breech-loading rifle of large caliber, and in the other were the reins of a spavined paint pony with a top-knot cut like bangs to fall over a pair of wall-eyes.

Foolishly, Beau had left the Sharps in the wagon. While he was pondering how to get at it, the strange Sioux turned at the rustle of a leaf and stared at him, long and hard. Beau dropped the cottonwood, discovered. But the Sioux did not throw up the breechloader and fire, as Beau expected. Instead, he went on with his scrutiny of the wagon's contents, murmuring to himself in a quiet happy monotone. He fondled a broken clock, he pushed experimentally at the keys of the harmonium, he ground the handle of the corn-sheller, murmuring all the time in his soft voice. Finally, he selected a feather from a lady's ancient bonnet and stuck it in his hat. Only then did he wade back to shore, leading the walleyed pony, and put out his hand to be shaken in a whiteman's gesture that he seemed to have learned by rote, not quite understanding it, but happy to do so if it pleased.

"Glad to meet you," Beau said. In the few words of Sioux he knew, he asked, "What is your name?"

The man pursed his lips, thinking. With what appeared to be an extreme effort, he finally made the sign for *heart* and for *no*. It mean that he did not remember, or was not sure, or perhaps he simply did not want to tell. But suddenly his lined foolish face broke into a grin, and he slapped Beau on the shoulder and made a sudden obscene gesture.

"That's it?" Beau asked in English, startled. "Goosey?"

Goosey nodded vigorously.

"I—know—white—talk," he chanted. "Goosey." Again he slapped Beau on the back, grinning and gesturing. He clenched a fist and rotated it in midair, looking intently at Beau. It was the sign for *coffee*. It did not take any student of language to see the coffee-grinder churning.

Beau nodded.

"Sure. I got coffee." He pointed to the wagon, and to Goosey's pony and the rawhide rope coiled on the saddle-pad. "You help me get wagon out. *Then* coffee." He remembered the Sioux word they used for their horses; *shonk-a-wakan*. He said it aloud, and pointed at the pony and the rope again. "Pull wagon. Over there. Out."

Goosey nodded hard, and uncoiled the rope. While he knotted it around the axle, Beau climbed up on the seat and unlimbered the whip.

"Hoo!" he yelled. "Hoo—*hah!*"

Lunging into the harness, the fat thighs of the mules drove hard. Goosey's rawhide rope stretched like a fiddle-string, and he added his own piercing bawls and shouts to the din. Lurching, swaying, the ambulance heaved out of the hole in one tremendous surge, and in a moment they were on the far bank, grinning at each other in triumph. Goosey cranked his hand in midair again, coiling up the rope.

"You're damned right," Beau said. "That calls for a drink."

The man was an obvious simpleton, not at all dangerous. Beau squatted on his heels across the fire from Goosey, sipping coffee, noting the man's huge nose, the receding chin, the foolish good-natured stare. But with all this, there was a kind of native shrewdness that lay back of it.

"Are there Sioux around?" Beau asked. He made the sign for *where* and then the sign for Sioux. It was a particularly rich gesture, one that pleased him. The Sioux must have had a reputation for cutting throats, or cutting off heads, because the sign was simple and expressive; the index finger drawn sharply across the throat.

Goosey stared at him with sudden guile. Then he laughed, a good-natured chuckle, and shrugged. He asked for tobacco, still chuckling, and Beau brought out an old pipe of Gammill's and a pouch of powder-dry Lone Jack. But before he handed it to Goosey, he asked again, "Where are the Sioux?" He made the sign for *big* or *many,* and waited, the pipe and tobacco held behind him.

Wrapping his long arms around his knees, Goosey turned sullen. He grunted, and made a vicious gesture with thumb stuck out between index and second fingers. There was no mistaking *that* sign. It meant *go to hell,* if not something much worse. But Beau went on wheedling and cajoling, and finally Goosey gave in.

"Two-three day's journey," his signs said. "That way. West. Many camps. Women and children. Big camps." He took the pipe and stuffed tobacco into it. Snatching a coal from the fire between his fingers, he lit the pipe and settled back, puffing.

This was fascinating to Beau, this talking with the fingers. Occasionally there was a sign that was unknown to him, but when he looked puzzled, Goosey always managed to use another and more recognizable gesture. When the Sioux told about women in camp, the sign was unmistakable—both hands drawn down from the top of the head toward the ears. Long hair, that was, worn combed like a woman's. *Many warriors, many women and children, many guns and horses.*

"Wait," Beau signed.

He went to the wagon and found the shell breastplate that Roach-Head had given him. Even after the months of being put away, wrapped in an old rag, the oddly-shaped shells glowed with an iridescent light. When he held it up for Goosey to see, the pipe dropped from Goosey's loose-lipped mouth and spilled burning tobacco down his shirt-front and burned holes in it.

"You know this?" Beau asked.

"Gottam!" Goosey said, looking at the burned holes in his shirt. "Gottam! Gottam!" He did not meet Beau's eyes. It was evident that the shell gorget had upset him.

"A friend gave me this," Beau said. "A brave young man who was killed."

Goosey rolled his eyes and said nothing. He picked up the spilled pipe and lit what tobacco was left in the bowl. Sucking hard on the stem, he scowled and fidgeted, ill at ease.

"All right," Beau said. He put the breastplate away, wrapping it carefully in the scrap of gingham, and slipped it into his pocket. Maybe there was something *wakan* about it. "Who is the chief?"

Goosey pulled hard at the pipe, brow furrowed.

"What is the chief called?"

"Many chiefs. Not one man. Many."

Beau shook his head, exasperated. A plan was beginning to form in his mind, but Goosey was not of much help.

"Chief," he repeated. "Great Chief. Who?"

Anxious to be helpful, Goosey screwed his eyes shut as if lost in thought. He rattled off a string of names, jabbing the air with the pipe each time. Sometimes he made sign, so that Beau caught many of them. *Yellow Fox. Kills in Winter. Fast Horse. Scraper.*

"These men, all great chiefs?"

Goosey nodded vigorously. With a sweep of his hand, he said, "All."

Beau went to the wagon. He took out the corn-sheller, three broken clocks, an old box filled with ladies' shoes, a sack of sugar. He indicated the harmonium, and the rest of the junk that filled the back of the wagon.

"All this is a present to the great chief of the Sioux who has many warriors and many horses."

"All?" Goosey's jaw sagged

"All."

The Sioux put his hand over his mouth at the untold wealth that was a present for one man.

"Who?" Beau prodded.

Goosey rubbed his long jaw.

"Why do you go to these people? They will kill you."

"Do you know them?"

Goosey nodded. "They are my people." He crossed his bony wrists and pressed them to his heart. "My people."

"Do they kill a man who brings them gifts?"

Goosey was uncertain. "Maybe."

"You tell them I am their friend. I will live with them. I will hunt with them. I will eat with them. I am their friend."

"Why?"

Beau decided to make a clean breast of it. The signs gave him trouble, but he managed to make himself understood. An enemy was chasing him, a white man who would kill him. The white man had many guns, and Beau but one. Beau did not like this white man. Beau would take presents, and go to the Sioux who would be his friends. But he must talk to the great chief of the Sioux band which went west, before him. "Who?" he repeated.

Goosey had one last question.

"You are not a soldier?"

"Soldiers wear blue." Beau indicated his ragged shirt and jeans, his boots. "Is this a soldier?"

Goosey cackled in sudden laughter.

"No. This is not a soldier." He took a last drag at the pipe, and handed it to Beau, indicating for his friend to take puff. "Iron Nose," he said. He pointed to the presents. "These are for Iron Nose. Iron Nose is a great chief. There are many chiefs of this band. Iron Nose is the one chief. The chief who gets all these presents. He will be pleased. He will not kill you. He will greet you and protect you. He is a great man, a good man."

"I am glad." The sign came to Beau almost without effort. Thumb and forefinger curled over heart, then hands sweeping out palms up. *Daylight in heart.* He felt as if a tremendous burden had lifted from him. "Lead me to Iron Nose. Tell him I am his friend. All these gifts are for my friend Iron Nose."

Goosey was pleased. He reached for Beau's hand and shook it solemnly in the white man's gesture. When Beau got up on the seat and picked up the reins, Goosey was already riding ahead of him, toward the west. The Sioux raised an arm, a solitary figure outlined against a sea of clouds, and rode his horse over a grassy rise. Beau whipped up the mules and followed him.

In Custer City, Lael Corotis opened her door a crack and called, "Who's there?"

A man's voice answered.

"Mrs. Corotis? I am a detective. My name is Samuel Shadduck. I must talk to thee—now. Will thee open the door?"

She was frightened, remembering the man in Denver with the summons. But the voice went on with quiet persistence. "I am looking for a man named Mannix, madam. Beau Mannix. I have been informed thee might be able to give me information."

Almost, rather, she would have wished it to be the man with the summons, looking for Lael Corotis. Almost—but not quite. She opened the door farther, letting the lamplight stream into the hall. The man was small and pinch-faced, wearing a worn fur cap, which he quickly removed when he saw her looking at him. He did not seem dangerous.

"You may come in," she said.

He brushed past her so quickly and silently he seemed almost to have no substance. Looking at the open trunk, the tightly-strapped valise, the clothes piled on the bed, he said, "I got here just in time, madam. It looks like thee is moving."

"I am on my way to Deadwood."

"I have been there recently," he said. "It is a Godless place."

"Whom were you looking for?" she asked, sharpness edging her voice. "I am in a great hurry, Mr. Shadduck. The stage is leaving in another hour, and places on the stage are hard to come by. I should not want to be delayed."

He ran a small hand over the fur of the cap in a thoughtful gesture.

"Madam, thee does not know Mr. Mannix?"

She shook her head.

"I know no one by that name."

"But I was told that man answering his description had come into Custer City with thee, madam."

She turned her face away from him, folding a nightgown with great care.

"I paid a man fifty dollars to bring me to Custer City. I do not know his name. I do not know where that man is now. I do not think that he was the man you are looking for." Patting the folded gown flat, she laid it carefully in the trunk. "Why are you looking for him?"

Shadduck's voice was patient.

"He committed a murder in San Francisco, and he fled to Chicago. I am a detective. I was sent to bring him back. Out of Cheyenne, on the Union Pacific railroad, he escaped from me."

"That is very unfortunate," Lael said. "I am sorry I can't help you."

The tiny miniature Beau had painted of her lay on the table, the lamp glittering on the gold paint with which he had edged it. The detective picked it up, casually.

"This is a very good likeness, madam."

She felt herself trembling with discovery, and too quickly she snatched it away from him and held it to her. Shadduck smiled.

"Beau Mannix is a very remarkable man. It is the devil's own shame he did not put his gifts to better use. I have seen him catch a likeness in half a dozen strokes of a pencil, madam. Think of that! Half a dozen—no more."

"This—this—picture—" She stammered in confusion. "A man in Denver did it of me, a long time ago. Yes, a friend of my late husband. He was a fine artist."

She slipped the miniature into her bosom.

"If you will excuse me—"

"Thee is lying, madam!" he said.

Moving close to her, he caught her wrist, and twisted it, hard. His hand was like a steel trap. Crying out in pain, she tried to pull away.

"Take your hand off me, or I'll scream!"

"Tell me," Shadduck said into her ear. "Tell me where he has gone, madam."

For answer she bit him, hard, clean, and accurately into the wrist. He dropped her hand and looked down at the wound, oozing small beads of blood from the neat tracery of tooth-marks.

"You get out of here!" she hissed. "Now! Quickly, before I call for help! I don't know your Beau Mannix, and if I did, I wouldn't tell you. Now go!"

He dabbed at the red with a soiled handkerchief.

"Madam," he said, in a voice that was somehow wondering and amazed, "I—I ask pardon. Believe me, I have forgotten myself. It is a thing I would never have thought possible. If—if thee will forgive me—"

He looked baffled and beset, and in spite of herself she felt a wave of pity for him. He was so like a child punished for some transgression he did not understand—a penitent child carried away by an emotion he did not fully comprehend.

"I forgive you," she said.

At the door he turned. His face was haggard and worn, the rays of the lamp casting his features into sharp planes of shadow.

"Madam," he said, "he will not come back to thee. He is not that kind of a man. He is very remarkable, and some day I will catch him in spite of that, but do not believe in him. He is not worth it. And he will not come back."

For a long time after he was gone, she stood frozen, looking at the open door. Then she moved softly forward and closed it, carefully and deliberately, as if the mechanism of a door were strange to her.

When her luggage was packed and ready for the stage, she called the clerk and had it taken down and loaded on the Deadwood stage. She paused at the desk, pulling on her gloves, and spoke to the clerk.

"If anyone inquires for me—" She hesitated, uncertain. "No, I mean if a man—" Again she hesitated. Then she decided to tell the truth. "If a Mr. Mannix inquires for me, will you please tell him I've gone to Deadwood. I—I'm in business, and they tell me things are better there."

The clerk inspected the nibs of his pen. "Yes, ma'am."

"He's a tall man," she said, flushing, "with wavy dark hair. He may be using some other name, even. But I should want him to know where to find me."

"Yes, ma'am."

At the door she paused, still working at the buttons of her gloves. "You won't forget?"

The clerk shook his head. His bald dome shone in the lamplight.

"I won't forget, Mrs. Corotis. And it's been nice having you here."

She smiled at him, and went out to the stage. As she climbed in, helped by the driver's solicitous arm, she saw Samuel Shadduck across the street, leaning against the wall of the livery stable. He watched the progress of the stage until it had passed around a corner and was lost to his view.

Item 8.  Watercolor on square of scraped rawhide, app. 10 ×
12 inches. In fair condition although colors faded
and water-stain in one corner. Long-tailed white
stallion standing on rise overlooking Indian camp.
Probably legendary *Great White Ghost Horse of the
Plains*, often encountered in plains Indian mythol-
ogy. Painting evidently not completely finished.
Not signed, but from brush work and colors obviously done by Mannix.

For the next several days, Beau doubted Goosey's trustwor-
thiness. He was almost positive they had left the great trail
he had first blundered across, and now were following a myriad
smaller and indistinct trails which had turned generally south-
ward, in the direction of the Platte. To all his inquiries, Goosey
turned his foolish side, and pretended not to understand Beau's
anxious queries. The tension between them grew, and Goosey
became alternately alarmed and then sullen. But he rode stubbornly on in the direction he had chosen, and there was little for
Beau to do but follow, or risk an open break with this, his first
contact with the Sioux nation. At last, as he was on the verge of
breaking off with his guide, driving him away at gunpoint if need
be, they came to the camp Goosey was seeking.

The camp was a small one, numbering not more than two or
three dozen *tipis* pitched in several small circles at the edge of a
creek. The moon had not risen, and in the dusk the lodges glowed
from the fires and candles within like big tapered lanterns.
Although many soldiers were out after these bands of Sioux,
trying to enforce the orders of the Black Hills Commission, the

camp of Iron Nose lay peaceful in the night, a fairyland stumbled across in a forest glade. No sentinels were posted, no dog barked at their scent, no shout was raised in alarm.

"They seem awful careless," Beau said to Goosey.

The Sioux turned on his pinto, and made a confident sign in the starlight.

"They know we come."

They were almost at the outer ring of *tipis* when a shift of the wind brought their scent to the camp curs. A wild yammering started, a yapping chorus that shrilled and grew in volume. From one of the lighted *tipis* a man stepped, and was outlined in the door flap for a split-second until the light behind him winked out. A piercing whistle cut the night, and in the flicker of an eyelid Beau and his wagon were surrounded by Sioux. He felt, rather than saw them. A lacing of smell was in the darkness—bodies and animals and smoke and gun-oil. Beside him, on the seat, Sammy raised his hackles and growled, and when a brown hand was laid on the reins, he snapped at it.

Goosey, however, was unimpressed. He swung down from his pony and lit Beau's lantern. Only when it had caught and glowed brightly did he appear to notice the warriors surrounding the mules and wagon. He held the lantern high, searching among the faces, and finally he found a friend.

"Hau!" He gave a roached and painted man a friendly shove in the chest. "Hau!"

Holding the lantern high so that all could see Beau Mannix and the manner of man he was, Goosey launched into an oration in Sioux. Beau did not catch too many of the words, but the import was clear. This was a good white man, an excellent white man. He came to seek the protection of his red brothers because of an evil spirit which pursued him. Now all must go to Iron Nose, the *wakicunza,* the civil leader of this camp, and lay the matter before him. While all might look at this man, and admire the fat mules and the brightly painted wagon, still the business was rightly between Iron Nose and the white man, and to Iron Nose they would go. This time, however, Goosey did not use the word for *white man,* but made the sign for *friend,* two fingers held upright with the others curled into the palm. He was doing his best for Beau Mannix.

Though the mules snorted and reared, the Sioux grabbed their cheekstraps and pulled the animals toward the lighted *tipis.* The rest of the warriors fell in around the wagon, chattering and joking with Goosey. Although he did not appear overly bright, Goosey was a great favorite, and well-known to them. When he answered a question in a droll high-pitched falsetto, the Sioux yelled with delight. Beau took comfort from their good spirits.

The *tipi* of Iron Nose was larger than the others. It was actually two lodges put together, a cross-pole linking the place where the two sets of lodge-poles came to their apex. Alongside the combined *tipis* stood stacked *travois,* the drag-sleds the Sioux used when they traveled, and a rack piled high with drying meat was next to an outdoor kitchen of willow-boughs. A smell lay heavy about the camp, an amplification of the smell that the Sioux laid about Beau's wagon. It was a not-unpleasant smell of smoke and sweet grass and animals and men, a smell no white man would ever forget. It was the smell of the Sioux nation, and it lay over the Dakota Territory and the west that summer like a warning; a warning that fighting men lived here, and that this was their country from long times past. Beau thought of the Fourth Infantry, swarming the streets of Custer City. How long before those soldiers would know the Sioux smell, know it much better?

When Iron Nose came to the door of the *tipi,* the murmurings and the chatter of the crowd stopped abruptly. There was nothing but the shine of firelight on brown painted faces, and the sound of breathing. In the yellow glow from a trader's oil-lamp within, the camp chief was an imposing man, broad-shouldered and deep-chested, with a massive and simple dignity. His dress was simple, too; a single feather stuck at an angle in his black hair, braids wrapped in otter-fur, a white man's flannel shirt of bright red, long leggings with fringes of hair. Blinking in the light, Beau could not clearly see the *wakicunza's* face, but the voice was deep and measured, filled with serene power.

"Friend, who are you?"

In spite of the danger of his position, something in the scene appealed to the artist in Beau Mannix. Not the many faces, the lighted lodges, the flicker of firelight, the smell of the camp, the muted growling of the dogs; though these were important, and he would never forget how they were, that first night, something else appealed to the quick improvisation in him, the gift for seizing the initiative and taking things into his own hands. There was drama in the sudden silence, the lift of the wind, the softness of the summer night. He had always loved the stage. Savoring the silence to the full, exploiting it to the full, he waited until the tension was strong, and then he made his fingers fly in the Sioux signs.

"I have no name. Once I had a name, among the white men." He pointed behind him, using the thumb in the Sioux way to guarantee he spoke truth. "I left my name there—in the white man's city called after Custer, after *Pe-ttin Hanka,* Head Hair Long. I left it there to fool an evil spirit that was after me, an evil spirit that put a spell on me." From the wagon he threw down the corn sheller, a handful of rusted jackknives that were still serviceable, three clocks, an ornamental glass lamp. "I bring these gifts to Iron Nose, to show my heart is good."

A group of the village elders and the war-chiefs stood beside Iron Nose, advising him in whispers. They were not friendly. One of them was a short powerful man in a bonnet of crowfeathers, his face painted in blue dots with a broad blue line across the forehead. His scarlet trailing breech-cloth, a foot wide, reached from his belt to the ground, and on his arms and chest were painted the red dripping disks that meant wounds inflicted by the enemy. Scowling, he whispered into the chief's ear.

When no one moved to touch the gifts, Beau felt the sweat break out on his body like tiny cold needles pricking at his skin. Thinking hard, his heart pounding, he remembered the sign for *big medicine* or whatever they called it—*Wakan Tanka,* that was it. The first two fingers near forehead, palm out, and then the hand swooping gracefully upward in a spiral. *Wakan Tanka,* supreme spirit, big medicine, whatever you wanted to call it. Pock-Mark and Droop-Eye and the rest of them had used it conveniently to describe anything they did not quite understand.

"I have another gift," he said. "This is for the chief Iron Nose. It is sacred. It is only for a chief. It will bring great harm to any other man who is not worthy of it." Climbing into the wagon again, his back prickling, he dragged out the repaired harmonium and set it in the circle of firelight. The wood had been good—better than the bellows—and the harmonium glowed with a deep richness in the flickering light. He pushed lightly on one of the pedals with his boot, and held down a key. The harmonium tootled, and the sound died away as the air pressure in the bellows dropped. Mouths dropped open, and feet shifted nervously. "This is *wakan*," Beau said. "But I give it."

No one spoke. A feeling of decision was in the air—a considering. It might go one way, it might go the other. All it took was a little push.

"You call these gifts," the man with the blue-painted face sneered. "All these things. We could take them from you. Then they would be ours. We would owe you nothing."

As he spoke, Beau felt a sudden icy tide flow in his middle, and his stomach seemed to turn and knot within his belly. The peering small eyes, the pitted skin under the heavy layer of paint, the sardonic smile on the man's lips—even the voice plucked at a deadly string in his memory. The nose, the broken and mashed nose, with the scar of the whipping manacle across it—he stared wide-eyed at Pock-Mark. Beau could almost hear again in his mind the boom of the big fifty from the rocks, the squirm of

Droop-Eye's struggling beneath him as Beau plunged the lance-head into his chest. He remembered, too, with a fatal clarity, the sight of Pock-Mark flogging his pony in retreat, a fleeing figure growing smaller and smaller in the distance. Now this was Pock-Mark, full size again, and a more considerable enemy. The odds would never permit a thing like this to happen, and yet it had happened.

Beau looked into the glittering eyes.

"Iron Nose is not a thief," he said. "He may have among his people those who would steal, or those who are cowards and run from battle. But Iron Nose is not a thief. Therefore, these are gifts I give him."

Pock-Mark's breath drew in with a hiss. At a sign from Iron Nose he drew back, glowering, pounding on the ground with the gaily-decorated coup-stick he carried in one hand.

"True," Iron Nose said. "I am not a thief. The Absaroka are thieves. Many of the Rees are thieves. But the Sioux do not steal. They want only what is theirs."

Pock-Mark reached forward and prodded Beau with the coup-stick, contemptuously.

"I know this man. He has killed Sioux before. No, friends, this man is like all the others. He is not to be trusted. Before long he will lead the soldiers to us, and they will make us go away and live with Spotted Tail or Red Cloud on a little bit of land where we can not hunt, and where we would get sick and die." Pock-Mark spat in Beau's face. "Friends, I say we must kill this man, quick."

Somewhere a bow-string twanged with a *tcchk,* and an arrow tore through the wagon-canvas beside Beau's head. He felt a quick looping dizziness, a mad impulse to turn and run, but he did not move. In the midst of his indecision, a thought came to him. Pock-Mark was too anxious to get rid of him. Things began to fit together in his mind, tumbling into place with a promising neatness. He reached into his pocket and brought out the shell gorget Roach-Head had given him, holding it up into the light.

"Where did you get this?" Iron Nose demanded. His composure was broken. He snatched it from Beau's hand, and held it cupped in trembling palms. "Who gave you this?"

"A young man of your people gave it to me," Beau said. "He was a good young man, a brave young man, and he was my friend. I was captured by a war-party, and he was with them. I speak the truth. I do not have reason to do otherwise."

The *wakicunza* raised his eyes from the gorget and stared at Beau. His eyes burned with coal-like intensity.

"This belonged to my son. It was my gift to him. He went away from here with Kills-First—" He nodded toward Pock-Mark. "It was his first raid. I did not want him to go, but he had to go. It was a very bad thing. No one came back from that raid but Kills-First."

Pock-Mark—Kills-First—spat, and pounded his coup-stick defiantly on the ground.

"Do not listen to this man! He stole the shells from Little Fox's body, after we buried him. I have told you the reason for our troubles on that raid. *Iktomi* misled us. *Iktomi* is one god who is a trickster and a fool. Besides, I had a vision that I was not to touch anything made of iron to my lips before that war-party. I have explained that many times. My woman gave me meat in an iron pot, and with an iron spoon."

His voice rose to a shout. "*Iktomi* led us into a trap, with a hundred white men waiting for us, with cannon and many guns. We fought bravely, but the rest were killed. I buried Little Fox with my own hands. That is the truth!"

Iron Nose looked at Beau.

"Is this true?"

"No." Beau shook his head. "I will tell you the truth. Kills-First captured me. They took me with them for a long distance, because I knew tricks with the cards that made them laugh." He took out the soiled deck, and fanned them out in the air with a quick hissing. He collapsed them, and put the deck in his pocket again. "Little Fox liked me. He was my friend. I liked him. He died when Kills-First attacked a small party of white men in a canyon. But he gave me the shells one day, and told me he was my friend. He smoked a pipe with me."

"This is all a lie!" yelled Kills-First. He advanced on Beau, waving the coup-stick, but Iron Nose pushed him back.

"At a later time," Beau said, "the three who were left attacked a small wagon, with one man and a woman in it. Kills-First was careless. He was so glad to see a small wagon with only a man and a woman in it that he rode away and left me unguarded. I took a gun and a mule and fought them from behind. The people in the wagon killed one man, and I killed another. Kills-First ran away as fast as he could go. That was the last I saw of him until this night. Now this is the truth, friends. I have spoken the truth. Little Fox gave me the shells. That is the truth."

There was a general intaking of breath. People stared at Kills-First with disgust. "A woman!" someone said. A laugh broke out, a small tittering laugh. Kills-First was furious.

"This is all a lie! Friends, do not believe this man! No white man tells the truth! He is sick, diseased—"

Beau knew an advantage when he saw one. Kills-First had tried to fill an inside straight, and had missed.

"This man," he said, "is my enemy. I came to Iron Nose seeking protection, but there is no protection here, not with this man, my enemy. I will fight him here, now, to see who is right. Or if the *wakicunza* wishes, I will go away and ask the Absaroka or the Rees or the Shoshoni for help."

Iron Nose looked down at the string of shells.

"He was a good young man. I am too old to have another. He was my son. Now he is dead. I do not know whether he should have died. Perhaps it was *Iktomi*." He looked at Kills-First. "Perhaps it was not. I do not know."

Sentiment was still divided. An old woman in a tattered dress stepped forward and ground a moccasined heel into the glass face of one of the clocks that lay on the ground. The glass broke, and the clock chimed a final tinny stroke. An angry murmuring arose.

"Friends," Iron Nose said. He held up his hand. "This is a thing for the Great Sixteen to decide. If the gods wanted Little Fox to die, this is all right. Now, if the gods want this white man to die, that is all right too. It is not for us to decide. But I say this. It is bad for any man to come to my camp and ask me for help, and for me to say no. But I tell the white man this. If you come into my camp, my people's camp, there will be blood. Kills-First will kill you, and that is not good, for a chief to have a killing in his camp. But if I tell you to go away, that is not good, because you came to me and asked for help, and I did not give it." Deliberately, he put the beads in a leather pouch that hung from his belt. "Friend, I say this. You go away from my camp, and take your big rifle that is on the seat of the wagon. Kills-First will follow you, alone, on foot, with his gun. You two fight away from my camp. Then it is up to the two of you. Whoever comes back, that is all right."

In the silence that followed, Iron Nose made the sign for *finished*—fists clenched before his body, thumbs up, then moving them apart and together, several times.

"*Hopo*," said Beau.

He reached for the Sharps, and put a handful of the big metal-cased cartridges into his pocket, aware that Pock-Mark was watching him with eager eyes, eyes in which was a lust for Beau Mannix's blood. Moving deliberately, he stepped out of the circle of firelight, into the night.

In the waning moonlight he traveled away from the camp, loping on long legs through the thick grass. He bore generally eastward, going by the Big Dipper low over his head in the sky, remembering a spread of high-piled black rocks Goosey had led the wagon through. In the maze of black rocks, he might find a niche where he could lie undetected and duel with Pock-Mark at a distance. With the Sharps, they might be on even terms.

He was leaving a trail in the wet grass that a blind man could follow, but he did not care.

When he finally reached the rocks, the scattered fingers of cloud were lit from beneath by the sun hidden below the horizon. Their undersides were ruddy and golden, and as he climbed higher and higher in the rocks, the first rays of the sun slanted across the dark rocks and burned into his face with a welcome warmth. When he had climbed partway up, he looked back over his shoulder. The plain lay ghostly and still in the half-light below, a gauzy mist settled on it. In the far distance was a tracery of dark vegetation that marked the watercourse where Iron Nose's people were camped. As his hand groped upward to pull his body higher, a rattle sounded, and he drew back in alarm. A slither, loud and deadly in the quiet, and a fat heavy body writhed away into a crack.

Higher and higher he climbed, his breath coming hard now. Finally he reached a shallow cleft near the summit, a protected fissure where he could crouch beneath an overhanging ledge and scan the grassland below.

Laying the cartridges in a neat row on the rocky shelf, he examined the action of the Sharps. Here he would be hard to get at. If Pock-Mark tried to follow him, dodging in and out among the fingers and slabs and ledges of dark rock, the fight would be an equal one, and that was all Beau Mannix wanted. Wishing he had had the foresight to bring water, he licked his lips and stared down, closing his eyes to slits against the heat that began to radiate from the dark walls of his fortress.

At noon, so far as he could judge from the sun, he saw a small dark dot in the distance, between him and the camp of Iron Nose. It was almost like a trick of his eye, but it crawled steadily toward him, and in another hour or so he could make it out as a man on horseback. He watched, licking his dry lips, and finally when the figure neared the base of the high rocks, he could make out that it was Pock-Mark. The Sioux was still out of rifle-shot, even with Gammill's big old fifty. He rode a pony, and he carried a coup-stick. Beau's eyes widened in astonishment. While Pock-Mark might carry other weapons, he had no rifle. Feeling vaguely uneasy, he watched Pock-Mark stop far below, staring upwards. For a moment he had a wild impulse to rest the heavy barrel on the ledge and squeeze off a shot, but the distance was too great for anything but a lucky shot, and he had only a dozen or so cartridges. He might need them all.

Strangely, Pock-Mark appeared to be in no hurry. He tied the pony and sat in the shade of a thicket of cottonwoods. From time to time he came out and looked upward. Once he shook the coup-stick in defiance. That was all, and the sun passed overhead and started to slant down the long hill to the west.

Early in the afternoon Beau was driven to seek water. Leaving the cartridges lined on the ledge, he took the Sharps, with a shell in the chamber, and climbed stiffly out of the crevice. There had been rains—quick drenching summer showers—and he hoped to find a shallow pool with water still in it. Keeping one eye warily on the cottonwoods below, he climbed upward, and suddenly stopped in alarm.

Above him, on the summit, was a faint gray haze of smoke, a thin veil he stared at in disbelief. As he watched, the wind whipped it away, but he got a quick sniff of it as it passed. Someone was up there, *above* him, cutting off any retreat; perhaps signalling to Pock-Mark below, showing him where the brash white man had hidden in the rocks. For a moment he stood paralyzed, mouth gaping, cursing himself for not having expended the extra effort to climb the last few hundred feet and gain the crest, where no one could flank him.

He was standing like that, stupid and foolish, when the heavy slug caught him in the neck, whirling him around with the force of its flight, and slamming him down into the rocks. The Sharps flew out of his hand and clanked down after him, and he lay stunned, feeling his whole right side suddenly numb and wooden. Reaching across with the other hand, feeling where the shoulder joins the neck, his hand came away wet and sticky and red. Strangely, he did not feel fear. Instead he was filled with violent and angry disappointment. Pock-Mark had out-thought and out-generaled him. While Beau lay like a cornered animal in a cleft in the rocks, keeping his eye on the patient Sioux below, a confederate had simply skirted the base of the hill, climbed above him, and now brought the affair to a close. He swore, gritting his teeth, and reached where the Sharps had fallen. The barrel was lodged in a crack, but he finally managed to drag it free with his left hand. Well, what were the odds? Not very damned good.

Where he had fallen, he could not see below, but he was sure Pock-Mark was running toward the rocks, climbing triumphantly upward. From somewhere above, a man was working down, also, rifle at the ready, slipping from rock to rock on moccasined feet.

Still half-stunned, Beau rested the barrel of the Sharps on a flat rock, pointing the barrel upward. In spite of the shock of the wound, in spite of the faint nausea that made him giddy, his mind tried to grapple with the problem. If Pock-Mark were coming upward, it would take him time to get there. The man above was not too far away—*could* not be too far away. The immediate danger was still from above. He lay back, resting his head against a ledge, and maneuvered the Sharps with his left hand so he could pivot it on the ledge, swing it from right to left and back again. Listening, waiting, he lay there, even sniffing at the air in an effort to locate his pursuer.

It did not take long. He was so silent, had lain so still, that the half-naked Sioux stood for a moment above him, not seeing

Beau sprawled below. When his ear caught the scrape of gun-barrel on stone, the man tightened all over, like an animal ready to spring. He swung the rifle toward Beau with desperate haste but the heavy slug hit him dead center in the chest, and he threw his arms wide and fell. The body caught for a moment on a projecting boulder, and then rolled a few yards down-hill to bring up looped around a scrawny bush that grew from a cleft. That was all.

Beau pulled himself upright, fighting at the giddiness that flowed over him like a fog. He had only the one cartridge in the Sharps, and it was gone, and the big gun was useless. He dared not go down below again for the other cartridges, lined up like idiots on the shelf where he had left them. He searched for the dead man's gun, and found it near the body. It was a good one; a seventeen-shot Winchester, and the magazine was full. It did not weigh as much as the Sharps, either, and that was good. Dragging it after him, he climbed laboriously upward, right arm hanging limp, keeping the rocks between him and Pock-Mark. This time, he would *stay* on top, if he could make it. Glancing downwards, he saw the bright red drip of his blood on the rocks. He did not care too much.

Near the summit, he found the coals of a small fire, along with a blanket and an empty water canteen. Damned fool Beau Mannix, not to figure the odds better than he had! And Pock-Mark had all the aces in *this* deck! He leaned back against a rock, fighting the way his eyes seemed to get fuzzy and fail him, drifting maddeningly out of focus. In a few more moments he would faint, a thing he deplored but which he realized was possible. He could not engage Pock-Mark in a scramble through these rocks. He might manage to lift the Winchester with one arm, and get in one shot, but he could never work the lever for another. If that first shot missed, he was dead.

In sudden inspiration, still playing the odds, he wedged the Winchester in a split rock, and levered out half a dozen shells. He threw them into the coals of the fire, and stumbled away, dragging the gun by the barrel so that the stock left a wavering line in the sandy earth and light rubble. A small diversion, that was what he needed. Something to distract Pock-Mark. That was the only way out, the only chance.

He succeeded in dragging himself to a flat shelf of rock that overlooked the campfire and the blanket and the place where the empty canteen still lay. Rolling over on his stomach, he propped the Winchester on the edge of the rock, sighting it in on the small clearing in the rocks.

There was no sound but the whistle of the wind around the sharp corners of the rock. A small gray lizard whipped across the ledge in front of his nose and dived into a crack. Above him in the blue cloudless sky wheeled a bird, soaring on stiff motionless wings.

Light-headed from heat and the loss of blood he yelled curses at his enemy, and his voice cracked ridiculously. He laughed, and when the sound had died away, he realized it was a ridiculous laugh, too; a sobbing desperate noise that echoed all around in the rocks.

Something moved in the rocks that surrounded the little amphitheatre where the fire smoldered. It was a small movement, but one that caught Beau's eye against the background of the unmoving rocks. In that flick of an eye he knew that Pock-Mark had come to the campfire, seen the blanket and the canteen and the red drops of blood leading still upward, and was now climbing after him. Beau let his head drop until his cheek was against the stock of the rifle, unable to fight the drowsiness that came over him. He had one small chance left.

If Pock-Mark got behind him, he did not have the strength to get up and fight. All he could do was lie in his rocky grave and wait for the stroke of the knife, or the ball from the revolver, or however Pock-Mark chose to bring it to an end. Droop-Eye and Bow-Legs were revenged. He laughed, and did not know why.

The coup-stick was the first thing he saw. It stuck from behind a rock below him and to his left, like the long neck of an ungainly bird. It was strung with feathers that whipped in the wind, and tufts of hair. Instantly it was withdrawn. Then he saw Pock-Mark run from that rock to another, so quickly that Beau could not have squeezed off a shot even had he been able to swing the Winchester around and fire.

Like a stalking animal, Pock-Mark flitted from one cover to another, running low. Beau watched the dashes with curious detachment, seeing the drawn revolver, the coup-stick, Pock-Mark's bent and hunched body, hearing him slip once and go to his knees in a patch of shale.

When the shots came, they were deafening. They rolled around the rocks like thunder, and one slug screeched over his head and spanged into the rocks, grinding into leaden rain. For a long moment after the echoes died there was silence. Then Pock-Mark stood up, disdaining cover, and looked around him, puzzled. He swung his head from side to side, sniffing. Then, caution forgotten, he sprang back down the rocks, jumping from one to the other like a mountain goat, revolver drawn, steadying himself with the extended coup-stick. He came finally to the clearing and for one moment—one moment too long—stood before the blasted campfire, looking down at the scattered ashes, the coals, the blackened ends of twigs that had been thrown wide. In that one moment, Beau squeezed the trigger and caught him in the face with the Winchester. The coup-stick fell, too, and lay flat in the sand, while Pock-Mark's blood soaked into the feathers and made them sodden and red.

Goosey found Beau in the rocks, and gave him water. He crushed an aromatic bush into powder and plastered it over the wound, all the time shaking his head and muttering.

"That was a bad man, that Kills-First. He took a horse. Also Walking-Bear. He was a friend to Kills-First. They were both bad men." He shook his head, and spat through his teeth. "Both bad men. Iron Nose did not know I knew, but no one believes me. They think I fool." He got Beau's good arm around his neck, and began the long descent, still muttering.

There was an amazing resilience in Beau Mannix, a resilience he had sometimes suspected after a hard drinking bout or a long night in a tough game. Now it came to his aid, and when they reached the copse of cottonwoods below, he felt almost cheerful. With Goosey's aid, he got a leg over the painted wooden saddle of Pock-Mark's pony. He still held on to Pock-Mark's coup-stick with an iron grip, and refused to give it up.

When they came at last into Iron Nose's camp, it was night, and the *tipis* glowed again like waxen tapers. Gammill's wagon—*his* wagon—still stood there, gay and painted. They rode slowly between the curious faces, some friendly, some merely interested, others reserved and doubtful. Pushing aside Goosey's proffered hand, Beau slid off the saddle. He pushed aside the door-flap of Iron Nose's lodge, and stood there for a moment, looking at the *wakicunza* who sat silently across the fire.

"I have no name," Beau said. "I left my name back there." Once again he gestured with his thumb, the left one this time. "But I have come to live here, if Iron Nose will let me. I will be known by the name the Cut-Throats choose."

He drew his finger across his throat, and sat down, cross-legged, inside the doorway. He sat for a long time, silent, until Iron Nose rose, dropped a coal into a carved stone pipe, and handed it to him.

**Item 9.** Canvas in oils, app. 20 × 35 inches. Winter scene of
Sioux boys coasting down slope on buffalo-rib sleds,
whipping tops on ice, etc. Done on square cut from
wagon-canvas, name of maker still in one corner.
Signed B/M.

For a long time, it seemed, he lay in the brightly-painted
wagon. That time was never too clear to him, afterward, but
he remembered being attended by Goosey and by a tall shiny-
braided woman who brought him food. Someone had stuck the
captured coup-stick in the whip socket of the wagon, and he lay
watching the tufts of hair fly in the wind. At night the ribbons on
the stick whipped in the wind, and sometimes only rustled. His
wound was very serious, and became inflamed. He remembered
feeling hot, and then very cold, and when he shivered the woman
put blankets over him. When he went out of his head, she held
his flushed face to her cheek, and talked to him in a soft musical
voice.

One day the fever was gone, very suddenly, and he woke feeling filled with life, the sap of being. Getting to his knees, holding
his neck stiff because of the wound, he got as far as the seat of
the ambulance, holding on with hands that seemed to belong to
someone else; hands thin and clawlike, with long bluish nails.
That far, he knelt for a moment, peering into the sunlight, hearing the clamor and the noise and the shouting and the laughter of the camp, smelling meat cooking in an iron pot, seeing
colors that hurt—reds and greens and browns that shimmered
and writhed before his sensitive eyes. A man sat before a lodge,
squinting into a hand-mirror and picking at the hairs of his

chin with a clamshell tweezers. Beside the wagon a small and determined band of boys skirmished back and forth, obeying the commands of a stripling in a tattered cavalry overcoat. Shouting so loud he had to cover his own ears with his hands, an old man wandered the camp, calling out news. And on the turf beside the wagon, leaning against a wheel and filing arrow-points from a discarded sheet-iron skillet, squatted Goosey.

"Friend," Beau called down, "I am glad to see you."

Goosey's eyes popped. He dropped the file and threw his old hat into the air, whooping. From all corners of the camp the people came running—men, women, boys, girls, toddling infants, even a crippled old man riding in a kind of a litter carried by two slender youths. In the doorway of the great chief's *tipi* across the way stood Iron Nose, watching. Then he disappeared within, joining some strange Sioux for a conference. They were men Beau had never seen before, and they looked important in their bonnets and bright four-point blankets.

"He lives," Goosey told the crier. "The white man lives. Go and tell all the people!" In a hurry, he seized the old man by the shoulders, and propelled him on his errand. "Go, Gottam! Go!"

"I live," agreed Beau in a hoarse voice.

He looked down at the brown faces, the curious eyes, heard them laughing and gossiping, fingers pointing. His white skin must have the pallor of a lily, he suspected. Putting up a hand to touch his cheek, he felt a tough and wiry growth, and recoiled in such alarm that the spectators shrieked with laughter, and mimicked him. But it was for the most part good-natured laughter, and he grinned back at them, and waved, and fell exhausted into the wagon. It was good to be alive, to come back from wherever he had been to this present time. He went to sleep again, lulled by a muffled chant from Goosey of *Gottam! Gottam!*

He did, indeed, live. Living, he returned to obligations. Not the same obligations put on him by a white man's society, but others more binding. The black-braided woman was delighted to see him well. Her name was appropriately simple; *Tall Woman.* Almost as tall as he was, her skin was delicate, with a roselike glow behind the soft transparent brown of her cheeks. She was shy and well-brought-up, coloring modestly when he spoke to her. Now that he was better, she sat for most of the day cross-legged in the shade of the wagon, graining beaver-skins with a tool made from a gun-barrel.

"I am grateful to her," he told Goosey, sitting on the wagon-seat and feeling the tides of life flow again within him. "I was very sick and she took care of me. How must I thank her?"

Goosey looked puzzled.

"Thank her? Friend, how do you mean?"

"I want to give her something. A gift."

Goosey snickered.

"Only one thing you can give her to make her happy."

Beau began to feel uneasy at the turn of the conversation, but Goosey went happily on.

"This is a wife's duty, to take care of her husband. When you are better, she will come to your bed in the wagon. Right now you are still a little bit sick, and she—"

"Stop," said Beau. He held up his hand, feeling dizzy. On a grassy patch a few hundred yards removed from the camp a band of young men raced their horses, laughing and shouting. They were stripped to their breech-clouts, and the hair and tails of their ponies were tied up. Beau watched them fly along the course, rope bridle in one hand, the other lashing with a wooden quirt. "My wife?" he asked. "She? Tall Woman?"

Goosey was practical and convincing in his explanation.

"She belonged to Kills-First. Now she belongs to you. She is very happy, because Kills-First was mean to her. He was a bad man. We are better off now that he is gone. We are all very happy."

Beau swallowed hard. Beside him on the seat of the wagon, Sammy watched him anxiously, and whimpered.

"You sit up too long," Goosey said. "You sleep now for a little while. Soon you are well again." He went back to working the marrow from the leg-bone of an eagle, making a whistle. Beau crawled back to bed, pale and shaken.

The Sioux were encamped along a tributary of the Belle Fourche. Now, early in September, autumn began to steal upon the land, like a warning of an early winter and a hard one. The days were hot and dry, with a soft haze enveloping the peaks. The grass was luxuriant from summer rains—the Sioux called it "two-day grass" because a bellyful of it stayed a pony for that long—around the camp lay a dense growth of grapevines, wild plums, and bullberries. Game of all kinds was plentiful, and the streams were alive with trout, although the Sioux did not care for fish. Beau sat on the seat of his wagon, Sammy curled beside him, and watched the life of the camp flow about him like a colorful river, strange and new, and with unplumbed depths. It was a time of storage for him; a time of registering in his mind the forms and colors and perspectives, of learning to live with the sharp new outlines and angles and hues and shades and tints. As soon as his wound healed, and the strange stiffness left his arm, he would begin to paint.

Between Tall Woman and Goosey, the apparently haphazard organization of the camp began to make some small sense to him. Iron Nose, the *wakicunza,* was a camp chief, or civil chief, chosen for his ability as a planner and organizer, rather than for prowess in war, although as a young man he had distinguished himself in combat with the Rees and the Absaroka. The real power, in these troubled times, lay with the war chiefs, men like Three Horses, Red Knife, and Man-Who-Ate-The-Wolf. These were saturnine, dignified men who sat most of the day before their *tipis,* painting new devices and affixing new ornaments to the ceremonial sashes that denoted their rank in the warrior societies of the Hunkpapa. From time to time strange Sioux rode into camp, often in a great hurry, and Three Horses and Red Knife and Man-Who-Ate-The-Wolf and Iron Nose conferred with the visitors in secrecy.

"This is a very bad time," said Goosey, with a shake of his head. "Someone is going to get hurt, Gottam! There is going to be a big gravy-stirring. The soldiers are getting very angry because no one comes into Red Cloud Agency to talk to them."

"Why not?" Beau asked. "It does not hurt to talk."

"Oho!" said Goosey. "When the fox asks the rabbit to come into his den and talk—" He shook his head again. "If we go in there, what happens? They take our guns. Gottam! They put us in jail. Gottam! They try to make us live on a little piece of ground where we would get sick and die." He leaned forward, chuckling, and dug Beau in the ribs. "Do you know what Sitting Bull told Louis Richaud? He told him 'Are you the Great God that made me, or was it the Great God who made me that sent you?' He said 'We do not go to the reservation. There is plenty of game here for us. We have enough ammunition. We don't want any white men here. If the white men want to see us, let them come here.' That is what he said."

Beau looked around at the young men playing their endless games of "hand" with a pebble, betting, wrangling. In the river, boys splashed with their ponies, shouting and laughing, breaking the fractious mounts in the Sioux way, chest-deep in the water, so that their movements were restrained and they quickly grew tired, and submitted to the rope bridle.

"If the rabbit talks big to the fox," Beau said, "the rabbit should have a gun."

"*Sha!*" Goosey chuckled. "*Sha!* Good! Excellent!" Then he sobered. "That is what they talk about in the big *tipi*. Every day come messengers from Gall and Sitting Bull and the great chiefs. They want us to join them and fight the soldiers in a big battle. But Iron Nose is a wise man. He says 'We leave them alone, they leave us alone'. He does not want to fight. But pretty soon Red

Knife and Man-Who-Ate-The-Wolf and Three Horses get us into a fight. You will see."

The warm golden period of the year faded into an early autumn. The trees wore mantles of color, the nights grew crisp and cold, and before dawn the cold bit like a steel spike, blue and hard. Ice rimmed the creek, ice that disappeared before the noonday sun, but came back thicker and wider each night. The women worked hard, working against time, drying buffalo-meat and buffalo-tongues. In expectation of a hard winter, some of the poorer mounts from the horse herd were killed and the meat cut into strips, dried, and packed into *parfleche* panniers to be smoked. The children, Beau's especial favorites, gathered buffalo-berries, wild cherries, and wild plums, and the women pounded the fruit into scraps of dried meat to make *toro,* tasting like the plum-pudding Beau remembered from Christmas long ago. It was a busy and a prosperous scene, a savage harvest-time.

Sammy arrived at an uneasy truce with the camp dogs. Hundreds of them had the run of the camp, for the most part short-haired snarling curs of uncertain disposition. Some of the larger ones were used as pack-animals, dragging stacks of fire-wood on miniature *travois.* The smaller ones were often seized, skinned, and boiled in an iron pot. Dog-meat was a delicacy, on a par with hump-ribs or deer-liver. When eating time came, Beau kept Sammy by his side. Tall Woman often cast a calculating eye on the dog, but Sammy gave her a wide berth. The breach between them widened when she displaced Sammy among Beau's blankets in the wagon.

"You are ready," she said one night, crawling into the wagon and wriggling under the old buffalo coat that covered him. Her body was warm and naked, and the touch of it sent a galvanic tremor through him. "I am ready, too."

He propped himself up on one elbow and stared at her. In the dying light of the cooking fire, her eyes were large and moist, and her lips curved in a smile.

"Do you like me?"

He touched her cheek with his finger.

"Very much," he said.

In that simple society there was no harlotry, or celibacy, either. Tall Woman spent the night with him, simply and without shame or self-consciousness. From that time on they were man and wife. They were very happy. She was proud of her new husband, and she was proud also of her own family. Beau met many of them, including the uncle, Man-Who-Never-Walked. He was the grizzled ancient with withered legs who was borne about in a litter, a wizened man with cheeks and brows and jaws so prominent that his head looked like a mediaeval carving, or the head of an expensive walking-stick. Man-Who-Never-Walked was a respected historian of the tribe. He enjoyed telling the white man about the Sioux wars, and the peculiarities of their enemies.

"The Flatheads do not fight good on horses. They are scared of horses. On foot with guns they fight good. But if you get them running you can beat them. The Rees are good fighters. The Shoshoni are the bravest and best warriors."

Tall Woman sat beside Beau, holding a mirror and giggling as he tried to shave with a rusty razor he had found in the wagon. Beau wiped the blood from his chin, and looked at his scraped face in the mirror.

"How are the white men?" he asked. "Are they good fighters?"

Man-Who-Never-Walked was uneasy.

"They have many guns."

"Do the Sioux fear their guns?"

The old man waved his eagle-feather fan.

"We do not fear them. But we do not want to fight them. Iron Nose is wise. If they do not bother us, friend, we do not bother them. There is plenty of room out here for all of us."

Beau squinted into the mirror.

"In Deadwood and in Custer City and in Fort Fetterman and Fort Laramie there are pony soldiers and many walking soldiers.

I do not think there would be so many unless they wanted a fight with the Sioux."

The old man's eyes glittered.

"I hope they do not come here to fight us. We do not want to fight. Let Sitting Bull and those big talkers fight if they want to. I am an old man, and I know war does not bring good to anyone. But if Three-Star and Head-Hair-Long come out here with soldiers, there will be a big fight."

Beau thought of the mournful captain in the Dakota House in Custer City, the talk of the expected war, the almost eager speculation about the trouble that would come if the Sioux did not travel to the reservations, where someone could keep an eye on them.

"I hope," he said, "there will not be a big fight."

"Friend," the old man said, "I hope there will not be a big fight." He made a quick, savage gesture—the palm of the right hand passed quickly over the left. There was no mistaking that sign. It was more eloquent than any words. It meant *wiped out*. "Like that," Man-Who-Never-Walked said. "We have great generals, too; Gall, and Crow-King. We will wipe them out."

In the camp, sentiment was divided. Iron Nose was moderate, a cool-headed and foresighted man who wanted no trouble, and who was convinced his people could get along with the whites. Red Knife and the Man-Who-Ate-The-Wolf and Three Horses were hotheads; fire-eaters and doers. Moreover, Iron Nose was only the *wakicunza*, the civil chief, and in matters of war was at a disadvantage when the war chiefs spoke. But he was also a crafty man, and a politician, and during the autumn months he managed to preserve an uneasy truce in spite of the extremists who wanted to mount a quick raid against the nearest troops, then fall back to join Sitting Bull and Gall and the rest of the warlike Sioux.

In the warrior societies, the question was debated. At night, men of the various societies met around the ceremonial fire.

They sang songs, they pounded the red drum, they argued and wrangled. When Beau asked Tall Woman what was going on, she was noncommittal.

"The men talk."

"What do they say?" he asked.

She shrugged, and smiled at him.

"I do not know."

Unnoticed, he sneaked one night to the edge of the circle of firelight, and listened. Although he got along passably well in the Sioux tongue, it was one he feared he would never be able to master completely. Languages in general he had always been good at; a little Italian, some Spanish, even a smattering of German. But in these tongues there was always some common grammar and structure. Sioux was like nothing he had ever heard before. Each word, each phrase, each sentence, had to be learned by rote, and bore no resemblance to any other word or phrase or sentence. The sign language was different; he had an instinctive feel for that.

Bay Horse was speaking. He was a stocky forceful man, proud of a bead necklace from which hung a silver cross, clusters of beads and shells, and a half-dozen dried forefingers of as many Ree and Shoshoni.

"Friends, I say we should listen to Iron Nose."

A murmur of disapproval arose, but Bay Horse waited until it subsided.

"I like a good fight. It is all right that we fight the Rees and the Shoshoni and the Absaroka and steal their horses. That is the way it has been for a long time. That is good. But fighting white men is different. There are many of them, too many. They keep coming out of the ground like corn."

Someone jeered, and Bay Horse became angry.

"I am not afraid of them. I am not afraid of anyone! I have been on this earth a long time. Whenever I went on the warpath, I looked out for the enemy and did something brave. I studied all

I saw, and tried to understand it. I now have good will to all people. I tell no lies; the man who lies is a weakling. I keep an even temper and am never stingy with food. In this way my name has become good." With a dramatic gesture Bay Horse pulled aside his breech-clout and displayed his genitals. "I have many children. Some are almost as old as this man who laughs. So do not listen to him, but listen to me."

Where the begetting of life was so essential to survival of the race, the declaration of potency did not seem exactly a boast. It was more a dedication to the gods who made the Sioux, the great Sixteen—Sun, Thunder, Rock, and all the rest. They made the Sioux; in consequence, they were anxious to have their Sioux children continue to walk the earth, and prosper.

"I have done many things," Bay Horse said. "I was elected Drum-Keeper of the Fox Soldiers. I have danced the Sun Dance. I have counted coup on more Rees and Shoshoni and Absaroka than I can remember. I do not even remember anymore. So listen to me, friends. Do not do a thing you will be sorry for."

There were muffled grunts of approval from some of the men. "Hau! Hau!" Others were dubious. Bay Horse put a coal in his pipe, sucked deep on the tobacco, and then blew smoke high in the air, following it with his eyes. He handed the pipe to the man on his left, and the carved stone pipe went the rounds, while all of them thought over the sentiments of the speaker. When the next man rose and held up his hand for attention, Beau slipped away. He sat for a long time in the wagon, playing solitaire, until Tall Woman came silently to him and put her hand on his knee. After a while, she asked, "You do not feel good?"

He knocked the dottle from his pipe, watching the sparks fall into the grass and glow brightly before dying.

"My body is well," he said. "My heart is not."

He had always loved children, with the especial and tolerant affection of a man who had known little family life. Now they came to watch him paint. The first day, he tacked a remnant of canvas to a board, and set up the makeshift easel in the shade of a stand of cottonwoods. Before he had laid out the brushes, the pots and bottles of paint, the rags and the rest of the paraphernalia, he was aware of dark eyes that watched him from the concealment of the wild grapes nearby. Whistling, making believe he did not see them, he mixed paints on a shingle of wood for a makeshift palette. Bit by bit they emerged from their concealment. There were several of them, mostly boys with two soft-eyed and naked small girls following discreetly behind. He had thought to do a kind of panorama of the camp—something to hold this carefree time in his mind, when he should have forgotten exactly how it was—but he was so captivated by the smaller of the girls that he changed his mind. She was a sparkling-eyed sprite, with long uncombed hair and a round little belly, sucking her thumb, and in the other arm cradling a carved wooden doll with great care and tenderness. Unafraid, she pushed past the others and came to stand beside him, looking first at the easel and then at him.

"You are very beautiful," Beau said. Talking to her softly, conversationally, he managed to hold her attention while he worked colors onto the canvas. Mixing like mad, daubed with color himself, he went at furious speed, delighted he was catching the glint of an eye, the soft roundness of the baby chin. "Some day soon all the boys will want you for a wife. They will give many of the best horses for you."

One of the small boys spat, and said "Girls are no good." The rest of them looked at each other, and grinned sheepishly. An urchin with an buffalo-tail on a stick reached over and shooed away a fly from Beau's nose.

"Friend," said Beau, "I thank you."

Entranced at the face growing on the canvas, they crowded him until he had hardly room to lift his elbow. He did not mind. Something had happened to him in these months that he had not painted. Even with the stiffness from the wound in his arm and fingers, he had caught a spark. The small solemn face glowed back at him, from the canvas, and he looked first at the girl, and then back at the canvas, feeling an elation he had not known for a long time. If he could do as well with other subjects—. He felt a growing excitement. There was no limit to what he could do out here, with these people, with paints and canvas.

"This is Chipmunk," one of the boys volunteered. He pointed at the painting, and then at the small girl. "Paint me," he said. "She is small. I am much bigger."

Beau whooped with laughter. He tore the canvas from the easel, still wet, and handed it so the small sober girl, still chuckling. There was something so strange in his glee, so unnerving, that the children fled, looking back over the shoulders in alarm. Chipmunk, however, did not drop the canvas. She stood on the edge of the thicket of grapevines, still watching, the doll in one hand and the painting in the other.

The portrait of Chipmunk created a minor sensation in the camp. Women brought him their babies, begging for "pisher." Man-Who-Never-Walked demanded an immediate sitting. Red Knife dressed in full regalia for him—shirt of mountain sheepskin with trailing fringes, quillwork across the shoulders and chest, tassels of hair on either side. The flexible elkskin uppers of his moccasins were covered with designs in dyed porcupine quills, and his leggings of buckskin had a broad stripe of beads down the leg, and a heavy twisted fringe from knee to ankle. He would not, in spite of Beau's repeated entreaties, take his war bonnet from the painted rawhide case he carried in one hand.

"Not till we fight," he insisted. "I do not take it out until there is a fight."

He did, however, let Beau look in at it. It was a handsome upright crown of plumes from the golden eagle, with a beaded browband and a tail of feathers a good six feet long. There was a chinstrap, and a beaded belt to tie the long tail about the waist.

"I put this *pisher* in my *tipi*," Red Knife said. "It will be good for people to remember me sometime when I am not there. I have been useful and renowned among my people. It will be good for them to look at this *pisher* and say 'That was a good man. I must be like him.' "

Beau grunted, tongue in one corner of his mouth.

"Move *that* way," he said, gesturing with the brush. "There is bad light on your face."

One night a light snow fell, a delicate powdering of the hills that disappeared like mist before the morning sun. Before it was gone, the snowy dusting was crossed and crisscrossed by the hoof-marks of unshod ponies and the wide scars of *travois* poles. A small band of Sans-Arcs had come to visit Iron Nose, a cheerful and happy brood led by a man called Turkey-Leg, as near as Beau could make out the name. It was not unusual for small bands to travel the land and visit out of sheer sociability, to exchange gossip and rumor and news, especially at this time when the pony soldiers were said to be out to enforce the edict of the Black Hills Commission. Turkey-Leg's band included a white man, a grizzled and verminous man in a grease-shiny buckskin coat. Beau caught him behind one of the *tipis* swigging from a dark bottle. Iron Nose disapproved of liquor.

"Where you from?" Beau asked.

Quickly the newcomer stuffed the bottle in his coat.

"Around." He wiped a hand across his unshaven chin, not taking his eyes off Beau Mannix. "I come from almost anyplace." His eyes narrowed. "My name's Smoke. What's yours?"

"Mannix."

Smoke nodded, his eyes still fixed on Beau. Almost as if lost in thought, he went on talking, aimlessly.

"Been travelin' with Turkey-Leg. Here and there, around and about. Married me one of his women one time. I like to visit the kids every so often. I—" He broke off, licking his lips in a wide area that left a lighter portion around his mouth, almost like a circus clown. "Now I got it! Mannix! Why, sure! You're the feller that detective was looking for!"

"What detective?"

Smoke grinned.

"No need to play dumb with me, mister! I guess I know about you. I hired out to this Shadduck in Deadwood, see? He was certain you was out in the bresh someplace, hidin' from him. He bought an outfit and we sashayed all over hell lookin' for you. Never did find you. I guess the detective got tired and went home. Anyways, I never seen him again after that night he left Turkey-Leg's camp down on the Inyah Kara." Smoke laughed. "Didn't even say goodbye. Just pulled out."

"Where did he go?" Beau's mouth was dry.

"*I* dunno. But I tell you one thing. I ain't ever about to get a pesky little man like that on *my* trail. I tell you he don't *never* give up, that man. If I was you, I wouldn't sleep nights, not with him chasing me. He's a pleasant enough sort of man, well-spoke and polite—but he reminds me of some kind of a hound dog, the way he sticks to a trail."

"What are you and Turkey-Leg doing here?"

Smoke took the bottle out of his jacket, and held it up to the light.

"Ain't more than enough here for just one drink." He looked at Beau, but Beau shook his head and Smoke turned the bottle gratefully upward and finished what was left.

"Fourth Cavalry," he said, tossing the empty bottle into a bush. "Two or three companies. Looked to me like they was comin' this way. They didn't bother us none—Turkey-Leg told 'em we was from Spotted Tail, jest doin' a little huntin', and we meant to go right back before snow fell. 'Course, that's a damned lie, and I reckon they knew it, but we was too small an outfit for them to bother with. Iron Nose is a different case. They ain't agonna let this many Sioux stay out here in one bunch all winter. I'd guess there's agonna be a little gravy-stirrin', like the Sioux call it, if they come this way."

Beau looked around him at the camp.

"It doesn't look to me like Iron Nose is going to run from them."

Smoke belched luxuriously.

"Hell, Iron Nose has camped here in winter for the last ten years. He *owns* this place! He ain't agonna move."

Neither of them spoke for a moment. Instead they stared together at a bank of leaden clouds that drifted slowly and ominously over their heads. Finally Beau asked, "What happens then?"

Smoke examined the cuff of his buckskin coat, and cracked a louse between his fingernails.

"Stirrin' gravy," he said. "By God, I never heard a better name for it." He blew his nose on the sleeve of his coat, nodded to Beau, and moved away in a haze of liquor fumes, walking with slightly off-center dignity.

When Turkey-Leg's band pulled out early the next morning, Beau was in the wagon with Tall Woman. She stirred drowsily at the neighing of horses and grind of the *travois*-poles in the dirt, and Beau pulled the old buffalo-coat up over her and went out with Sammy to watch them leave. At the front of the column rode the man called Smoke, beside Turkey-Leg.

"If you ever get into Custer City," Beau said, "there's a woman there. A Mrs. Corotis. If you see her—" For a moment he floundered, and his face turned red. "I mean—well, if you see her, just tell her I'm all right, will you? Tell her everything's all right."

Smoke reined up, and the small column trailed past in the bitter morning cold. The blood-red sun hovered on the icy hills and lit the scene with a glow that had no heat in it.

"I'll tell her," Smoke said. "I'll sure tell her." He leaned forward, his breath steaming, and gave Beau a friendly clap on the shoulder. "Any message for that old hound dog? That Shadduck?"

"No," Beau said. "No message. Not for him."

Smoke laughed uproariously, and clapped heels to his pinto. They dashed away, the pony's hoofs drumming in the frozen grass. Beau watched the little band until it had passed into the red eye of the sun. Then he climbed back into the wagon, and pulled Tall Woman's warm body against him. He was cold and shivering, but she did not flinch at the chill marble of his flesh.

"Your is heart is bad?" she asked.

"No," he said absently.

He had forgotten the unpleasant news of Samuel Shadduck. He was thinking with pleasurable anticipation of an old crone he had seen yesterday, making *toro* before her son's *tipi*. He must get her on canvas the way she had been; proud, obstinate, stubborn, tenacious. Gradually his eye focused in the wan light, taking in the weave of the canvas wagon-curtains over his head. He was running out of canvas, but *there* was canvas—a lot of it. If he cut that up, he had plenty of canvas.

**Item 10.** Man's painted buffalo robe, Siouan in style. "Black warbonnet" pattern, concentric circles with radiating figures representing feathers. Colors brown, red, and yellow, probably from iron-containing clays. Rolled, in rawhide case; very fragile.

That winter he looked like a scarecrow, pacing the camp in his old buffalo coat, cracked boots patched with a crazy-quilt of rawhide. Tall and thin, so absorbed in his painting and sketching that Tall Woman could rarely tempt his appetite, he was a kind of magnifying glass, hungrily drinking in the sights and people and occasions, filtering them through his own eyes and brain and being, putting them down on canvas. The Sioux regarded him with amused tolerance, not professing to understand him; knowing only he was a brave man, a man who liked children and spent endless patient hours doing sleight-of-hand for them. Tall Woman's eyes followed him as he went about sketching and talking, finding delight in some new face or tribal ceremony. When he tumbled into the wagon, full of plans for a new canvas, she was always there, quietly sewing, or scraping skins, or doing any of the thousand wifely duties. She was pregnant with his child.

They had found a name for him, too: an affectionate and sometimes envious name. He was Many Fingers, because of the way his long bony fingers flashed in the sign talk. The old men of the tribe prided themselves on the skill and fluency and fluttering grace of their sign talk, but Many Fingers was their peer. For countless hours he sat with them in their *tipis*, passing around the pipe, listening to them argue tribal politics, tell old stories, or reminisce about the deeds they performed when they were young men. When it came time for him to speak, there was always a rustle of anticipation, because Many Fingers had a great store of fantastic but interesting stories. Of course, his tales of horse-cars and gas-lights and great houses that went on the water were patently false, but the old men told stories that were not meant to be taken literally, either, so they listened, and grunted approval, and later tried without success to match the flashing speed of his hands.

The warm smoky interior of the *tipis* became a delight to him. The camp of Iron Nose lay in a hollow along the creek bed, already protected to some extent from the winter winds. As additional shelter, windbreaks of poles and brush were erected around the *tipis,* often ten and twelve feet high. Inside, a double lining of sewn hides made a kind of curtain, and the space between this *ozan* and the outer skins was filled with hay and dry grasses. In the larger *tipis* an underground passage had been dug, connecting the base of the fire with the outer air. In this way a constant supply of fresh air entered the *tipi,* was warmed, and heated the interior as well as a Franklin stove.

The wagon was not quite so comfortable. Its gay colors were hidden under a cover of poles and brush Goosey had built over it. The winter snows had piled over the rude covering until the wagon was little more than a snow-covered hillock, with a small dark hole at one end to go in and out. Beau thought occasionally he might do more to make a proper dwelling for Tall Woman, but he was so busy that he had little time. She did not seem to mind, as long as he was there at night, to lie beside her.

"See?" Whispering in his ear, she took his hand and laid it on her swelling belly. "It grows, like a seed. Sometimes when I sit in the wagon sewing, when you are gone, I feel something move in there. It is a man, I know it. A man who will be tall and graceful like you, with long black hair and soft eyes and a very strong spirit inside."

*"Sha," he said. "Sha."*

"In the spring he will come, and that is the best time, because everything comes into life then, and grows. A child born then is the best kind of child—strong and honorable. Like you."

"Like me?" he asked drowsily.

She nuzzled her face into the hollow between his neck and shoulder. There was a scar there—the scar from his battle with Kills-First. It was a hot ridged scar that pained him still on damp days. But it had not affected his hand, or his fluency with the brush.

"Like you," she said.

In the dead of winter, with the temperature hovering far below the freezing mark, horsemen came to their camp from Crazy Horse and Sitting Bull on the Powder River. They came bearing messages of impending trouble, new and fresh trouble with the white men, the persistent and wrong-headed white men. These white men were angry at the Sioux, very angry, and now there was going to be real trouble. All talk was over. Unless the Sioux came in to the reservations before the thirty-first of January—came in and *stayed* in—they would all be considered hostile, and dealt with accordingly by the soldiers.

To date, this had been a battle of words, with little blood shed except that of incautious miners who had come rashly into *Pa Sapa*—the Black Hills where the Animal People lived. Now things were approaching a climax. Sitting Bull and Gall were organizing their forces. All the wandering bands were to rendezvous on the Powder, to discuss the danger, and take steps to guard against the crazy white men. Come in to Standing Rock and the other reservations, indeed! Drag families and possessions through snowdrifts and blizzards and bitter cold—for what? There was no food at the agencies. In Iron Nose's camp were agency Indians who had fled there to get food!

For three days the visitors conferred with Iron Nose and the war chiefs. Pipes were smoked. The camp buzzed with speculation. Finally, the visitors went away, their ponies' hoofs crunching in the snow and nostrils blowing steam. They looked very stern, and dignified. No one spoke as they left.

A summons came to Beau from the *tipi* of Iron Nose. He had never been in that *tipi* since the day, months before, when he had returned from slaying Kills-First, and smoked a pipe with the *wakicunza*. Now he respectfully squatted inside the door, across the fire from Iron Nose. It was a dreary iron-colored day, the sky filled with low-scudding clouds that warned of more snow. Behind the *wakicunza,* in the other half of the great double-*tipi*, Beau saw the harmonium occupying a place of honor. Iron Nose's war-shield leaned against it, in its white buckskin case. His breech-loading Springfield was propped against it, and on top lay the chief's medicine bag, a small leather sack, decorated with paint and quills.

For a long time they sat there, neither speaking. The fire burned low, and the embers became covered with a gray ash. Finally Iron Nose spoke.

"Those men. They want us all to come to the Powder River. They want us to fight with them against the white men. They say there will be one big battle, and then that will be all. They will drive all the soldiers out of the country. They will drive them into the big water that lies out there someplace—" He waved a lean arm. "They will kill them all, and then things will be the same as they used to be. Plenty of buffalo, plenty of good times. We fight the Rees and the Shoshoni, we steal their horses like in old times, we dance, we smoke pipes. Everything will be good for us again."

Beau had learned much of Indian deportment. He grunted and stared at the fire.

"I do not like white men," Iron Nose said. "I do not hate them, as some do, but I do not want to fight with them, either. They do not fight as we do. They want to fight all the time. If you beat them one place, they do not go back to their camp the way we do, and sing and dance and pray. No, they keep right on coming. They keep fighting. That is the wrong way to fight, but they do it. It makes things very hard when they do not understand the way to fight."

The *wakicunza* put tobacco into a pipe and dropped a coal into the bowl. Sucking deep on the stem, he blew smoke to the four quarters, and up into the smoke-blackened cone of the *tipi.* Then he handed it to Beau.

"You are a white man. What does Many Fingers think?"

Beau repeated the process, taking his time, and then laid the pipe aside.

"There is plenty of room out here for everybody. I have many friends among the white people, and among the Sioux. I do not want to see them fight." He sat silent for almost five minutes, cross-legged, hands folded in his lap. A small animal ran across the tightly-stretched skins of the *tipi,* and the skittering sound was loud in the silence. From a nearby tree a load of snow fell to the ground with a slithering thud. "I do not know," Beau continued. "There is not an easy answer. You cannot go in to the reservation in weather like this. It is even a long way to the Powder River. It is hard to go there, too. I would like to have the wisdom to say 'This is the thing to do.' But I do not know. I am sorry."

For a moment the winter sun shone, and a soft delicate light filled the *tipi.* The *wakicunza's* strong features were cut into deep lines, and etched into his face were sorrow and concern. Over these past uncertain months, he seemed to have aged and eroded. His serenity was gone, and in its place was a haunted responsibility he did not quite know how to handle. He bent his head until the eagle-feather almost touched his knees.

"It is easy for Three Horses to say," he murmured. "Red Knife and the rest—they like a good fight. But there is more to this than one good fight. It is many fights, a great fight for *Pa Sapa.* It is more than that. It is whether our people live, or die. The whole people. I do not know what to do." He waved his hand in a gesture of dismissal, wearily. "Friend, thanks. Many thanks."

As Beau lifted the door-flap to go, Iron Nose called to him.

"Wait a minute, friend." He got to his feet as if the action called for a great effort. Going to the harmonium, he looked down at it, and touched one of the yellowing keys with his finger. "This is *wakan,*" he said. "I know that. Once, a long time ago, I was at Fort Laramie, and saw one. It is truly *wakan tanka,* because the white people used it to talk to their gods too, and sang songs around it, and prayed." He turned to Beau. "Are you *klischun?*"

For a moment Beau groped for the meaning. Then he understood.

"Yes. I am a Christian."

"Can you make it go?"

Beau nodded. "A little."

"Then make it go," Iron Nose said fiercely. He pounded on the harmonium with a clenched fist. "The white men are all *klischun*! I do not understand how it works, but it has helped them. Friend, you make it go, and I will sit down here and try for a vision. Maybe it will help me too. Anyhow, I will try!"

He sat before the dying fire, burying his face in his hands.

"Make it go," he ordered.

A rawhide drum made from a hollow log stood in the shadows. Tufts of hair and bright quillwork decorated it, and perhaps it was a *wakan* drum, also. Taking a chance on sacrilege, Beau placed it before the harmonium and sat down to play. Pumping the pedals to build up air, he was relieved to see that the repaired bellows still held. He struck a few experimental chords.

At the strange sound, Iron Nose's shoulders trembled. For the rest, he sat like an image carved from stone, face still in his hands, calling up his medicine. Beau remembered a song he had once heard a girl sing in a Frisco music-hall. Lulu was not a good girl according to the usual lights, but she had a fine strident voice and a fantastic memory for the words of songs, mostly bawdy. The words were best forgotten, but the melody of one came back to him—a plaintive strain from the easy lady's own Kentucky hills, called *The Little Mohee.* He played it through passably well. From *The Little Mohee* he went into a tricky jig he remembered from a black-face show at the Bella Union, and when that was done he concluded with *Rock of Ages,* played simply but with great effectiveness.

When he slipped from the *tipi* into the dusk, Iron Nose still bowed motionless over the dead fire. His body showed no movement, not even the slow rise and fall of breathing. He was deep in a vision. Outside, the *tipi* was ringed with silent people, faces grave and troubled. Beau pushed his way through them and went to his wagon. Tall Woman was bent over the remnants of his shirt, trying to piece it together again with strips of soft buckskin.

"I heard the music," she said. "It was very strange."

The stub of the candle burned low. It was the last one they had, and he did not know where they would get another. In the flickering light her braids were sleek and shiny, and her full breasts lay ripely on the growing burden in her belly. Her face shone with love for him, and concern. She would not understand his feelings, however. He turned on his side and tried to sleep, but again and again the question came back to him. Just what was he any more? A white man? Or a Sioux? It was the first time he had ever put the question into words, although not the first time he had wondered about it.

The idea of the Winter Calendar came to him through Goosey. One day when it was cold, so cold that the trees groaned and cracked in the tightness of the cold, and the air was still and clear so they could hear sounds from a mile away or more, Goosey mentioned the Calendar. Beau, lying on his back in a pile of robes, was interested.

"Friend," he asked Goosey, "what did you say? When was that?"

Goosey sat cross-legged in the warm smoky clutter of the wagon, reloading shells for his old rifle. He was very fond of Tall Woman, and seemed to be distantly related to her. But he was very correct in his relations with her. Wild horses could not drag him into the wagon unless Beau was there. Tall Woman found this very funny, and teased both of them about it. Now, however, content to be a member of the happy small group, Goosey wrinkled his brow and tried to remember what he had said. Unsuccessful, he signed that he did not remember, and went unhappily back to his shell-loading.

Beau burst out laughing at the rueful look on his face.

"The hundred white men—" he prompted Goosey.

Goosey's broad foolish face beamed.

"The Hundred-White-Men-Killed Year. Yes, that was when it happened. It was that year my father killed the grizzly bear. I will tell you all about it. My father—"

"Friend," Beau said, "your father was a great chief. I know this. You have told me. He had many horses, and he gave them all away to show how generous he was. But what is this Hundred-White-Men-Killed?"

Goosey frowned.

"Now you are trying to mix me up. I want to tell you how my father counted *coup* on that grizzly. He—"

Beau appealed to Tall Woman for an explanation.

"It is like this," she explained. "It is a way of keeping time. The old men in our camp know all the years. The Hundred-White-Men-Killed Year was a lot of winters ago. I was a girl then."

Looking at her, he rubbed his nose with his pipe.

"Sixty-five, sixty-seven—along in there someplace?"

"I do not know numbers like that," she said gravely. "But it was the year our people killed a hundred white men at a place where the walking soldiers were, near what they called Riviere de la Prete."

His excitement grew. He was always taken by a new idea, a new bit of knowledge.

"That must have been the Fort Fetterman massacre!"

She looked at him, dark eyes puzzled.

"*Mass—a—ker?*"

"Never mind," he said. He turned to Goosey. "Tell me some more years. What did they call them?"

Goosey was sullen with the pride of the very simple.

"I do not know the name of all the years. What am I—a wise man, a medicine man? Gottam! Go ask the old men. They are the ones who know. Who am I?" He raised his eyes in exasperation to the wagon bows over his head, and went back to measuring powder into a shell.

"Do you know?" Beau asked Tall Woman.

She smiled at his excitement, and touched his cheek with a brown finger.

"I am only a woman. I cook, and mend clothes, and sleep with my husband. That is all."

Not bothering to put on the scabrous buffalo coat, he pushed up the curtain and jumped out. Bounding like a gaunt animal through the snow, falling and floundering as he broke through the stiff crust, he came to the *tipi* of Man-Who-Never-Walked. He shook the door-flap politely, and when he was bidden enter, he ducked his head and went in, arms wrapped around himself, shivering. He squatted inside the door, remembering his manners. Man-Who-Never-Walked lay on his stomach across the fire from him, groaning with pleasure as his wife rubbed his back.

After long minutes, the old man waved his woman away and propped himself upright. He pressed tobacco into the bowl of his pipe and handed it to Beau.

"It is bad to be old," he said. "A man's back hurts when he is old. There is a devil in my back. Tomorrow I will make some medicine in a little bag—some sweet grass and feathers and red dirt. This must all be mixed with the urine of a very young girl— a virgin, certainly—and then put into the bag. When I wear this around my waist, the devil will go." He nodded with satisfaction. "You will see."

"What girl?" Beau asked.

The old man shrugged.

"A young girl. The daughter of Long Bear. She is a good girl. She will help me."

"She is young," Beau agreed, fishing for the information he needed. Man-Who-Never-Walked would talk all day if he were let alone to do it his own way, but he regarded direct questions as impertinent. "I do not know when she was born."

The old man looked wary.

"It was the Winter when Kills-Often Was Brought Home."

"Sha," Beau chuckled.

"I remember it very well," the old man said. "Do not think you can fool me on a thing like that."

Beau blew smoke into the upper darkness of the *tipi,* watching it curl among the smoke-darkened poles.

"I did not know she was that old. She looks much younger."

Man-Who-Never-Walked smiled in triumph.

"You are thinking of her younger sister. That one looks like her also, but she is not a virgin. I know that. No, the younger one was born the Winter When the White Woman Was Rescued."

Beau bent his head in token of the old man's superior knowledge.

"Father, I am wrong. The times get all mixed up. The white man's way of keeping time is different."

Man-Who-Never-Walked grinned, his leathery face breaking into a network of wrinkles. The skin around his toothless mouth was so wrinkled and cracked his lips were almost lost in the maze.

"I have heard of the white man's way of keeping time. It is done with numbers." He held up ten fingers. "That is so many fingers. That means a number to white men. They hold up their fingers many times, so—" He waggled his hands. "That is the way they remember things that happened. So many hands of fingers. But what does that mean? Numbers do not mean anything. But the Winter the War Bonnet was Torn—now *that* is a time!

Everyone remembers that time. There is not any mistake. The Winter the War Bonnet was Torn—that means the same thing to everyone. Numbers—pah!" He spat.

"*I* do not remember that time," Beau said.

The old man shrugged.

"That is easy. Ask me. Any man here can ask me. That is why the old men are important. They remember these things, so they can tell people. The things we do not remember from having seen them ourselves, we remember from our fathers and our grandfathers. This is the reason for us old men."

Beau nodded respectfully, hard put to conceal elation at the plan that was forming in his brain. This was a history of the Sioux nation, this way of keeping time! The Winter the War Bonnet was Torn, the Winter the White Woman was Rescued, the Winter a Hundred White Men Were Killed, the Winter When Kills-Often Was Brought Home; he saw them in his mind not as a measure of time, not as history, even, but as a series of pictures—canvases for the painting. He had paints, he had canvas.

"Father," he said, "this is a good way to keep time. It is better than the white man's way. But the white man's numbers go back further than the Winter Calendar. Numbers—" He raised his hands, fanning out the fingers with a snap of his knuckles. "The white man's numbers are better to go far back."

Man-Who-Never-Walked was indignant.

"Why do you say this, friend? Are you trying to make me angry?" He folded skinny arms across his chest. "Our calendar goes back farther than any white man's numbers! We were here a long time before any white man came. Listen to me!" He began a litany of the years, reciting the Winter Calendar of the Dacotah people. The Winter the Girl Saved Her Brother's Life, the Winter the White Ghost Horse Was Seen, the Winter *Iktomi* Fooled the White Men, the Winter the Bird People Came Down, the Winter the Silent Eaters Killed the Shoshoni. Eyes closed in a kind of trance, the old man droned on and on, and Beau lost count. The Winter Calendar stretched back and yet farther back, past the War Between the States, past the War of 1812, into the Revotionary War and beyond. The old man chanted the years, drumming with one fist on his thigh as he sang. Finally he stopped, and opened his eyes. He seemed dazed, caught in a net of antiquity. Blinking, he stared at Beau.

"There are more," he said. "It is late. I am getting tired, friend."

Beau made his respectful thanks.

*"Hie. Hie."* He got to his feet and backed toward the door-flap. *"Hie,"* he said again, bowing his head, and turned and loped away through the snow. His brain prickled with the concept of the Winter Calendar, and his face felt hot and fevered. Not caring that the night was cold and that he wore only a shirt and jeans and moccasins, he came to a stop in the starlight, one hand grasping his long chin in a gesture of thought. In his mind's eye he could see the whole project—a magnificent series of canvasses, one to illustrate each Winter of the Calendar. He would start as far back as the memory of the old men went, because when they died something was always forgotten—some small bit of the Dacotah history. In a way, it would be his gift to them; thanks for the generosity with which they had received him, and treated him, given him their food, shared their life.

He did not know how long he stood there, too wrapped in thought to know it was cold, that his feet were numb and block-like, that he shivered till his teeth clattered and his lungs hurt from the bite of the cold. Suddenly he was aware of a light, and someone pulling him and someone else pushing, and both of them very angry with him. Tall Woman and Goosey had found him. Between them they made him go into the wagon and lie under a mountainous stack of robes. Goosey pulled off his moc-casins and rubbed his feet while Tall Woman tried to force a horn spoon of broth between his set lips. He brushed her hand away.

"I need canvas," he said. "Lots of canvas."

They thought he was delirious and tried to hold him down. But he insisted, growing almost violent, and finally Goosey took out a knife and cut a square from the wagon-canvas.

"Gottam!" His tone was withering. "Now what do we do? It is cold." Shaking his head, he stuffed straw and blankets into the hole, shivering. "Me, I am crazy. They all say that. But I am not as crazy as Many Fingers. I do not cut holes in my *tipi* on a cold night like this." Still grumbling, he climbed out of the wagon, and a moment later they heard him piling brush over the hole in the canvas.

Tall Woman slipped out of her clothing and came beside him under the robes. "I am here," she said. "I will get you warm." She wrapped her smooth soft legs around his, and pressed her bare breasts tightly against him. She was hot and soft against him, fragrant with a woman-smell. But he did not move, only lying rigidly beside her, one hand holding the square of canvas Goosey had handed him. Finally he felt her taut body relax and sag away from him.

"You are angry with me?" Her voice was puzzled.

For a moment he did not speak, and there was disaster for her in the small space that lay between them. Through the strange spell that had gripped him he sensed her hurt, and felt much less than a man. He rolled the canvas carefully, and stood it in a corner of the wagon. Then he pulled her to him, and she lay contented against him, head pillowed on his shoulder.

"No," he said. "I am not angry. I am foolish, that is all. Sometimes a devil gets hold of me and makes me foolish. But I love you, and you are a good wife to me."

Her voice trembled with relief.

"My uncle is Blue Horse. He is a man who knows all about devils. Tomorrow we will get him to make a charm for you to wear. No devil will come near you when you wear medicine that my uncle Blue Horse has made. Sun, Thunder, Rock—he speaks to them all, and they tell him what to do."

In the darkness, he smiled to himself.

"No. I have a medicine for this devil."

The next morning, he cleaned out the wagon in preparation for the great project. Tall Woman he sent off to stay with her uncle Man-Who-Never-Walked. Sammy was banished from his favorite lair in a corner of the wagon. Fingers tingling with anticipation, Beau set up his paints and selected brushes and fastened the square of canvas to a makeshift easel which Goosey fashioned for him from water-hardened rawhide strips, laced together with sinew. He squatted cross-legged before the canvas, thinking to start with the Winter A Hundred White Men Died, the Fetterman massacre. He knew a little of it from books and newspaper accounts.

For a long time he had watched some of the old men at work, painting robes. The women painted, too, but there was a queer division of labor that intrigued him. Only the men might paint living things; people, horses, plants, trees. The women were restricted to ceremonial designs, abstract combinations that were almost geometrical with squares, triangles, neatly stair-stepped lines, and ornamental borders. So he borrowed from them those of their techniques and materials he liked; the colors mixed from ochre and berries and colored earths combined with buffalo fat, the porous buffalo-rib bones into which they sucked color and then rubbed over the scraped hides, the odd, almost childlike tricks of perspective that were at once so simple and naive, and yet somehow powerfully effective.

The Winter A Hundred White Men Died grew rapidly under his hurrying hand. It was a curious mixture of Philadelphia art school and Sioux, and he was pleased with it. The scene showed a boiling mass of mounted Sioux bearing down on a party of woodcutters, and it held a quality of imminent conclusion and physical shock that he was proud of. The colors, too; they flashed and glowed, but as a light wash over the whole scene he used a dead gray that muted the whole to a somber mood. The gray he had gotten by pounding a light volcanic stone to powder and mixing it with water. That was a good color. He nodded in satisfaction.

Goosey, however, was not satisfied. He put his head into the wagon and watched Beau for the better part of an hour. Then he said, *"Gottam,"* and walked away. Shortly he was back, carrying Man-Who-Never-Walked on his back. The old man settled himself at Beau's shoulder and stared at the first scene of the Winter Calendar of the Dacotahs. Beau waited in silence while he inspected the canvas with stony unblinking eyes.

"It is good," Man-Who-Never-Walked said at last. "I *think* it is good. I do not know for sure." He made the sign for *two hearts,* fist against chest, first two fingers extended, then turning the hand over and back again, rapidly. It was a convenient sign to the Sioux. It could mean anything. *Perhaps. I do not know. Maybe. I am thinking about it.* "But you made some mistakes." He pointed to a horse. "That is not a Sioux pony. That is a white man's horse. It is too big, and it is black. A black horse is unlucky. We do not ride black horses. And here." He stabbed at the canvas with a bony forefinger. "You do not use your eyes, my son. All Sioux ponies have their nostrils slit. Have you not seen? That way they breathe better when they run fast." The old man chuckled, and signed for Goosey to lift him on his back. "Also," he said, "I think you make too many Indians and not enough white men. It was a good fight that time. It was not so easy. You make it look too easy for us."

That night Beau slept as if he were physically exhausted. He lay motionless all night in the wagon. Once, when the moon was flat and cold in the western sky, Tall Woman came to the wagon and pulled the robes up over him again, but when morning came he had forgotten it. It was like a dream. He went furiously back to his painting again, and the stew she brought him thickened and congealed in the wooden dish as he worked. He was too busy to eat. He was almost too busy to notice the sounds of distant rifle-shots, a faint pattering that drifted in on the east wind.

**Item 11.** Canvas in oils, approximately 10 × 14 inches. Meeting Fox Soldiers, Sioux warrior society. Ring of men around fire in *tipi*, some men carrying whips as dance-leaders, others carrying lances. One man sits before a large red drum supported by four ornamental sticks making a kind of stand. Another blows an eagle-bone whistle while men dance within the ring. Diagonal tear in lower right corner. Paint cracked and peeling over lower half of the surface. Otherwise good. Signed B/M.

I f it had not been for two boys out on a lark, the camp of Iron Nose would have been caught completely unprepared. Green Shirt, a grandson of Man-Who-Ate-The-Wolf, and a boy named Fool Horse had made a sled of buffalo-ribs, and took it out to a nearby hill for its first flight. The day was cold and still, and the sky glowed with bluish and leaden intensity. A mile or more from the camp, the two boys climbed the hill, chattering gleefully at the prospect of the long fast slide to the bottom.

No one had given any thought to the imminence of horse soldiers. In the first place, the sentiment of the camp was divided. No one knew whether to give in to the white men and go to the Red Cloud reservation, or stay where they were and try to reason with the Black Hills Commission, or adopt the plan of the extremists and join Sitting Bull on the Powder River right away. Since the matter was still under discussion, it was not fair for the horse soldiers to bother them. Besides, it was very cold, and the horse soldiers would not move in that kind of weather anyway. Too, there was plenty of meat and coffee and tobacco; it was pleasant to lie on one's back in the *tipi* and pass around the pipe and reminisce about stealing horses from the Absaroka in the old days. The Absaroka were maybe the best horse-stealers there were, and to steal horses from *them! Wagh!* The idle talk went on. *Now I will tell you about my grandfather, and how he counted coup on the Grease People with his bare hand. Listen, friends!*

Later, they knew it was three or four companies of the Third Cavalry that had hit them. They knew that from the dead bodies and papers found on the soldiers they had killed. But when Fool Horse ran shouting into camp, dragging the blood-spattered sled behind him, no one knew anything. The whole thing had come as such a shock, such an unbelievable and unjustified thing, that the young men and the old men and the women and children merely clustered around the boy, mouths open, unwilling and unable to believe.

"Where is Green Shirt?" someone asked.

Fool Horse pointed to the blood on the sled.

"They killed him. He was on the sled. A big man in a fur coat rose up from behind a bush and shot at us."

In the same unbelieving voice, someone said, "Fool Horse, you are hit, too."

The boy looked down at the hole in the blanket that he wore kilted around his hips. In silence he folded the blanket back, and looked at the wound in his belly. From a diagonal rip in the stomach wall protruded a rope of blue-gray bowel, like an evil animal, a worm, a snake.

"True," Fool Horse murmured. "That is true." He sat down in the snow, pulling the blanket around him. Tears were in his eyes, although he tried hard not to let anyone see. "We wanted to ride down the hill on the sled," he said. "That is all." In a high-pitched young voice, he began to sing a death-song, singing very loud.

Suddenly, like the breaking of ice on a frozen pond, they fell into the real truth and meaning of the event. For precious minutes they had all been gripped by a paralysis, but now they knew what to do. As in all emergencies, the warrior societies took over. The Keeper of the Red Drum sent off men to reinforce the guards on the horse herd. The Silent Eaters took their guns and bows and lances and ran toward the hill where the boys had been coasting. Man-Who-Ate-The-Wolf herded the old men and old women and the sick toward a deep gully a quarter of a mile away, where they would be safe. Red Knife got his war-bonnet out of the painted rawhide case and put it on.

"We will kill them all!" he yelled. He whacked on the canvas of Beau's wagon with his bow. "*Hopo,* friend! Let's go!"

Unaware at first of the meaning of the clamor, Beau climbed out of the wagon in his shirt and little else.

"What has happened?" he asked.

Behind him, Tall Woman put her dark head through the flap.

"What has happened? What is all the noise?"

Beau stared down for a moment at Fool Horse, squatting in the snow at his feet.

"Friend," Fool Horse said, "I am very sick."

The pony soldiers broke through a thicket of frozen willows along the creek, coming at a gallop. Big men, all of them, riding big horses and looking even larger because of the bulky canvas overcoats and fur collars and fur caps they wore. In that horrible frozen moment Beau could see every detail with painful accuracy; plunging hoofs breaking through crusted snow, the steam-snorting nostrils, the raised carbines from which little jets of flame spurted, even the sweating red face of a yelling mustached man on a bay. The dark wave sped over the frozen ground toward him, and behind it was another dark line.

"Go away!" he yelled at Tall Woman. He waved wildly at her, almost as if to push her to safety from that distance. "Run! Hide!" Pulling at Fool Horse's arm, he dragged the dying boy under his wagon. As he straightened, he saw Tall Woman's frightened face, and felt the cold metal of the big Sharps she thrust into his hand, loaded. It was then that the big plunging horses hit them, and one soldier put his hands to his face, dropping his carbine, while the black he rode shouldered into the painted wagon and knocked it over on its side, the wheels spinning.

The Sioux did not habitually plan for war. Once it came about, either thrust upon them or as the exasperated consequence of their depredations on the white men, they fought with magnificent courage, and skill. Now that they were slammed headlong into this engagement, they went to work like the professional hunters they were. Later, from the stories of the Sioux men who fought there, it was calculated that the Third Cavalry was outnumbered, and should have been beaten anyway. But at the time the pony soldiers had a heavy advantage in their surprise attack, and the outcome was in doubt.

Beau dove behind the wagon. The black horse was half-pinned beneath it, and a frightened driving hoof caught him in the knee with numbing force. He struck the animal in the head with the butt of the Sharps, and it shivered heavily and then ceased to struggle. Across from his upturned wagon he saw Iron Nose struggling with a mounted soldier. The *wakicunza* gripped the bridle of the soldier's horse, and with the other hand attempted to beat the man to the ground with his lance. But each time Iron Nose tried to strike the horse reared and plunged, and neither could get in a telling blow.

There were screams, and shouts of anger, and the heavy thud of hooves and the blast of guns and the curses and whoops of the cavalrymen, mingled with yells of defiance from the Sioux. A pall of smoke came quickly on the scene, and then a heavier darker smoke as a soldier put a torch to one of the *tipis* where dried meat and corn were stored. The skins caught like tinder, and a sheet of flame licked upward, roaring toward the crossed lodgepoles.

Beau jumped over the wagon and struck the cavalryman across the back with the butt of his Sharps. He could have propped it on the wagon and shot the man as he wrestled with

Iron Nose, but he did not. Instead, the man fell on him and they rolled together like fighting bears in the muddy snow, cursing and tearing at each other. Suddenly the man lay limp, gasping, and a film spread over his eyes so that they became dead and glasslike. Iron Nose shook his lance, and the red on the blade stabbed at the sky.

"*Onhey!*" he shouted. "I have killed this one. Thanks friend!"

Another *tipi* burst into flame, and then another. The *tipis* burned with a hollow roar, and the meat and skins and fat in them bubbled and boiled and sent off slanting clouds of rich smoke, whipped high by the wind. The camp was dark with the plunging mounts and big bodies of the pony-soldiers. Iron Nose, running toward a dismounted soldier who knelt with a torch at the *wakicunza's tipi*, was ridden down from behind; as the carbine-butt came down on his head, his face seemed to sag and come undone, and he fell down in the snow. Red Knife kicked the soldier sprawling from behind, and as the man fell he jumped forward and ripped off the fur cap.

"*Onhey!*" he shouted. He slashed at the man's head, and ripped loose the scalp. "*Onhey!*" Holding it aloft, he made a howling sound, and when the scalped man tried to rise, he buried the reeking knife three times, to the hilt, in the furred back. The man struggled to his elbows, looking dazed at the pool of red mud in which he lay. Then he collapsed, and was still.

"You have killed Iron Nose!" whooped Red Knife. "I have killed you, soldier! *Onhey!*"

In sudden panic, Beau turned to look for Tall Woman. She had been in the wagon when it went over. The wagon now burned brightly and fiercely; the paints and canvases must have caught. Horrified, he saw a soldier with a torch who lumbered around the wagon, a furry bearlike creature, pausing in his dance only to set a new fire and then rush on.

"Stop that!" Beau screamed at him, his voice breaking into a shriek. "Don't do that!"

For a moment he stood paralyzed. The soldier, startled at the command in English looked at him with open mouth. Then he dropped to his knees in a well-trained gesture and raised his carbine. Beau looked for an eternity down the barrel of the gun that pointed directly at his face. He saw the black hole of the muzzle, and the cheek bent fondly and professionally over the sights. Still carrying the Sharps in the crook of his elbow, Beau threw himself sidewise, firing at the same time. In the same instant, the slug from the carbine went over his head.

He thought he had missed. The soldier still teetered on his knees, aiming the carbine. Then, after an eternity, he struggled to his feet, curiously bowed in the middle, like a jointed toy that is in need of repair. He tottered forward, holding out the carbine like a cane, trying to support himself. He came faster and faster, tottering and toppling, his body going faster than his booted legs. Finally he fell. He got one knee under him, and tried to rise, but the leg slid sidewise in the mud, and the man rolled over on his back and lay still.

"*Onhey,*" Beau whispered.

He did not know why he said it. The word came unbidden, and surprised him. Walking forward, he saw that the man was still alive, looking up at him. In the face he saw hurt, and bewilderment; a kind of rage at being so taken advantage of.

Beau was jerked back to consciousness, and the realization of his danger, by a yell from Goosey. Carrying a broken carbine, his own weapon lost, Goosey charged past Red Knife and the rest and ran headlong at a beleaguered knot of horse-soldiers, taking shelter behind Beau's flaming wagon.

"*Onhey!*" he shouted, drunk with excitement.

A blast of flame bloomed in his face, like an unfolding flower, but he was not hit. Miraculously he ran on, shrieking and swinging the broken weapon like a club. When he came to the wagon, he hit a man in the face with the butt, and the man went down, hands groping at his broken face. Still whooping and yelling, Goosey dodged away, and reached shelter without being hit.

"*Onhey!*" he yelled in Beau's ear. "I have a spirit in me! No one can hit me!"

The cavalry had mortally hurt the camp, but they began to realize now that they had overextended themselves. Many of the soldiers lay dead in the snow, looking like buffalo ready to be skinned. The Silent Eaters had gotten in behind them, and the remnants of the soldiers were caught between two fires. Somewhere a relief column was coming up to rescue them; Beau heard the faint metallic voice of a trumpet in the distance. Two or three dozens of the horse-soldiers formed a square in the middle of the village, some mounted and some on foot, others lying behind horses that had been killed. Order and discipline were still apparent in that group, and death came in sheets from their guns.

Beau's wagon still burned, and he did not know where Tall Woman was, but there was no time to wonder. The reserve of the horse soldiers hit them then, and for a moment all was confusion again. It was the dying convulsion of the battle, the end of an ill-planned attack. The reserves were anxious only to rescue the survivors of their men, and to get them out of the camp. Riding two and sometimes three on a single staggering mount, the horse soldiers burst out through the ring of Sioux, yelling and shooting. The violence of the charge took them out of the camp, as it had taken them in. After a few moments there was only the crackling of burning *tipis* and the blood on the snow, the hoof-beaten mud and still bodies; that, and the thin wavering thread of a trumpet-call in the distance. The Third Cavalry was gone, most of it They had recovered most of their dead, and all of their wounded, too.

"Stirring gravy," Beau said, half to himself. He did not recognize the hoarse croak of his own voice. He looked down at his lean naked legs, spattered with mud. In one hand he still held the Sharps.

Goosey clapped him on the back, feeling good.

"Friend, did you see what I did to that soldier? Gottam!"

He pushed Goosey away, and leaned the empty Sharps against a tree. His paints, his canvases—all of them were burning in the wagon, but he did not care. With a bemused detachment, he realized that Tall Woman and Red Knife and some of the rest were ripping off the burning wagon-canvas, trying to save some of Many Fingers' *pishers* and the tool he used to make them. Walking over to the body of the man he had killed, he knelt and looked down at the white face.

When Tall Woman came to him, he pushed her away.

"Go away." His voice was angry. "I—I must think about this."

It was a decision he had never wanted to make; one that had been forced on him. He had shot a man. A white man, one of his own kind. It was an irrevocable and a complete decision, too, with no dangling strings. He was Sioux whether he had made up his mind before or not; committed to living their life, sharing their meat, fighting their battles. He felt dead, like the fierce-mustached boy lying before him.

Tall Woman knelt beside him, eyes filled with sadness, and pity. "They will have to move the camp. We must all go now."

"Go?" He looked at her, frowning. "Where?"

"To Powder River." She pointed. "That way. To the camp of Sitting Bull. Red Knife and Three Horses and Man-Who-Ate-The-Wolf say that is all we can do now. They have sent a war pipe. I do not know. I am a woman."

He shook his head, wearily.

"I do not know what I will do."

She lowered her eyes. Squatting beside him, she was uncomfortable with the burden she carried, the burden he had put there.

"If you want to stay," she said, "I will stay. Whatever you want to do."

He got to his feet and gently raised her by the elbow. Not looking back, he went to the wagon with her.

"We will go," he told her. "There is noplace else to go."

A good name for that winter was "The Winter When Many People Died." Iron Nose's people did not know that, when they started for the Powder River, and the camp of Sitting Bull. Even if they had known, there would have been no other choice. Most of their food was gone, and their winter robes. All the dried meat, the fruits and berries, the corn and beans they had traded for, much of the ammunition and powder; all these were gone in the holocaust of the burned village. The skins that covered the *tipis* were gone, and the lodgepoles; these last were hard to come by, and the Sioux had gone a long way to the east for them. Now there were no lodge-poles to make *travois* from, but there was little to carry on the *travois,* anyway, except the sick and the old and the very young.

"It is good," Tall Woman said with resignation. "A heavy load on a *travois* grinds off the ends. All the time they are shorter and shorter, till you have to get new ones." But in spite of her calm-ness, Beau could see fright in her eyes. The baby was not too far away, now, and it would be hard to have a baby on the march to Powder River. Divining his thoughts, she buried her face against his chest, and said in a muffled voice, "I do not care. It does not make any difference to me. I have told you that. As long as I am with you, I am all right."

Man-Who-Never-Walked was pessimistic. Huddled in a fur robe, he watched the bustling activity of the camp, heard the shouts of the many leaders, watched the confusion and flurry and the many false starts.

"I do not like this," he said to Beau. "I do not like this at all. When Iron Nose was here, he could keep everything moving quick and fast and good. He knew how to talk to all the people. He knew what food we had, and how many guns, and where to get more, and when. He could look many suns ahead, and when a thing had to be done, it got done, friend." The old man rubbed his toothless gums with a finger, and watched Red Knife and Three

Horses argue with Man-Who-Ate-The-Bear about the disposition of the pony herd. "Those are brave men," he said. "They talk too much, though. That is the way with many brave men. To be brave does not take much thinking."

Beau's wagon had been gotten upright again, and the burned canvas patched with scraps of skin and part of an ancient gingham dress. The mules were in fair shape, although a little gaunt from winter forage. They would not eat the cottonwood bark the horses relished, and there had not been much hay.

"True," Beau said.

The old man chuckled, and placed a bony hand on Beau's arm.

"I do not mean you, friend. You are a brave man, but you are a smart man. You think a lot. I am glad you are with us, but it is not going to be a happy time." He dragged himself into his litter, and clapped his hands for the boys told off by the Fox Soldiers to carry him about the camp. He looked very old and bowed as he jogged away.

Goosey was an active part of the confusion of the camp. For his exploit in counting *coup* with a broken carbine, he took an immediate high place in the councils. He did not quite understand how this sudden elevation came about, but he was proud of it.

"Think, friend!" he said to Beau. He struck a pose in the new four-point blanket an admirer had given him. "Red Knife came to me today and asked me to count the sacks of meat in the camp. He asked me to do this, because it is very important, and because I am a great warrior."

Beau grinned, and said nothing. Goosey's face sagged.

"I counted *coup* on that horse soldier. You saw me do it."

"I did," Beau agreed.

"Then why do you laugh at me?"

"I do not laugh." Beau wrapped a broken harness strap with sinew, and tied a hard knot. "You were very brave."

Goosey's face split in a grin. He threw the blanket around him with a flourish.

"I did not think I could be so brave. I tell you, a spirit came on me, and I could do anything. I wish there were more battles like that one, so I could show them all what I could do." Then his face collapsed into melancholy again. "No, that is not good. Iron Nose is dead, and other people. No, I do not wish that." He looked across the snow at the tree where they had put the *waki-cunza*. The body lay stiffly outlined against the sky, at rest on the pole platform his people had made for him to sleep on. A feather bonnet fluttered in the wind, and an inquiring bird wheeled away in fright. "No," Goosey said, "I do not wish that. Iron Nose was always good to me."

Beau threw the harness on the off mule.

"Friend," he said, "reach around my mule and hand me the other end of that strap."

Goosey's face took on a cunning cast. He looked at the dangling strap. With a thumb stuck between first and second fingers, he made an insulting gesture.

"I am not a woman," he said. "I do not do work like that. Gottam! Go get Tall Woman to help you. That is woman's work. I am a warrior." With magnificent *hauteur* he stalked away, head thrown back, looking at the world under lowered eyelids. Beau's face was sad as he watched him go.

In the Moon When the Wolves Run Together, the camp moved off toward the Powder River, and their allies, the Sioux and Cheyenne who waited for them there. As they passed the tree where the body of Iron Nose lay, the women cried out in anguish, and gashed themselves with knives. The long column wound by like a wounded snake, halting and disorganized even before it had gotten well under way. The Fox Soldiers rode back and forth, trying to keep the village in order, but there was a feeling among the people that things were not starting out very well. To add to this feeling, the south wind started to blow. It was well known that the south wind brought sickness, and that the south was a land of death. But there was nothing else to do but go on, away from this place where the *wakicunza* had been killed by the horse soldiers. A baby started to cry, and that was the only sound; that and the soft sighing of the wind, the scraping of the *travois* poles on the crusted snow, the shuffle of feet.

From a long way off, Beau looked back at the tree. He drove his wagon, Tall Woman sat beside him, huddled in a blanket, her breath frosty.

"Do not look back," she said. "It is bad luck. Do not even say his name. That is bad luck too."

The body of *wakicunza* had been given back to the elements; the four winds, the rains, the winged things of the air. Tied to the *tipi* pole stuck in the ground beside his tree-platform, his drum and sashes and rattle moved in the wind. Without him, the village moved on.

**Item 12.**  **Shell gorget. Fine example of Plains Indians shell-work. Three rows of iridescent freshwater mus-selshells in graduated sizes, strung together with sinew. Some stained; dark rusty stains that could be blood.**

---

The journey to Powder River turned rapidly into a nightmare. Lack of food brought into sharp relief the lack of leadership, and the lack of leadership aggravated the lack of food. Three Horses and Red Knife and Man-Who-Ate-The-Wolf wrangled for hours on end about minor matters of precedence, or about a lost or stolen horse. During these arguments, the long column came to a halt in the snow. Small fires were lit, and the people huddled around them, cooking whatever small store of meat and grain they had. The weather was cold; so cold that all game seemed to have vanished from the face of the land, and the hunters came back empty-handed and angry.

They had few lodgepoles, and when they camped for the night, the best shelter they could manage was to plant willow-shoots and branches in a circle, covering the makeshift rig partway up with blankets. With a small fire in the center, it was not too bad, but some of the older people grew sick, and babies cried all night. Beau and Tall Woman shared the wagon with their friends, and one night it grew so crowded and noisy that Beau slipped silently out and spent the night huddled in a blanket at the foot of a stunted tree. When he came back in the morning, Tall Woman smiled at him.

"You are a good man. The people like you."

Holding a half-frozen bit of hump-meat in his mouth, he snicked a bite free with his knife, and handed the rest to her.

"You do not like people to think you are a good man," Tall Woman said. "You like to look fierce, and maybe crazy. But you are still a good man."

When he did not answer, she put her head against his arm and said, "In the Sun Dance they teach the men to be brave, generous, and strong. They say a man must endure pain and suffering without weeping, and that he must be able to make a lot of children for his wife. Did you go to a school to learn all these things, that you do them so well?"

"Eat your meat," he said roughly.

He did not fool her. She smiled all that day, and sang old songs to him. Even when the wheels of the wagon fell into chuck-holes and jolted over rocks, she continued to sing, although the baby was not far away.

It did not snow much, not right then. The land stretched endlessly ahead, yellow with winter-killed buffalo-grass and bunch-grass, with a sprinkling of sage. There was little water, because the small streams and rivulets were uniformly bad; brackish and alkaline. When it froze into ice, it was difficult to cross, because it was rotten and dangerous. There was little wood for fires, and the wind howled all day and all night, sucking the warmth from their bodies as if they had been plunged into cold water.

Day after day the hunters went out and came back empty-handed. One of them found a small amount of fresh buffalo-manure, and told his companions he was going to stay out and find some meat. That night the rest of them came in, but the man who had found the buffalo-manure was never seen again. Maybe he had run into a party of Rees or Absaroka, or maybe the horse-soldiers got him. No one knew. His wife gashed herself, and put white paint on her face. When it came time to leave the camp, she would not move. Tall Woman went to her and bent over, heavy and awkward, trying to raise her. But the woman struck her, and would not move. The camp went on without her. For a long time they could see her sitting motionless in the trail, head bowed. Then they passed behind a bluff, and they did not see her again, either.

No one knew how far they had gone. Red Knife said he remembered the country quite well, but he and Man-Who-Ate-The-Wolf fell into an argument about the trail, and almost came to blows before Three Horses pulled them apart. Goosey added to the altercation by stating publicly that they were both wrong. In his new mantle of importance, he made ridiculous statements with confidence, and turned ugly when anyone crossed him. Even the gentle Tall Woman began to fear him, and shrank against Beau when Goosey rode down the column on his hammer-headed pony, wrapped in his new blanket. So far as Beau was concerned, however, Goosey confined himself to glowering and muttering. He did not trust Many Fingers any longer, Goosey confided to Red Knife. It was possible that Many Fingers was putting some kind of a spell on the village. Beau shrugged, and said nothing. They were all jumpy and nervous, beginning to show the effects of lack of food and water and warmth.

One night they came upon an abandoned village, where they camped. The frameworks of drying racks for meat were still intact, and a rough palisade had been built about the camp, probably against the incursions of the Absaroka, who raided on the Sioux when the Sioux were not raiding on them. Much cottonwood lay about, felled as food for ponies, which relished the inner bark as winter forage. There were many graves, the corpses wrapped in their best blankets and robes. It was a good camp; the water was good, after the ice had been broken, and there was grass in the nooks sheltered by the wind. For the first time in a long while, they were comfortable at night, although still without much food. But when morning came, the sky was leaden, and as they were getting ready to move on, a stinging snow whipped out of the northwest.

Tall Woman was sick. All that night she had been wakeful, and when morning came, her face was feverish and her eyes unnaturally bright. Red Knife came to the wagon, and knocked on the side with the butt of his rifle.

"It is time to go."

Beau looked out at the swirling snow.

"My woman is sick."

Red Knife shook his head.

"A lot of people are sick. We have to go on. We will never get to the Powder River if we stay here. It is starting to snow. We will get stuck in the snow here and maybe never get away. Friend, I say we have to go."

Beau climbed out of the wagon and pulled Red Knife away, so Tall Woman would not hear.

"What is this you say, friend? A lot of people are sick?"

"Many people." Red Knife looked baffled, and angry. "They are hot, and the woman of Old Bear has spots on her face and her neck and her chest. Friend, I tell you we are having bad luck."

Beau took Red Knife by the arm and said, "Listen. This is bad. There is a sickness that starts this way. They call it the smallpox. It is a very bad sickness. It comes quick, and a lot of people die."

Red Knife was a good man, and a brave man, but the many problems of the march were too much for him. He sat down cross-legged on the frozen grass, rifle across his knees.

"I am going to pray," he said. "Friend, I do not know what to do. Maybe someone can tell me. *Iktomi* is making fun of me. He has brought all this on us. I will pray to him, and see what he wants me to do."

"*Sha*," Beau said. "That is a good idea."

Beau left him sitting there, and hurried away to find Old Bear and his wife. The woman was sick, and her face was covered with small pustules. He put a hand on her head, and felt the heat coming from her. Old Bear pushed him aside, and tried to drag the woman to a *travois*.

"Wait a minute," Beau said. "This woman is very sick. If you make her go on, she will die."

Mute, the woman looked from her husband to Beau, and back again, patiently waiting.

"There are others who are sick, too." Beau said. "We must stay here. If we try to go on in this snow, everybody will be sick. We will all die."

Man-Who-Ate-The-Wolf stalked back to them, waving his bow.

"What is the matter here? Why are you all waiting?"

Goosey was with him, and he was angry, too.

"Why do you talk so much?" he asked Beau. "Many Fingers, you talk too much. We will handle this. We know how to decide things."

"I say this, friend. I have seen this sickness before. It is a bad sickness. I think my woman has it too. We must stay here and let them rest. That is the only way. If we try to go on we will all die." The wind snarled, and a gust of white flakes blotted out the anxious faces for a moment. The branches of a tree threshed wildly in the wind, and made a cracking sound. "I speak the truth," Beau said. He made the ritual gesture with his thumb. "This is a bad thing. Listen to me."

Man-Who-Ate-The-Wolf was uncertain. He took off his bonnet of crow-feathers and scratched his head, looking at Beau with sharp bright eyes. Holding out the edge of his hand, he sawed at his stomach with it, making the sign for *hungry*. "We do not have very much food. The animals have all gone away from here. If we stay here we will starve."

"If you go on," Beau said, "you will all die of this sickness. I tell you, friend, it is worse than to starve. It is a very bad way to die. But if we stay here, maybe we can find some food. The sick people can rest, and maybe they will get better."

Goosey drew close, looking suspicious.

"What are you talking about?" he demanded.

Beau ignored him.

"These people are my people too," he said. He waved his arm at the long line, patient in the snow. Young men and old, women, children, horses, *travois,* boys with their feet wrapped in skins, girls shivering in the cold, Man-Who-Never-Walked in his litter. "Friend, this is the best thing to do, to stay here and take care of the sick people."

Red Knife walked gloomily up, eyes averted.

"I could not get a vision," he said. "Something is wrong. Friends, I do not know what to do."

Beau could feel the indecision in them, the lack of a leader, the purposelessness of their desperation. The fire-eaters were silenced. They looked uncertainly at one another. "Kicking Horse is very sick," Red Knife volunteered. "His woman is too, and his small children."

"Then we stay here," Beau said. He waved at the people. "Go back. All of you, go back. We are going to stay here. We will take care of the sick people till they are well again, and then we will go on. But now we camp here for a while."

For a moment Tall Woman did not seem to know Beau. Naked, she lay on a buffalo robe, and she made hurt whimpering noises as she moved from side to side. He held her by the shoulders, looking down at the speckling of pustules on the brown fullness of her breasts. Feeling his hands, she opened her eyes and looked at him.

"Who is it?" she whispered. "I do not know you."

Her body was radiant with heat from the fever, and she fought him as he tried to cover her with the robe. Finally, exhausted, she lay still and let him cover her.

"It is you," she said. "I did not know."

When he was silent, she asked, "Am I sick?"

He nodded.

"You know so many things," she said. "Give me something to make me well. Do not the white men have things to give people when they are sick?"

Helpless, he squatted beside her, holding her hand in his.

"I have nothing," he said.

"This is enough." She held his hand against her cheek. This is all I want."

During the day, others fell ill. By nightfall almost a third of the camp had developed the fever, the watery blisters on the body, the dry racking cough. The small store of food was carefully saved for the sick. The doctors went from shelter to shelter, carrying their medicine bags. Their faces were painted blue, and some of them wore buffalo-horns attached to their heads. They knew what the trouble was; an evil spirit had been left in the camp when they drove the horse-soldiers out, and now it was traveling with them and had entered the bodies of the sick. The best way to drive it out was for a doctor to fill his mouth with water and spit it out on the sores of the sick. It was also known that a bad spirit was afraid of a rattle, and the doctors shook their rattles all day and all night. But three people died during the night.

Tall Woman still slept when Beau awoke. Her sleep was uneasy and troubled, but to the touch of his fingers her face did not seem quite as hot. The pustules were still there, though; they had spread, and covered her neck and part of her face. He sat for a long time watching her, and bathed her face and body with a cloth dipped in water. That was all he could do. After a while he left her, still sleeping, and went to see Man-Who-Never-Walked.

"What must I do?" he asked, squatting on his heels in the makeshift lean-to. "I do not want her to die."

In the early light of morning, the old man's face was gaunt and troubled. "I do not know what I am doing here," he complained. He pushed away the handful of corn his wife offered him. "I do not need to eat. When a man is as old as I am, he should go away and not come back." For a while he was silent, and then he said, "All people die. It is not so bad."

Beau put his hands in his face to compose himself. Then he said, "I have been thinking about this all last night. There is only one thing to do. I will go to Deadwood and find a doctor there. I will bring him back with me."

The old man snorted.

"You talk crazy. They think we are all bad. They will not do anything for us. A doctor would not come with you."

"Then," Beau said, "I will buy some medicine from him. Good medicine. I will bring it back here and give it to everyone." He pointed at the worn sole of his boot. "In here I have money, plenty of money. It will buy a lot of medicine."

Man-Who-Never-Walked scratched his head with his eagle-feather fan.

"Maybe," he said. "It is a long way to that village, and the winter is hard." His face softened, and some of the hard lines seemed to melt and disappear, like candlewax softened by the flame. "It is a good thing to do. It is an honorable thing. But maybe I will never see you again."

Beau touched the old man's withered knee.

"I will come back. I will come back soon. No one can stop me."

Man-Who-Never-Walked seemed not to hear. He rocked back and forth, eyes staring into the distance.

"Listen," he said. "I have been here for a long time. I will tell you how to be a good man. Study all you see, look it over and try to understand it. Do not tell lies, because a man who tells lies is a weakling. Keep an even temper, and never be stingy with food. Always keep your horses. If you have a mare, keep her till she has a foal, and if the foal will make a good gelding, train him for running buffalo. If the foal is a mare, hang on to her. Someday your neighbor may need help and you can give her to him. That is the way to be useful and renowed among the people." He blinked watery eyes. "I tell you all this because you are like a son to me. You should know these things so you can help the people."

Beau nodded.

"You are good to tell me these things. I will remember."

When he left the shelter, he was puzzled. He did not understand why Man-Who-Never-Walked had made such a point of passing on the information. And he did not understand why the old man's wife was weeping.

That night two more died. Tall Woman seemed better, however. The watery blisters were still there, and had spread a little, but she was rational, although very weak. She watched his preparations for the journey—the little pemmican he had been able to put by, cartridges for the Sharps, a wooden cup, flint and steel.

"I do not want you to go," she said, and turned her face away from him. "But I know you must. A man must do many things that are not good." She tried to laugh. "A woman has an easier life, I think."

He pulled her to him, and she lay against him for a long time, neither of them speaking. Finally she went to sleep that way, and he held her gently until his arms ached and were numb, and the legs doubled under him lost almost all sensation. Then, moving carefully, he laid her down and pulled the robe around her. Listening to her breathing, he thought that it sounded rough and shallow in tone. But she would get well. She had a magnificent constitution, like most of the people. Besides, he would soon be back with medicine. He sat beside her, sleepless, throughout the night.

When morning came, she was still asleep. He did not awaken her. Instead he looked down for a long time at her face, and then kissed her on the forehead. When he climbed out of the wagon, the camp was quiet in the frosty dawn. Everyone was either sick or attending the sick. While he was putting a saddle on the stronger of the two mules, the wife of Man-Who-Never-Walked came to him. She was a fat woman and old, her face red and swollen with crying. Now her fat hung on her in thin folds, and her moccasins shuffled in the snow. She was called *Chahumpi*.

"I will take care of Tall Woman," she said. "You go, Many Fingers, and bring help for us. I will take good care of her."

For a moment he felt dizzy, and leaned against the mule to steady the reeling world. He had not eaten, he calculated, for the better part of two days.

"I will get someone else," he said. "Man-Who-Never-Walked needs you."

She shook her head.

"No. Not him. He is gone."

"Gone?" He smiled, wondering what she meant. The old man could not have gone far on his withered legs. "Gone where?"

Chahumpi turned, pointing to a wide smear in the snow which lead from their shelter out into the brush-dotted plain. It was a curious kind of trail, as if someone had dragged a dead animal away from camp. Before she spoke, he knew.

"Out there." She folded her hands before her, and looked down at them. "Last night. After you went away. He said he would whip me if I followed him. He said it was a thing a man had to do. He ate too much, he said, and there was little food. He said he was an old man, and he went away."

Beau started toward the trail, but the woman snatched his arm and laid her weight against him.

"No!" she pleaded. "He will be very angry with me. He will be angry with you too. He said he could not fight, his legs were no good for fighting. But he said he could do this, and he would do it."

"But—"

"No!" Chahumpi said. "No! It would shame him! Let him go!" She sobbed, and swallowed, and caught her breath so that her voice was again firm. "If I can let him go, you can let him go."

He stood irresolute for a long time, staring at the dark track in the snow. Finally he turned away and busied himself with the saddle. "All right," he said. "It was something he had to do. It was very brave. No man with good legs could do anything braver." He touched her arm, and said, "Go to Tall Woman. Take good care of her. When I come back I will bring you a bright red dress. You will look beautiful in it."

Bulky in his buffalo coat, he rode through the camp. It was silent, and looked deserted. A man would have thought it abandoned, except for a woman's muffled weeping, and the cry of a baby. It had snowed the night before, a brief, windless snow, and the whole world, as far as he could see, was white. The sun did not shine but flat harsh light came down from the sky and made his eyes hurt when he looked out over the whitened plain. Deadwood was almost a hundred miles in that direction. The dead land lay endless before him, untouched by the track of the smallest animal. It was too cold; his breath crackled and froze in his beard until his mouth and lips were rimmed with frost.

He rode for days, through the Sun Dance Hills, around misshapen buttes studded with timber, down long table-flat valleys, across frozen streams. The cold was on him like a physical pressure, a giant hand weighing on him constantly, something that had to be fought, to be pushed against, always to be reckoned with. It did not snow again; the weather was too cold for snow. Beau ran out of dried meat, and the small amount of *toro,* too; the plum-pudding-like mixture of dried meat and buffalo tallow and dried berries.

Hungry and half-frozen, feet numb and hands like blocks of wood, he pressed on, only hoping the gaunt mule would continue to carry him. The ribs of the mule stood out in sharp outline, and occasionally it stumbled and took a long time to recover, standing in its tracks as though thinking. But the mule had endurance; it had long been eating the rich grass fertilized by hundreds of generations of buffalo on these plains.

On the Inyan Kara, not too rational from lack of food, Beau saw the deer. It was a thin, shabby creature, and it nosed at the frozen water, thirsty. When the deer saw him come, it did not run. It stood, patient and baffled, with a ludicrous crown of snow on its black nose. He half-slid, half-fell off the mule, and knelt in the snow, holding the Sharps in shaking hands, hands that suddenly found the familiar form too heavy to bring upright. Struggling, he managed to raise the heavy barrel and looked down the sights, but his eyes would not focus.

"I need you," he whispered in the Sioux way. "Please go into my lodge. If you do, I will give you red paint." Waiting till the front sight swung past the dun body, he jerked at the trigger and fell backward in the snow. When he crawled to his hands, and knees, the deer lay gracefully propped on its bent forelegs, still looking at him with the same quizzical stare. Blood pumped from its shattered ribs, and as he watched it fell over and lay still.

With the last of his strength he cut the liver out of the doe and ate it raw, tearing at it like an animal. Beau was sick, then, from too much meat, and vomited it all. He lay in the snow, too weak to move, but after a while he got to his feet and managed to build a fire. The day was almost gone, and high dark clouds raced in the sky. It looked like snow; there was a fresh cold clean smell in the air that he knew meant snow. He burrowed down in his buffalo coat near the fire, mouth filled with raw meat. He would wake early, he knew. The Sioux had a way of rising at any desired time. When he first understood how it worked, he was delighted at the beautiful simplicity of it. All a man had to do was drink more or less water before sleeping. More water, rise earlier. Less water, rise later. He scooped up a handful of snow and ate it. Deadwood could not be more than another two or three day's ride.

In a short while, so it seemed, it was full morning, and the rising sun was like molten brass, the light crackling on new-fallen snow, making him blink and rub at his eyes as he rode away.

That day he went snow-blind. His eyelids became so red and swollen that he could not see. Sliding off the mule, he groped his way to a rock, and sat down. Man-Who-Never-Walked had told him what to do. He broke open a cartridge and poured black powder into the palm of his hand. Spitting into it, he made a kind of paste, and smeared that on his eyes, rubbing it well in. For a few moments he thought he could not stand the pain, and he rolled in agony in the snow, afraid he had blinded himself for good. But after a while he could see again, short blinks that reassured him, and after that the swelling went down. For the better part of the day he sat motionless in the sun, letting the makeshift medicine do its work. It was almost evening when he was able to see clearly again. He blinked, not believing his eyes. Not a mile away was a road, a rutted track through the snow. There were wagons on it, and men on horseback. It was the road that led from Custer City to Deadwood.

**Item 13.** Several pencil sketches of nude woman. Studies of hand, arm, leg, structure of hips and thighs. Done on backs of sheaf of Notes Payable, blank. No signature, but presumably work of Mannix.

A momentary thaw had come in the icy grasp that gripped Deadwood. Splashing through pools of sucking wet mud, splattered by the wheels of passing wagons, Beau looked for the office of a physician. Mud was everywhere; hoofs and boots and wheels churned it into a vapor that penetrated every corner of the town. It settled on hands and faces and clothing, it permeated the lobbies of inns and hotels, it got into the food and drink and whisky and tobacco, it descended on all with the same impartiality. It was only to be endured because, with the setting of the sun, it froze again into dun-colored ice. No one appeared greatly to care. It was considered a constituent of the air they breathed, and so beyond comment or objection.

The town was saturated with soldiery. Beau tried to avoid them, but they were as ubiquitous as the mud. Something big was brewing, that was evident. From observing the regimental insignia, the number of high-ranking officers, the long trains of blue army wagons, from listening to scraps of conversation as he passed, it was evident that a strong campaign against the Sioux was being mounted. He quickened his pace.

The shingle of a Dr. Duffy flapped from a rusted bracket over his head.

DR. MARCUS W. DUFFY, PHYSICIAN AND SURGEON. SOLE AGENT FOR DUFFY'S GALVANIC ELIXIR. Anxious to escape the harsh winter sun that followed him everywhere, Beau opened the door and went in. A bell on a coiled spring tinkled softly, and he stood motionless for a moment in the gloom of the inner office, trying to accustom his eyes to the dim light.

Several patients sat in the anteroom. As his eyes adjusted, he saw a plump woman with a little boy, a blonde girl with a heavy bust and a high-crowned straw hat ornamented with ribbons. Several miners were there, silent muddy men in high boots. One had a bandage at a rakish angle on his head, and another held a dirty kerchief to his eye. The room was laced with the smell of ether, and also with something else. They looked at him, all of them, with doubt and suspicion. He did not appreciate why until he caught a glimpse of Beau Mannix in a pier-glass that stood against the far wall.

He might as well have been a hostile, perhaps Gall or Red Cloud himself. The lanky figure that stared back at him from the glass was strange, even to him. Long and unkempt black hair, skin of the face burned brown and weathered, split and shabby boots so many times patched that they looked like the high moccasins the Sioux wore—even the scabrous buffalo coat had been so torn and worn and pieced out with skins that it looked more like a robe than a proper coat. There was also, he suspected, a smell of some kind about him. The young lady with the heavy bust waved a lacy square near her nose, and looked faint.

"Is the doctor in?" he asked.

They were the first words of English he had used in a long time, and came out with an odd inflection that made him even more of an outlander. Uneasy, almost frightened, he took a step back and reached for the handle of the door, but the fat lady said "Yes," and he sat down, gratefully.

"Yes," she said again. "He's in there. Drunk again, I suspect, but he's the only dad-blamed doctor we got, so there ain't much choice." She settled herself again into a stolid and massive contemplation of the opposite wall.

"Thank you," Beau said. "Thank you, ma'am." He had almost said *hie, hie*—the Sioux words for *thanks*.

The inner door swung open, and the assembled heads swung like linked mechanical toys. Doctor Duffy was a bony man with a veined red nose and a mat of kinked grayish hair.

"Take the powders twice a day," he said to the young girl with the painted face. "And stay away from men, you hear me? Tell Mrs. Cool I said you're out of service."

"Sure," the girl said. "Sure, doc." She ambled past the staring patients, swinging her hips, and Beau smelled a strong perfume as she passed. She looked down at him, and winked, and went into the winter afternoon.

"Who's next?" Duffy asked.

"I am," said Beau.

There was an immediate outcry; rage, suspicion, and doubts of his ancestry from the miners. Beau took Doc Duffy's arm and pulled him into the office, latching the door against intruders.

"Doc," he said, "I need medicine. A lot of medicine." Struggling with the long unused words, he became nervous, and he spoke jerkily, in oddly accented sentences. "Not for me—I'm all right. But a lot of people are sick. They've got smallpox."

Duffy opened his mouth, and scratched at the corner of it with yellowing fingernails. "Smallpox? Who? Funny I ain't heard of it before. Where?"

Beau sat down in a rocker and pulled off his boot.

"Look, I got plenty of money. Right here someplace. Just give me a second—"

Doc Duffy joined hands under his coattails and flipped them, the way a cat flips his tail when intent on some quarry. "Who did you say these people was? Miners, maybe, at one of the mines?"

Beau stripped out a tattered innersole, peering within the boot. "That's right. Miners. I've got the money in here someplace. Maybe fifty people in all. Doc, what's good for the smallpox? Give me a lot of it." He reached down in the toe of the boot, biting his lip in perplexity. "I always keep it in here someplace. Haven't looked at it in a long time, but it's got to be here someplace."

Someone knocked on the door, and an angry voice cried, "Doc, I was ahead of that feller! My eye's got a sliver of chisel in it!"

"All right," the physician said to the door. "Just a minute. I'll be out." He sat down at his cluttered desk, looking at Beau over steel-rimmed spectacles. "Mister, what mine is this you're talking about? The Hardscrabble, down toward Whitewood Creek?"

"Yes, that's it," Beau said. "The Hardscrabble."

Doc Duffy poured himself a drink from a bottle. He poured another for Beau and shoved it across to him. "That's what I thought you'd say," he growled. "There ain't any Hardscrabble Mine *I* know of! Now just kindly join me in a little drink, and settle down, so's I can see what I can do for those eyes of yours."

Beau looked at the ancient boot, turned almost inside out. He put his hand in it, felt, then drew it out. His fingers were greenish-looking, and small pieces of moist paper clung to them. He sat in numb shock for a moment. Then he muttered stupidly, "It rotted away."

Beau pulled his boot back on, and rose.

"Now wait a minute," Duffy protested. "Goddamit, a doctor takes an oath when he starts to practice! Just wait a minute, will you? Maybe I can help you."

But he was speaking to a closed door.

Outside, Beau floundered down the street, dodging under the necks of bullocks, cursed at by exasperated teamsters, and finally found shelter behind a livery stable, where a corral of horses and mules watched him with grave interest. He slumped gratefully in a pile of straw.

Money! That was the key to everything. He had to get money somewhere. There must be other doctors in town. If he could get some money, he was sure he could find a doctor that would sell him medicine for his people. But where could he get money? A lot of money? He reached in his pocket and took out a handful of tattered cards. Yes, that was it. That was the only way.

A suspicious gunsmith gave him eleven dollars for his Sharps. He spent a dollar in a bath-house, and came out clean, at least, long hair hacked to a semblance of neatness with a sheath-knife. There was little he could do about his clothing, but in this teeming frontier town there were many who looked worse than he did. With studied nonchalance he walked down the street, mentally classifying the gambling houses as he passed.

The Pride of the Pan-Handle had everything; faro, roulette, keno, poker. The room was loud with the clink of coins, the rattle of bottles, the voices of the bankers, crying "Make yer bets, gents; all's set." Beau bought a drink for fifty cents, and carried it around the smoky lamp-lit room till he found a small game with a vacant chair. This was what he wanted; a ten-dollar game, and he would work his way up, given a little time. He did not need luck. He would handle that himself.

The game was stud. If he had been content to let his winnings grow slowly, prospering by a dollar here and five dollars there, he would have succeeded in his plan. But thinking of Tall Woman lying sick in the wagon, waiting for him to return with white man's medicine, he was too eager. Up to that point, there had been no need to cheat. He was making small but consistent gains, and the few dollars he started with had grown to fifty, even though he had once bought drinks all round. Beau took another three off the bottom of the deck to join the pair he already was holding. He did it well, considering it had been months since he had handled a deck of cards, but he did not do it well enough. The buffalo-hunter sitting across from him scratched himself in the loins, and said, "Mister, put that last card back."

"What card?" Beau asked.

The other players had not seen his deception, and for that moment there was only the tight words between the two of them. But in an instant the feeling mushroomed into the smoky halls of the Pan-Handle, and people turned to look. The fat-hipped girl on the stage stopped her clowning; at the bar a man in a white apron took down a rifle from a hook beside the mirror. The jangle of the piano became more shrill, running uphill to end in startled tinkling. There was silence, and the sound of breathing. Gray smoke curled in and out, between and around the spectators.

"You know what card," the hunter said.

He reached into the breast of his buckskin jacket as if to scratch again. This time he brought out a long-barreled Navy Colt, and poked it toward Beau.

"You know damn well what card!"

Beau sat still. His knee was under the board frame that supported the table. If he could drive up with his knee and tip over the table, he might have a chance. He did not have a gun. The lamp was within reach of his fist. He might strike out at it as he kicked over the table, and perhaps it would dump oil on the table and catch fire. All these thoughts were in his mind, but he knew none of them was any good. He had cheated, and he had been caught at it. A bleary-eyed buffalo-skinnner, a lousy hide-hunter, had caught him at it.

"Listen," Beau said. "Listen, mister—"

He was never sure, afterward, exactly what he had intended to say, because there was never any need to say it. Someone put a hand on his shoulder, someone standing behind him.

"Teddy," a voice said. "I think you're mistaken."

The voice was tinged with a chuckle. Beau turned, looking at the man behind him. He was a tall man, wide in the shoulder, dressed in a neat black, with a small nugget swinging from a gold chain across the chest. His face was ripe with good living, and the ropy blond mustaches were carefully groomed and pomaded.

"Isn't that right?" the man insisted. "Aren't you wrong about this, Teddy? I've been watching the game for a while, now, and it seems to me you don't see so good anymore."

The buffalo-hunter let the muzzle of the Colt droop. He avoided the stare of the china-blue eyes.

"I dunno." He swallowed, and his face was baffled and infuriated. "I thought I seen him palm that last card off'n the bottom of the deck." He turned to the other players. "Didn't any of you fellers see him pull that shenanigan?"

The miner with the gold-dust shrugged. The others examined the backs of their cards. The man called Teddy swore, and shoved the pistol back in the loose folds of his coat.

"All right," he said. "If you say so, Mr. Hanratty. Only there ain't no law says I have to play with a goddam card-sharper." He got up and stamped away, and suddenly the music started again and voices chattered. The girl in tights emerged from the wings and took up her song again. The piano tinkled.

"I'm obliged to you," Beau said.

Hanratty took him by the arm and pulled him to a side door. They went into the icy street together.

"This way," Hanratty said. There was no longer any joviality in his voice. "I'm doing what I'm paid to do," he said, pointing to a stairs that led up the side of a rambling structure of raw lumber. "Up that way."

"Wait a minute," Beau said. "Why do you want me to go up there? What's—"

"If you want," Hanratty said, "you can go back to the Pan-Handle again. I think Teddy's looking for you. He's got a skinning knife you can shave with."

At the head of the stairs, Hanratty let himself in with a key. They walked together down a dark hall, dimly lit by a cutglass lamp on a table at the far end. Halfway, Hanratty stopped and knocked softly on a door. A woman's voice answered.

"That you, Jim?"

"Yes, ma'am."

The door swung open. Lael Corotis stood within, smiling.

"Come in, Beau," she said.

Hanratty paused in the hall, uncertain, but did not enter. Finally he asked, "Will you be all right, Mrs. Corotis?"

"I'll be all right," Lael said. An edge of sharpness was in her voice. "I'll call you if I need you."

"Yes, ma'am," Hanratty said, and went away.

She closed the door and stood against it, body flattened, hands spread against the panels. In the lamplight her high-piled hair shone richly. Her eyes were not as blue as he had remembered; they were more smoky and dark. But the rest of her was the same. The air of confidence, the proud jut of her breasts under the lace-trimmed white blouse, the capable way she had always had about her.

"You came back," she said. "I knew you'd come back. I've had Jim Hanratty watching for you for months. He was all for letting Shadduck pick you up."

"Shadduck?" Trying not to let her see the fright in him, he sat down in a chair. Not fright for himself; he had lately faced worse perils than Samuel Shadduck. But he was afraid for Tall Woman and the rest if he did not get help for them and return to the snowbound camp. And the soldiers were making ready to march. "Shadduck?" he asked again. "Is he in town?"

Lael frowned. "Whatever is the matter with your eyes? We must get you a doctor."

"Damn the doctor!" he burst out. "Where is Shadduck? Is he here—in Deadwood?"

"Not right now. But when he finds you're here, he'll be back."

"I've got to go," he said. "I've got to get out of here." Unsteadily he got to his feet and wavered toward the door but she barred his way. "I've got to get out of here," he said again, and tried to push her away.

"No," Lael said. She was strong for a woman, or perhaps he was weaker than he had known. "You poor darling—you don't have to run any longer! I'll take care of you now. I'll take care of everything. You can rest, and know that everything will be all right."

He felt the pressure of her body against his, the softness of her pushing against him.

"Please," he said. "Please, Lael—let me go."

Suddenly her composure was gone and she clung to him, arms around his neck, reaching up to press her lips against his weathered cheek.

"Beau," she said. "It's been such a long time! I've waited for you. You can't know how lonely it's been." Her voice was broken with little catches, as a child's is after long weeping. "But you don't need to worry now. No one will bother you. I'll take care of everything."

He tried to pull her arms from around his neck but she only clung tighter. Finally, feeling trapped, he gave in. He would have to explain later, he knew, but right now there was no point. He was too weary to try.

"All right," he said. "You're the boss. But listen—"

"I won't listen." Suddenly gay, she looked up at him, unshed tears sparkling in her eyes. "You listen to *me*, Beau Mannix! I'm an important woman in this town, and people have to listen to me whether they want to or not." She pushed him down in the chair, poured him a drink from a bottle of whisky, but did not have one herself. Then she sat cross-legged on the rich carpet and took off his shabby boots. She wrinkled her nose, and tossed the split boots into a corner. "First off we'll have to get you some new clothes."

Feeling a lassitude creep over him, he stretched out his legs and lay back in the chair. A glow spread through him as the good liquor hit his unaccustomed stomach. He looked round at the brocade draperies, the framed oil paintings on the wall, the crystal and silver shade of the oil lamp on the table. The miniature he had painted of Lael was in a heavy gilt frame under the cone of lamplight.

"It looks like you're doing all right."

"This is a wonderful place to make money. I started a laundry, like I said. In a month I sold out for three times what I put into it. I put the money back into mines, then. I had a thousand dollars in the Golden Utopia when they hit the big vein. I bought half of the Tough Luck, and sold it the next week for ten thousand dollars. Jim Hanratty gave me a tip on the Blue Alice, and I bought in just before they hit thousand-dollar ore!"

He emptied the glass, and she filled it again.

"Who's Hanratty?"

She tossed her head.

"Don't worry about him."

"He saved my bacon in the Pan Handle."

"He'll be paid for it. I—well, he's just somebody that's convenient, that's all." She was suddenly grave. "We might need him again, though. I've got a lot of say in this town, but it may take more than that. Word's gotten out that a white renegade in one of the Indian camps killed a soldier. Maybe it was you—I don't care. You don't even have to tell me. But they're offering a thousand dollars for your arrest, and we have to be careful." She laid her cheek against his knee.

Suddenly uneasy, he sat up in the chair. "Lael," he said, "I want to tell you something."

"Oh, my goodness!" She sprang to her feet, the silken folds of her skirt rustling. "You must be starved." She pulled a bell-rope in the corner. "I'll have something brought up. Now you just wash up a little, and then close your eyes and nap till the boy brings dinner."

They ate together by candlelight. A Chinese boy brought champagne from the Grand Central, and roasted squabs, together with a box of fine Havana cigars. Thinking of his people starving in their *tipis*, Beau felt guilt, but the liquor had weakened his resolve. Crunching bones and wiping fingers on his jacket, he ate most of the squabs himself. Lael watched him fondly, contenting herself with sips of champagne. In the richly-furnished apartment, with good food, wine, and cigars, a beautiful lady opposite him, Beau could have been in the finest mansion on Nob Hill in Frisco, instead of in this raw frontier town. Lael was right; money could do anything. He lit a cigar, sinking back in his chair with a sigh of pleasure.

"Happy?" she asked.

The cigar did not taste the way he remembered. Indian tobacco, flavored with birch shavings, must have changed his taste. He looked at the cigar, frowning, and then stubbed it out, hardly smoked.

"It's no good," he said. "I've been trying to tell you, Lael. I can't stay here. I've got an obligation to the people I've been living with. They're over on the Belle Fourche somewhere. Most of them are sick with smallpox. I came to Deadwood to get medicine for them. They helped me when I needed help. I've got to get back to them."

"Indians?" Her voice was incredulous, and she put down the champagne glass. "Beau, you can't be serious. Medicine for Sioux Indians?" She laughed, and twisted a ring on her finger. It sparkled in the lamplight and cut at him with a thin sword of light. "Can you seriously think anyone would sell you medicine for *Indians*? Why, they're planning a big campaign against them in a few weeks! General Crook is going out from Fort Fetterman, and some other generals from Fort Abraham Lincoln and up on the Yellowstone. Before you could get there, they'll be wiped out!"

"It doesn't make any difference," he said. "I've got to go back to them. That's where I belong." He ran a hand through his hair. "I can't explain it to you, it wouldn't make sense. They took me in, those people, when I needed help. They gave me everything they had. They shared with me when there wasn't very much to share."

"But it's so foolish," she protested. "You're not an Indian! You don't have anything in common with them!"

"Listen," he said. "Listen to me. Did you ever hear of the Winter Calendar?" He took her hand in his, as if the physical link would make the communication certain. "It's the history of the whole Sioux nation, back over the years. I'm painting it. I've got a whole series of canvases. Some of them are a little burned, but I can fix that. I don't think I've ever done anything worthwhile in my life, but now I think I've got it It's a whole way of life that's disappearing, full of color and drama—the real stuff—and I'm right there to paint it."

She looked at their linked hands. "I won't argue with you now. You're tired. You've had a hard time of it, but I'm going to change all that for you. That's all I'm going to say for now, Beau, because I—I can't bear to fight with you. Not about anything. You're tired, and you need rest." She touched his cheek with her fingers. "You need to be saved from yourself. You always did."

"Lael," he said, "I'm sorry. If I could only make you understand—"

She pointed toward an inner room.

"There's a bed in there. It's where I put up guests. Sleep, darling, and tomorrow we'll talk this all over and arrive at what's best." Dismissing him, she turned away and picked up a ledger from a desk. A moment later she was dipping a quill in an inkstand and making entries in the ledger, quick and businesslike.

He made a hopeless gesture with his hands, and went into the bedroom, closing the door after him. For a moment he stood at the window and looked down. The hour was late but the streets of Deadwood swarmed with activity. An army wagon-train was making up, and the canvas wagon-sheets rippled in the wind. Soldiers ran to and fro in the light of torches, boots crunching in the new ice.

A lot of people were looking for him, but he was confident that he could escape and evade Samuel Shadduck and all the others. Now, in this warm and secure island of safety, he had time to formulate a proper plan. He sat on the edge of the bed, trying to think. Senses dulled by rich food and champagne, he stared at the crack of light under the door. Lael was out there. That was the only way out; that, or through the window that overlooked the street. But the street milled with soldiers, and the soldiers were looking for him, too. If he waited till morning, though, the wagon-train might be gone. Yes, that was it; he would wait till morning, and then he would leave. He would have to get back right away. Tall Woman's sick patient face came to him as in a vision. And the wife of Man-Who-Never-Walked—he had promised her a red dress. He had no money. How would he do all the things that were expected of him? He lay back on the bed, gnawing at his knuckles. From these troublesome thoughts he drifted into a sleep so black and dreamless that it was almost like dying.

**Item 14.** Pencil sketch on brown wrapping paper. Buffalo hunters at bar, searching clothing for lice. (Cf. Bourke, Vestal, et al. Custom for last man to find louse to stand round of drinks). Signed MF, probably for *Many Fingers*, thought to be name by which Mannix was known among the Sioux.

---

When he woke, it was daylight—early afternoon, judging from the slant of the sun. Light streamed in through the drapes; someone had pulled them wide, and the smell of coffee was strong in his nostrils. *Pazuta-sapa*—coffee. He rolled over on his elbows and stared around the room, blinking in the sunlight. Grinning broadly, the China boy from the Grand Central put down a tray covered with a napkin. Over his arm was a suit of clothes, and fresh linen. "She say I bring you breakfast. Then you wash up and put on clothe." Carefully he laid the clothing over a chair. "Very fine clothe. Cost a lot of money. She rich lady. Always buy good thing." The boy grinned. "You eat now?"

Stiffly Beau got to his feet and went to the window. It had snowed during the night. The deep wagon-ruts were softened into sinuous ridges by the blanket of white. The army train had gone. Across the street, where he now remembered he had stabled his mule, a mud-and-stick chimney puffed smoke, ragged shreds whipped away by the wind.

"Where is Mrs. Corotis?"

The boy took the napkin off the tray. A silver pot of coffee was there, and eggs. Beau had not seen an egg for a long time. It was not fair to treat him so, to ply him with good living. For a long time he had forgotten about coffee in a silver pot, and eggs, and good liquor. Feeling uneasy, he poured himself coffee, and sat on the edge of the bed, nursing the cup between his fists.

"I said where is Mrs. Corotis?"

The boy shrugged.

"She tell me not to talk to you. Say just bring food and help with clothe when you dress. No talk. No infamation."

The China boy never mentioned her by name, but the way he used *she* had the ring of a title to it. Lael Corotis had not boasted. She was an important woman in Deadwood. While he was licking the last crumbs of biscuit from his fingers, he heard voices from the outer room. A woman's voice, and the heavier voices of men. He went to the door and put his ear against it while the Chinese boy stacked the plates and flicked a napkin around.

"I don't know," That was Lael's voice, firm and authoritative. "I heard he was in town, too. Mannix—was that his name? Yes, of course I knew him once. You know that. He brought me to Custer City in his wagon. But I haven't seen him since."

The voice of the man was persistent, with a kind of tenor petulance. Beau had heard that voice before.

"Madam, this man is dangerous. In addition to his other crimes, he has killed a soldier out on the Belle Fourche river somewhere. I have warned thee, madame; do not trifle with the law."

Samuel Shadduck! He shook his head at the Chinese boy, signing to him to cease the clatter of the plates. Straining his ears, he recognized the voice of the second man. It was Hanratty.

"Mrs. Corotis has told you she knows nothing about Mannix."

There was silence for a moment, and Beau could hear the heavy thud of his own heart. Then Samuel Shadduck's steady voice said, "I do not think that is enough. For instance, sir, there is a muddy pair of boots in the corner there, looking as if a hunted man had recently taken them off." Shadduck's voice went up reproachfully. "Mrs. Corotis, thee is playing a very dangerous game. Thee—"

"Wait a minute," Hanratty said. "Are you intimating that Mrs. Corotis is shielding this man? Say what you mean, and stop this mealy-mouthed talk!"

Shadduck bit off his words like small fragments of metal.

"Sir, I speak only to warn this woman. I warn thee, too."

"All right," said Hanratty, and a chair scraped, as if someone had pushed it back and risen. "Get out, then! You have no warrant, or any authority to impose yourself on us any longer. Get out, and don't bother Mrs. Corotis again. Do you hear me?"

Beau could imagine the ghost of a thin smile around the detective's lips.

"I do hear thee, sir. And madam. But thee does not hear me, and it will be to thy sorrow, I am afraid. Madam, good day. Sir."

A heavy door opened, then closed. Lael and Hanratty spoke together, too low for Beau to hear. He went to the window and looked guardedly out, seeing the detective's small figure pass below him. Across the street Shadduck paused to speak to someone, and Beau recognized Smoke, the man who had once hired out to Shadduck to hunt Beau Mannix. So Smoke was after him too. Of course he would be, for a thousand dollars.

"You dress now?" the China boy asked. He held a basin of water, and soap and towels.

"All right," Beau said.

Later, when he looked at himself in the mirror, he saw a stranger. Clean-shaven, hair neatly trimmed, a conservative hound's-tooth tweed suit that fitted him well—even a silk cravat. He smoothed the fit of the waistcoat, pulling it down around his narrow waist, eyeing the mirror. Smoke would not recognize him. Perhaps Samuel Shadduck would not, either.

Well, there was nothing wrong with accepting the clothes. His own were patched and threadbare. Only the old reliable buffalo coat had any substance to it anymore. When he left town he would need warm clothing. Besides, he had not committed himself at all to Lael Corotis. He had told her simply and truthfully what the situation was. She had only herself to blame if she persisted in trying to hold him here. But when she knocked at his door and entered, he found himself again floundering in the sea of her will.

"Well!" Her voice was cheery. "Sleepy-head! Do you know how long you slept?"

"Where's Hanratty?" he asked.

She was dressed in a full dark skirt and a snowy white blouse with a black ribbon at the neck, looking modest—almost demure. He remembered how she had looked that night on the trail when she wore Gammill's old clothes. Even under the coarse shirt and woolen jeans her body had insisted on being seen, making itself known in strong perfect lines. He swallowed, and asked again, "Where's Hanratty?"

She moved gracefully and purposefully toward him, the sun catching glints in the high-piled brassy hair.

"You don't have to worry about Jim, darling."

"Where is he?"

"He's gone. I sent him away." Going to the window, she pulled the drapes. They swished off the late afternoon light with a rustle and a clinking of rings. "You look so different. Your face is pale where you shaved."

He rubbed a hand over his chin, not knowing what to say. "I guess so," he muttered.

"Now." She motioned him down onto the bed, and sat beside him in a rocker, serene. "Let's talk about our plans. I've got it all figured out, what we'll do. I'm getting tired of Deadwood. Things are slowing down here anyway. I've made a pile, and I've always wanted to see New York. Have you ever been there?"

He shook his head.

"Then that's where we'll go. Jim will arrange to get you out of town." She giggled, like a small girl with a secret. "He won't like it—he hardly ever likes the things I do. But he'll do it. For me."

"You always get what you want, don't you?"

"Why, of course." She fussed at his cravat, adjusting the knot. "I always have, ever since I was a little girl. There's no secret to it, really. If you want anything bad enough to pay the price, you can have it. I've paid the price for everything I ever got. No markdowns, either. They always held me up. But I paid. I married Mr. Corotis. I ran away. I risked my life when I had to. I was smart. I've got a brain, you know; a way with money, too, and men. I'm probably the wealthiest woman in the Territory since the Blue Alice came in."

With all she had gone through, she had managed somehow to retain a childlike way of looking at things, a direct and immediate approach that was somehow startlingly effective. It was the way of a child who reaches for all the toys in sight, ruthless and untroubled, until it is soundly spanked and sent to bed.

Clasping his hands between his knees, he leaned forward, his voice grave.

"Lael, this is all no good. I can't come with you. I must get away."

She kicked off her slippers, and tucked her feet under her, looking brightly and amicably at him.

"Yes, we must talk it all out now, and get it out of your system. It's probably an Indian woman, isn't it?"

He ignored the jibe, but knew he flushed.

"We've both been through a lot since we parted last. I—I can see you're different, changed. So am I. I'm not the same man. Let me tell you about it."

She smiled. "You must talk all you want to, darling. I'll warn you it won't convince me. My mind's made up, and I'm a very hard woman to convince. But I know it will be good for you to talk, and so I am prepared to listen."

"They took me in," he said. "I owe them everything for that. I was nothing—hunted and scared, and they took me in. I—I'm grateful to you, too, and I owe you a lot. But, Lael, these people are mine. I know that sounds crazy—me sitting here in these fine clothes and telling you I'm an Indian. But I mean it. Even here, in this room, I think like one, and I know I must go back to them. Women, men, children—I know them all, and love them, and have a debt to them. The only way I know to pay it is to paint them, to finish my Winter Calendar, to try to put them down on canvas before it's too late, before the soldiers get to them for the last time and destroy it all—the life, the color, the vigor. I want to help them to live, even if they were destroyed. Do you see what I mean?"

Rocking, she nodded.

"It does you credit, I'm sure, darling. But you're never be happy there. Not really happy, like we could be together. You're rash, in action and in thought. You know you are. You regret too many things later. Someone must help you with these things."

Steadily he kept on, not quite knowing where he was going, hoping only that he could somehow, by talking, dislodge her from her firm position. Looking at the faint outline of her breasts under the lacy bodice, he murmured, "They are a very remark-able people. They say that round things are always best. Their *tipis* are round. They pitch the *tipis* in a circle, always in a circle. Their war shields are always round. The sun is round. The earth is round. I think they're right. They're right about a lot of things, in a way that's hard for a white person to understand. But it all makes sense, and it hangs together in a logical way when you see it whole, with an open mind."

A knock sounded at the outer door, off the hallway. Beau stiffened, but Lael only went on rocking, and said, "Don't jump so. He'll go away."

"Who is it?"

"Probably Jim. He always comes by in the afternoon to give me a report on the mine. He's very conscientious." She reached out and touched his cheek with a finger. "He hates you. He hates you very much. But it doesn't make any difference. It's none of his business what I do. He doesn't own me. No one owns me but myself." She stroked the long line of his jaw. "You, too, I think. You own me. Did you know that?"

Boots shuffled in the stairwell, and the room was silent again. Sighing, he went to the window and looked out. It was late afternoon. Slanting shafts of sun lit the street, and in their beams the falling snowflakes turned to gold. A rich rain fell on Deadwood. He turned to look at her in an abstracted way, and finally she was uncomfortable, and shifted nervously in the chair.

"Don't!" he said.

"Don't what?"

"Don't move." He had been studying her, curled in the leather-upholstered chair—the way the dying light lingered in her hair, the curve of her shoulder, the planes of light and shadow that made up her body. "Have you got a pencil someplace? Paper?"

She nodded. "In the drawer there."

He lit the lamp, and found the stub of a pencil and a pad of legal forms. Enthused, he propped the pad on his knee and began to sketch. "Just stay like that, with your cheek on your hand. No, turn—just a little bit! There, that's right. Keep your chin barely turned toward me."

Obediently she posed for him, her face proud with a kind of secret knowledge. This was her man, and he was making her picture with love and skill and affection. Here, in this warm and intimate room, they were together at last. She rocked a little, just a little, and watched him as he worked feverishly, slashing at the paper with broad strokes of the pencil.

"How was it really like out there, where you were?" she asked. "What were they really like, the Indians? You make it sound so— so important. But really—"

"Are you sure you want to know?" He glanced at her, and then back at the pad. Holding it out at arm's length, he stared at it, and then went back to work on it.

"Why not?" she asked. "It can't do any harm now. It's all over, isn't it?"

"Well," he said, "they're fine people. They're different from you and me, but they have their own laws and their own ideas of right and wrong and their own code of conduct. They've been generally cheated by white men, but they still regard an agreement as binding. When they sign a treaty in good faith, they expect the other party to do the same."

"Savages," she said. "You make them sound interesting, but they're still painted savages."

"The horses," he said, shading in the soft contour of her body where it lay against the tufted leather of the chair. "It's funny about horses. A Sioux wouldn't have a white horse or a black horse or a gray horse or a brown horse. They like *pintos*—paint horses. If they can't get a *pinto,* they'll do the next best thing. They'll paint him up till he looks like a *pinto.*" He rubbed the cross-hatching with his finger, blending it into a smooth dark shadow. *"Berdache,* too. That's a queer thing."

She was becoming irked at the stiffness of her position, and fidgeted.

*"Berdache*—what's that?"

"Men that are really women. They're born men, but when they come into their youth, they have the wrong kind of a dream. It's the time in his life when a boy is supposed to take up the weapons of a man. But something happens in a *berdache's* vision. He reaches for the bow and the lance, and a mischief-making god snatches then away and hands him the woman's things—the needle and the cooking spoon. He's not a man any longer. He's a woman. He acts like a woman, and for all practical purposes becomes a woman. Everyone is very sad about it, but everyone understands, also. The Sioux treat the *berdache* kindly, try to make a place for them in the camp."

She shuddered. "It sounds disgusting."

"Maybe the way we treat men like that is more disgusting. We have *berdache,* too, you know, probably right here in Deadwood. The prostitutes use them for pimps and steerers. There were a lot of them in Frisco." He made a half-dozen more quick strokes, and finally with a sigh threw the pad aside and sank back in the chair, closing his eyes. "God," he said, "I'm tired."

She picked up the pad and studied it, and frowned.

"It isn't very good. I don't know—somehow I—I don't look like that, do I?" She held it out at arm's length and studied it, her face apprehensive. "Why, that looks barbarous! I mean—well, you've made me look like an Indian!"

Knowing he had displeased her, he tried to make amends.

"You are like an Indian in some ways. You're very direct, and honest. You say what you think. That's what they do too, among themselves. When they're with white people, they're uneasy, and they talk a lot, and orate. But with themselves they're honest and straightforward. It's one of the things I like best about them, and about you."

Only slightly mollified, and still suspicious, she sank back in the chair.

"What's all this about the Winter whatever it was? Whatever can it mean to a man like you to bother yourself with a heathen thing like the Winter Calendar?"

He looked down at the pencil still in his fingers.

"Because it means the Sioux to me. It's the whole Sioux nation, for hundreds of years—the battles, the great events of their lives—heroes and villains, the good times and the bad, starving and being lost and beaten, and then the victories and the scalps and the dances. The gods like Rock and Thunder, the wide lands, the rivers, the ceremonies, the color of their clothing, the sounds of their voices when they sing, the beating of their feet on the earth when they dance—".

He broke off and stared at her. "It doesn't mean a thing to you, does it? I'm just wasting my breath."

She was silent for a moment, and many emotions passed across her face. "Does it really mean so much to you?"

"It does," he said. "It's something that's great and powerful, but something that can't last. The Sioux don't see it. They can't see things like that. They're The People, the only people. Everyone else is nothing. They can't imagine The People ever being gone from this land. It's a high tide in a way—a great moment in their history and in ours. No one sees that. They can't. You can't. They're heathen to you and the people in the Territory, something to be wiped out so civilization can get on. The Sioux can't see it either. They've always been here. They know they'll always be here, after the last white man has been defeated and driven into the ocean. But I know. I know it can't last. Somehow or other, Lael, I feel important, for the first time in my life. I feel that I've been put here to record this last great time. Maybe it sounds like bragging, but I think I'm the only man can do it. I *want* to do it. I will do it. Nothing can stop me. I'm that sure of myself."

"Do you love me?" she asked. "Are you sure about that?"

It was one of her unpredictable changes of direction, and it caught him unaware. But he thought before he spoke, taking his time. "Of course I do. You—you're lovely. You can't know what it means to me, seeing you again, being with you."

"I don't mean that," she said. "You've had a lot of women. I can tell. Maybe some of them were prettier. But do you love me?"

"I've told you I did."

She pushed the rocker back, and stood up, proud and imperious in her bare feet. "Look at me! Look at me in the eye. Now tell me you love me."

He looked at her, the narrow waist swelling above with the fullness of her breasts, below with the ripe curve of her hips. He looked at the dainty bare feet, the flood of corn-gold hair, the fine straight edge of her nose, the firm set of her lips.

"I think you're the most beautiful thing I've ever seen," he said. He went to her, and put his arms around her, pulling her against him. "I never said that to any other woman, believe me."

Putting her hands against his chest, she pushed away from him so that she could look into his eyes. Before that level stare he felt guilty, and confused. Lael Corotis was a very shrewd woman; he had always known that.

"Beau," she said, "let's not play games with each other."

"All right."

"I won't let you go. I told you that. I know what's best for you. I never talk just to hear the sound of my own voice. I mean every word I say. Do you believe me?"

"Now, Lael," he said. "You're getting excited about nothing."

"I told you." Her voice rose a little. "Everything I have is yours. I haven't held back anything. But you've got to trust me. You've got to give me something, too."

"Lael," he said, "please—"

"I waited so long for you. Everytime I made some money, I said 'this is for Beau and me.' I planned it all. I said, 'when he comes back, this will buy a carriage for us to ride in, or a new suit for him, or whatever he wants.' Doesn't that mean anything to you?"

"A great deal," he said.

"I know it isn't just a woman you left back there. Believe me, I know. If it were, I'd know what to do. I'd make you forget her. I know how. But—this other thing, this strangeness—" She shook her head, losing some of her composure. "I don't know how to fight it."

"Lael," he said, "I'm not the man for you. I'm not the man for any woman. I'm married to painting. That sounds crazy. Maybe it is. But try to understand. I'm everlastingly grateful to you. If I wanted to marry anybody, it would be you. But it wouldn't work out. There isn't room in my life now for it. What's inside me now is deep inside, like wanting to live is with other people. I can't take a chance with it. I can't ruin anyone's life with a clear conscience, except my own."

Her fists clenched at her sides.

"Mr. Shadduck warned me against you, but I was too silly to understand what he was trying to say. Now I know. He said not to believe in you, that you weren't worth it. He said you were a very remarkable man, but not to believe in you."

He shrugged.

"Maybe he was right. But no matter what, I've got to go. I've got to go back." Going to the door, he put his hand on the painted china knob. "When I first went away from you, I owed you for a wagon and mules. I never paid that back, and now I'm going away owing you a lot more than that."

She turned on him like an animal, fiercely and expertly.

"Who do you think you are, that you can come in here like this and make a fool of me and then say goodbye? I'm the one that will say goodbye, and not till I'm good and ready! You're a wanted man. All I have to do is say the word and you're in irons on your way back to San Francisco. Or I could turn you over to the Army. *They'd* know how to handle a renegade that shot one of their soldiers."

Trying still to be tender with her, he blundered into inanities.

"I'm—I'm grateful to you. I wouldn't want you to think that I wasn't. Only—"

Her eyes became suddenly hard and bright.

"Is that all you've got for me? Gratitude? For an unpaid bill?" She flung herself through the door, past him, and into the outer room. Before he knew what she was doing, she grasped the bell-rope that hung in the corner. "You think I'm soft and mealy, like the rest of the women you've had! You think I'm like an Indian squaw, happy to take whatever you give me!"

Seeing the framed portrait of herself he had painted, she picked it up and smashed it on the floor. The glass broke into fragments, but she stamped on the small picture in an ecstasy of passion, grinding the pieces into the carpet until her white feet bled, and left dark stains on the rich pile.

"I'm as tough as any man! I won't let anyone hurt me! I'll turn you over to that detective. I won't let you just walk out on me!"

In three long steps he was at her, fighting for the bell cord. Clawing and biting at him, she still tried to pull it, but he held it high over her head.

"Listen!" he shouted. "You damned little fool, listen to me before you do something you'll be sorry for!"

"I'll scream!" she cried.

She opened her mouth, but he looped a turn of the bell cord around her neck and pulled hard, choking off the cry. For an instant she struggled like a drowning kitten, gurgling and tearing at him with her nails and making whimpering sounds. But the cord tightened, and finally her body sagged limp in his arms. He held her for an instant, gently, and when he had choked the fight out of her he let her sag to the floor.

"I'm sorry," he said.

Money. He had to have money. He went through the drawers, the closets, looking behind paintings on the walls for a safe, turning back rugs. Flinging open a closet door, he found nothing but a man's clothing on neat racks. Hanratty's. Looking down at Lael's limp body, he murmured, "You'll get along." Finally he found a metal box on a high shelf, and broke it open with the aid of an iron stand which held a fern near a window. The box was filled with neat string-wrapped bundles of currency. As he was filling his pockets, Lael made a gasping sound and rolled over, rubbing her bruised throat.

"Beau," she whispered.

He took a dark full cloak from Hanratty's closet, a magnificent garment which would have gone well at the Opera in Frisco. With the collar turned up and one of Hanratty's hats pulled low over his face, he might pass for Hanratty, and go unchallenged.

"Beau?" Lael pleaded. Still dazed, not knowing for sure where she was, she got to her knees, looking uncomprehendingly around her. "Beau! Where are you? Don't leave me! Don't!" The effort exhausted her, and she fell back, sitting on her bent legs, weeping.

Pockets filled with the beautiful money, he leaned over her and took her face in his hands. "Goodbye, Lael," he said.

He kissed her on the lips and went out into the hall, pulling the cloak around him. With an aplomb he did not feel, he went down the dimly-lighted hall and descended the stairs at the end, not knowing what he could find there, feeling a pleasurable excitement. He was on his own again.

No one noticed him as he walked through the lobby of the hotel below. They did not know him. They did not see him in the press of the crowd. Triumphantly he went to the livery stable, paid his bill, and rode out of town. He was well out onto the snowy plain, cloak wrapped about him against the cold, when he again thought of Lael Corotis, and her cut and bleeding feet. The Sioux women gashed themselves in grief when a loved one died. His name was never spoken again, and they cut themselves in sorrow and grief.

**Item 15.** **Portrait of young Sioux woman with child. 10×12 inches, canvas in oils. Practically destroyed by unrolling, although beadwork on woman's dress, and face of child, remain intact. Signed M/F.**

H e had gone far out of his way to throw any possible pursuit off the track, and now, jogging westward, the land was endless under the blanket of late snow, but he had no doubt of the outcome of his journey. He had bought sugar and coffee and cartridges from a passing wagon-train, coming from the south where he would hardly be known. Now, after weeks, the opera cape was tattered and rent, and the borrowed hat had melted into shapelessness, but his spirits were high. He was on his way back.

Spring was not far away. Even under the snow, the land seemed to struggle upward, ready to burst into flower. Harney's Peak and others projected to a great elevation, and their flanks were dark with pine and fir. The foothills, when warm weather came, would be thick with pasturage, the narrow valleys of the creeks a jungle of willow, live oak, wild rose, and plum. He sighed, thinking of the paints in his wagon. Where was the wagon, now? And Tall Woman, and the rest? Still on the Belle Fourche? He would find them wherever they were.

He was a long time getting back. When he finally reached the site of the camp on the Belle Fourche, the people were gone. It had been a permanent camp, used by many of the Sioux before them, but it had not been occupied since Beau's people left. Many new burials were there, with blanket-wrapped bodies in them, weeks dead. He searched among them but found not one he could identify. An unseasonable thaw had come, and short-lived but warm weather. Animals and birds had been at the bodies, and the heat of the sun also. Tall Woman's body was not there, he felt sure.

Signs lead him on across the Little Powder, past the high knob called Pumpkin Butte. The trail was broad and plain, although now weeks old, perhaps a month or more. On a day early in March he rode hunched over in the saddle, rain and snow beating into his face in the storm that came from the northwest. The scenery was dreary; the bluffs on either side of the trail were bare and somber prominences of slate, sandstone, and yellow clay. On his left reared the high wall of the Big Horns, and he kept them there, travelling up the Dry Fork of the Powder. Huddled in the cloak, he rode that day almost on top of a large military command, also going north.

They did not see him, perhaps because of the swirling snow, perhaps because a white man in an opera cape was hardly to be expected in this hostile country. He threw himself off the horse, pinching its nostrils in the Sioux way to prevent it from whinnying to the horses of the soldiers. For a long time the column passed in the sandy canyon just below him; hundreds of men in huge wrappings of wool and fur, many wagons, over forty head of cattle. The column moved silently, the only sound the clink of gear and the creaking of wagon-wheels. It was a battle-wise, efficient column, and it was on the same trail Beau Mannix followed.

When they had gone, he trailed them at a discreet distance. Once he found a box of bread that had fallen from a wagon, and that evening he dined on bread soaked in coffee from the small store he had left in his saddle bags. As he ate, he heard scattered firing ahead, and feared that the column had caught up with Red Knife and Three Horses and Man-Who-Ate-The-Wolf. But the shots quickly ceased, and he wrapped himself in the cloak and slept, satisfied it had been only a minor skirmish with some small war party.

When he reached Crazy Woman Fork, the trail of the soldiers went on, toward Fort Kearney. The trail of his own people, which Beau had long followed, was now completely wiped out, erased by hundreds of hoofs and the ruts of wagon tracks. So long as he followed the troops, they would be always between him and his people. For a long time he pondered; then he turned north, and rode up Crazy Woman Fork. There he fell in with a small band of Cheyennes. He did not speak their language. It was strange to him, harsh, nasal, and sibilant. But the hand talk quickly brought them together, and convinced them he was one of them.

"Friend, we have just had a big fight." They pointed north. "We fought Three-Stars," they said proudly, and Beau remembered that was the name General Crook was known by to the Indians. "We fought him hard, and he burned our lodges. But there is no sense to the white men. We almost lost the fight, but just when things were very bad, the white men went back where they had come from, and left us the village." They shook their heads, and marveled. "It did not cost us much. A few lodges, some men died. The soldiers all went away, and we kept after them, and shot some more when they ran away. Friend, do you understand this?"

Beau shook his head. This was the fine column that had passed him at Pumpkin Butte, two weeks or more past. Now the defeated column was probably on its way back toward Fort Fetterman. The Sioux and the Cheyennes were still in the field, victorious. He shook his head. They could not fight the whole United States forever. It had to come to an end.

"It must have been a good fight," Beau said. He looked at the horses, painted with stripes on the legs to show the number of times the owner had struck the enemy on that side. Horse-tracks were painted on the barrel of the horse, to show the number of horses the owner had stolen, and there were fresh scalps, too, fastened to the bridle-bits. "Friends," he asked, "have you seen the Hunkpapa chief Red Knife? The chief called Man-Who-Ate-The-Wolf? I left them in this country a long time ago. They were all very sick and I went to get help for them. Now I can not find them. They are all gone."

One of the Cheyennes wrinkled his brow.

"In two Moons' camp, when we fought the white men, there were a few Hunkpapa. They came from the river they call the Belle Fourche. They had been sick there, and had a lot of trouble. But I do not remember these names. Anyway, they went on toward the Big Powder River."

"I am glad," Beau said. He made the sign for *glad,* which was the same as *sunshine in the heart;* thumb and forefinger curled over the heart, then *daylight,* hands palm down before the chest and swept forward with palms turning over in an unfolding gesture. "Do you know of a Hunkpapa woman called Tall Woman?"

"No," the Cheyennes said. "But there are a lot of women in the big Sioux camp on the Tongue River. Maybe you can find her there. We are going to do a little more looking around, and maybe we can find some horses. Then we are going back to the Tongue River. We are going to talk to Crazy Horse and Sitting Bull and Gall about joining with them. We did not want to fight the white men, but when they came into our camp shooting, we had to shoot too. Now there is war between us. Two Moons sent a war pipe to Sitting Bull. Friend, there is going to be a big gravy-stirring soon."

They said their farewells, and the Cheyennes raced away on their ponies, whooping and shouting in pure animal spirits. Beau watched them go, wishing he could paint the fury and delight of their going, the spotted ponies, the lean brown figures, the waving lances and rifles. He went on toward the Tongue this time, but his pace was slower. He was tired from many weeks in the saddle, but the feeling came from more than fatigue. Something tightened around his heart, and he clucked to the bony horse, looking back over his shoulder.

When he came into the big camp on the Tongue, he thought he had never seen, nor would he see again, such a tremendous gathering of power. The *tipis* marched on and on into the spring sunlight. Where the eye failed in the haze and dust that lay in the distance, there was still more *tipis*. He drew rein for a moment, sucking in his breath at the sight. With their curious unmartial ways, the Sioux and Cheyennes in the camp had posted no guards. They never did. There was no concept of organization, or tactics, or of strategy. This huge camp could not successfully be attacked by any force now in the field, so what did guards or sentries or pickets mean? There was much meat, and good forage for the horses; dancing and telling of stories and time to sit all day in the sun and comb one's hair and paint suns and moons on buffalo shields.

He rode directly into the camp without being challenged. An old woman sat at a *tipi* door scraping the skin of a small animal.

"Mother," he said, "I am looking for the camp of Red Knife and Three Horses and Man-Who-Ate-The-Wolf. They are great Hunkpapa chiefs."

The woman pushed away a strand of gray hair. She was blind, and looked toward him with milky-white eyes.

"Down there," she said, pointing. "In the direction of the sun. The Hunkpapa are all down there, dancing."

Although he was a poor judge of numbers, he guessed that at least five thousand were in this great camp; Cheyennes and Teton Sioux, for the most part. There were many people that were different, to his eyes, in their dress and bearing. Oglala, Miniconjou, Sans Arcs. Presently, he saw his wagon, his painted wagon, at the edge of a circle of painted *tipis*. On a dusty plain surrounded by the circle of *tipis,* the Hunkpapa danced. He saw Red Knife and others he had known. Slowly, feeling very old and tired, he slid off the horse and stood for a moment, leaning against its bony ribs.

A fat woman came to him from a *tipi,* first holding aside the flap for a long time and watching him. Then she ran toward him, moccasined feet slapping in the dust. It was the wife of Man-Who-Never-Walked, called Chahumpi.

"Many Fingers! You have come back!" Her manner swung from delight to apprehension, and she looked at him and then away, digging her toe into the dirt. "The people did not think you would come back."

He took her by the hand.

"Old friend," he said.

"We waited for you." Relieved, she chattered like a magpie, fat cheeks wobbling and her small dark eyes alive with joy. "We waited a long time, and more people died. Finally Man-Who-Ate-The-Wolf said we had to go. He said if we stayed there in that place, we would all die. So we left that place, and came here."

She felt silent, and knew what he was going to ask. Before he could speak, she said, "Many people died. It is not good to speak of them. It will bring them bad luck, and us too."

"Tall Woman?" he asked.

She turned pale. Then she nodded, and turned away. He caught at her elbow. "The child?"

"He, too," Chahumpi said. "He did not live very long. I made a little tree place for him too, beside his mother." For the first time he noticed the ridged scars on her fat forearms. "I cut myself for both of them," she said. "I loved them very much. I did the best I could for them, but it was hard." Tears were in her eyes, and she bowed her head.

*"Hie,"* he said. He touched her bowed head. *"Hie, hie."* When she looked up, her many chins trembling, he spoke kindly to her. "Give this sharp knife to a crier, and tell him to go round the camp and tell the people Many Fingers has come back."

She took the knife and waddled happily away. When he called after her, she turned.

"I promised you a red dress," he said. "I am sorry. I could not bring one back."

She blushed, a dark flooding of her cheeks.

"No matter," she said. She turned and ran, holding a scarf aloft, shrieking at the top of her lungs.

Beau's return made him a minor celebrity in the great camp. This was no mean distinction when the camp on the Tongue held such great men as the Cheyenne chiefs Two Moons and White Bull; the Hunkpapas Gall, Crow King, and Black Moon; Chief Hump of the Miniconjous, and Spotted Eagle of the Sans Arcs. But Red Knife and Three Horses and Man-Who-Ate-The-Wolf were indefatigable in their praise of him. The criers went round the camp for the better part of three days, shouting with great volume the praises of Many-Fingers.

"We are a small band," Man-Who-Ate-The-Wolf told him, "But we have good men too. It is up to us to tell all these important people that we are important, too. Did you not ride into Deadwood in bad weather to get help for us?"

Beau grunted.

"I did not bring back any help."

Man-Who-Ate-The-Wolf scratched his head with his special painted scratching stick. He was under the power of a vision, a dream that he would be invulnerable in battle if he did not scratch his head with his fingers. If he touched only the scratching stick to his head, bullets could not harm him. Also, he must not touch iron to his lips, and so had to be very careful about things like spoons.

"Did you not escape from the devil who always chases you? The small devil in the fur cap, the one you told us about the first time you came to the camp of Iron Nose on the Belle Fourche?"

"He was a very small devil," Beau said.

"Small or not," Man-Who-Ate-The-Wolf pointed out, "he was a devil. A man does not overcome these things without being celebrated. I will make up a song about you sometime, when I have nothing else to do."

"*Hie,*" said Beau modestly. "*Hie, hie.*"

His fame spread through the camp. Many came to him seeking a charm or amulet, something touched by Many Fingers which would transfer to them a part of his power. They came from all the camps; from the *tipis* of the Miniconjou and the Cheyennes, the Sans Arcs and the Oglalas. Beau obliged them cheerfully, first requiring them to sit for their portraits, complete in war finery. His small store of paints was almost completely gone and he was forced to make his own from the colored earths and berry-juices and buffalo-fat that the Indians themselves used in decorating their *tipis* and robes and shields. Caught up in a kind of compulsion, he painted from first light of dawn until the shadows of dusk, aware always that there was not much time, that this was the golden moment; that this time had never been here before and never would be here again. The Sioux themselves grew to hold him in a wary respect reserved for those who are motivated by spirits. When they came to the painted wagon of the gaunt hot-eyed man, they made various protective signs and rolled their eyes at him in mingled respect and fear. Beau laughed at them, but gave them bits of canvas smeared with crosses and dots and jagged lines of red paint, and they went away happy with their new charms. Meanwhile, he had a growing stack of studies; sketches of hands and stern faces; details of beadwork and quill-work and the designs on war-ponies and the high-boned cheeks of the men and the fluttering of tufts of hair on the lances. All these he planned to incorporate into the Winter Calendar when there was time.

The woman called Chahumpi took good care of him. Now that she had no husband, she cooked for Beau, mended his clothing, fed him, ground paints for him, worked endlessly and uncomplaining. Disapproving of the sleeping arrangements in the cluttered wagon, she made a slatted mat of willow rods for him, suspended from the wagon bows like a hammock. She decorated his new woolen suit with porcupine quills one day while he slept, soaking the quills in warm water, drawing them between her front teeth to flatten them, and then dyeing them by boiling them with berries. She gathered lambs-quarters, poke shoots, and wild spinach, making savory stews with scraps of dried winter meat. Somehow she seemed to understand better than anyone else he had known that here was a queer and difficult person, a man with a driving and compelling urge that pushed him on like a tightly-wound spring. She did not ask for gratitude, and he did not give it. They understood each other completely.

Neither of them spoke of Tall Woman. Beau had sometimes a feeling of shame that he did not think more often of Tall Woman's grave serious face, of the love she had given him, of the generous and unstinting love that bore a child for him, and then died that time so far away now in his memory. But he did not think of Lael Corotis either, or of Shadduck, or of Deadwood. He did not think of anything but his painting. That, he now realized, was what he really loved, what he had never stopped loving. No woman was worth what he gave his painting. He became a man apart from all the people on the Tongue River, a queer bearded holy man who never stopped making *pishers,* and the Sioux treated him with a tender regard he did not even notice.

In the middle of June, a big war-party from the Tongue River camp fought another battle with the redoubtable Three-Stars on Rose-Bud Creek. The great Crazy Horse himself lead the Sioux and the Cheyennes. It was a good fight. The horse-soldiers had over two hundred of the hereditary enemies of the Sioux with them; hated Absaroka, each well-armed with a breech-loader and murderous hand weapons made from knives bound into long handles of wood and horn. There was plenty of chance for a man to count coup there. So far as the battle itself was concerned, it was a standoff. But Crazy Horse was masterful that day. He threw wave after wave of mounted warriors against Three-Stars, mauling the soldiers badly. At the end of the fight, Three-Stars stubbornly held the field, but what did the field of battle mean to an Indian? They recovered their wounded, all but thirteen of their dead. Then they rode laughing and singing away, waving fresh scalps and confirming each other's coups. It had been a good day.

With so many *tipis,* so many horses, it was not long until the valley of the Tongue was scoured bare of forage. Game was soon hunted out, and the grassy plain became hot and dusty. The first Beau knew about the move was when Chahumpi started to harness up the two spavined ponies which now drew the wagon.

"Mother," he said, "what are you doing?"

She went placidly on with her harnessing.

"We move. We go away from here. There is not grass any longer. No food. When we fight Three-Stars again, we have got to have good grass."

"Where are we going?"

"Up there." She poked her thumb northward. "There is a good river there, and good grass. The grass is so good they call it the Fat Grass River. That is where we are going."

"But I am painting!" he protested.

She took the pot of paint from his hand, and his brushes, and put them away. Gently she pushed him down in the wagon, a mother with a fractious child.

"You sleep," she said. "You are very tired. It is not good for a man to work so hard all the time. When we get to the Fat Grass River, there will be plenty of time to paint. Now you sleep."

He had not known he was so tired. The last thing he remembered was Chahumpi's broad back against the starlight, the rolling of the wagon, the sound of her voice chanting a quiet song that might have been a lullaby.

**Item 16.** Portrait in oils, done on scraped animal skin. About 6 by 10 inches. Fat middle-aged Sioux woman, identity unknown. Painted with great skill and sympathy; in spite of unlikely nature of subject, this is one of the best. Signed M/F.

---

The Fat Grass, which the white man called the Little Big Horn, was a rapid snow-fed stream which watered a plateau of undulating prairie. The rich grass would feed their pony herds for a long time, and so they camped there, the thousands of them. The Cheyenne allies led, raising their circle of *tipis* along the western bank of the Fat Grass. The Sans Arcs and Miniconjous were next, their circles closer to the river, and the Oglalas further to the west. The Hunkpapas, which included Beau's people, occupied the lower and southernmost circle. Pleased with their new camp ground and their recent victories, they held a social dance. Bands of young men went from one circle to the next, dancing with the girls until daybreak. That night Beau got little sleep. Napping fitfully in his wagon, pulled up in the circle of Hunkpapa *tipis,* he would no sooner doze off than a fresh party of young men would arrive, shouting and capering. Finally, despairing of sleep, he squatted in the wagon, peering out through the flap. Since his bout with snow-blindness on the way to Deadwood, his eyes had given him a great deal of trouble, suppurating and smarting. But he could see well enough to make out a pall of smoke lying over the valley, lit from beneath by the flames of great fires. The whole camp was one great party. In the flickering light danced the young men, singing in high falsetto voices. From time to time, one of them would make a rush and grasp a girl, pulling her into the prancing circle. Beau stored up the images in his mind's eye, trying to fix the precise shade of red that lit the sky, the way it softened and was made luminous by the drifting smoke. He wished there were some way he might put on canvas the sounds, too, and the smells; the singing, the acrid smoke, the smell of beaten grass, horses and men sweating. There was no way this could be done, though; he would simply have to suggest it somehow when he painted it. But no one would ever know, really. There was no way he could make anyone not there actually smell these things, or touch them. A picture was all he could make. The rest was up to the people who would someday see his picture. If he had done his work well, they would smell the grass and the sweat, too.

When dawn came, the young men went for a dip in the river. Then they lay down in the shade of the cottonwoods that lined the banks of the Fat Grass and slept, exhausted. The camp was quiet in the grayness of the dawn. Beau slipped out of the wagon, quietly to evade Chahumpi's watchful eye, and roped himself a horse from the herd. It was hard work, the milling mass of ponies blurring and swimming in his vision, but he finally snared one and got a leg over it. Naked from the waist up, long black hair over his shoulders, he might have been a born Hunkpapa. With some stubs of charcoal and a precious scrap of his diminishing store of paper, he rode away. On the day before, one of the Sioux warriors, an important man who was a brother of Circling Bear, had died of wounds received when they fought Three-Stars, and was buried in a valuable and handsomely-decorated *tipi* some distance from the camp. Beau had admired the lodge, the mystic and ritual decorations on the skins, and he wanted to make sketches of them for his Winter Calendar paintings.

On his way he came across the trail of horse-soldiers. There were many of them, very many. At first he did not see the trail, and it was only the skittish behavior of his pony that warned him. Sensing something wrong, he got down and examined the trail closely, peering with his nose almost in the pounded dirt.

From the sharp texture of the prints, it had not been long since they passed. He squatted, morning sun beating down on him, and finally touched a hoof-track with his finger. Horse-soldiers. Many soldiers.

Something else in the trail caught his eye. The soldiers had dropped a wooden box of hard bread. A canvas sack of some sort, too, had fallen from a pack-animal. He sat on the box of bread and picked with his fingernails at the knot that closed the sack. When he had it almost open, some extra sense caused him to peer quickly up the trail. A horse-soldier—a big man, with chevrons on his sleeve, was watching him open-mouthed. The man's carbine was still stuck into his saddle. Beau dropped the sack and sprang into the brush just as the carbine spanged over his head. Floundering in the undergrowth, he found his pony and threw a leg over it, pounding away with head low along the straining neck. He flogged the paint hard with his quirt, and when he galloped into the Fat Grass camp both he and his mount were lathered and spent.

"Horse-soldiers!" He pointed behind him. "A big party of them! They are coming this way. *Hopo!*"

Red Knife and Man-Who-Ate-The-Wolf ran from the *tipi* where they had been conferring. "How many?" Red Knife demanded. Man-Who-Ate-The-Wolf slipped the cover off his buffalo shield and waved it in the air, shouting "Tell the people the horse-soldiers are coming!" He caught a white-haired old man, one of the best criers, and pushed him away in the direction of the Oglala camp. "Go tell everyone! Tell all the people to get ready. Tell Gall the horse-soldiers are coming!"

In an instant the camp was in an uproar. The old man ran among the *tipis*, roaring his message. "They are coming!" He dashed about in a skittering run, head thrown back, baying. "All people get ready! The horse-soldiers are coming!"

A military man would have sent out a scouting party to probe the enemy, a small force to test them and find their number and intentions. But the Indians had no concept of the West Point approach to a fight. Knowing they outnumbered any force likely to be sent against them, they did not leave the camp. While the warrior societies sent the women and children to the top of the camp, away from where the onslaught was expected, the men struggled into their best war finery. They primped and preened, dressing their hair into a warrior's knot, painting their faces, looking into their hand-mirrors and squinting at the effect. Only when all this was done did they go to the horse-herd and get their ponies. To strengthen their mounts and get them into their second wind, they raced back and forth through the village, shouting gleefully at each other and waving their weapons.

Sitting Bull came from his *tipi* among the Hunkpapa to direct the defense. He was a heavy-set muscular man, held in great regard because he was the official host, receiving and enter-taining all visitors, and thus high in the councils of the Sioux, making their policies and agreeing on treaties with the white men and with other tribes. Gall was with him. While Sitting Bull only counseled the warriors, and talked with them, Gall rode back and forth through the camp, dressed in red and wearing his warbonnet, shouting and singing his war-song and exhorting the people to stand fast.

"No one will get hurt!" he cried. "I have had a dream! We will count many *coups* on them! Rock came to me in a dream and told me we would kill all the horse soldiers!"

Beau went to his wagon and sat in the hot dimness, gnaw-ing at his knuckles, uncertainty in his heart. Chahumpi found him there. She thrust a carbine into his hand, and a bandolier of ammunition.

"Go!" Her face was flushed and happy. "Go kill them! Kill them all!" Laughing, she took a handful of painted sticks from her bosom and pushed them into his hand. "Look! This is a great charm. It is *wo-ta-we!* My husband said it was given to him by a warrior of the Cheyennes who was very brave. No bullet can hit you if you put these sticks in your hair!"

He pushed her hand away, uneasy.

"What?" Puzzled, she started to cry, tears coursing down her fat cheeks. "Do you not want to fight? What kind of a man are you?"

"My eyes," he said sullenly. "They hurt. I do not see well."

She stared at him unbelievingly. "That is true. I know it. But what difference does that make? Man-Who-Never-Walked was once carried into battle on a litter. He counted *coup,* and he could not even walk."

"I do not care," he muttered.

"It is not that," Chahumpi said. "I do not believe it is that. It is something else."

"I do not know what it is," he said desperately. "I am *berdache,* maybe. I have become *berdache.*"

"No." She licked the salt tears at the corner of her mouth. "Not *berdache.* Not you."

"Mother," he said, "I—I have had a dream. It is wrong for me to kill a white man. Once I did, but I could not help it. Now I can go away, before they come." He nodded toward the north end of the camp. "I will go away in that direction."

She blinked watery eyes at him.

"That way? Where they have taken the women and children?"

Angry, he shouted at her. "I do not care where they have taken the women and children! The women and children have nothing to do with it!"

"You are not a white man," Chahumpi said. "Outside, maybe. But not inside. You are like us inside. You must stay with us, and fight. That is what you ought to do for us. We are your friends. Why do you run away, now, at this time?"

"Because I must!"

"I would not go," Chahumpi said. For the first time he noticed the revolver belted around her broad waist, and the hatchet stuck in her girdle. Her big breasts sagged over the belt, and were propped on the keen edge of the hatchet. "They wanted me to go away, too, but I am going to fight."

"Fight, then," he said, and went away to catch horses to draw his wagon.

When he got back, he saw the first wave of the horse-soldiers had broken on the lower end of the village. He saw Chahumpi running toward the sound of firing, fat legs wobbling, the belted gun slapping her thighs as she ran. "Chahumpi!" he called, but the rattle of guns was too loud for her to hear. She ran on, toward the cloud of smoke that began to form in the lower end of the valley.

It took him a long time to harness the fractious pintos. Not used to drawing a wagon, they reared and bucked and snapped at him with yellow-stained teeth. Finally he snared them, and they stood sullenly in the traces, looking back at him over their shoulders. The first time he urged them with the whip they stood block-still, obstinate and surly. The second time, they took the bit in their teeth and dashed away into a *tipi,* sprawling to a halt when a broken lodgepole wedged in one of the wheels. Cursing, tugging at the splintered lodgepole, he peered back at the south end of the village. A big fight was going on there. The sky was dark with drifting smoke, and the sound of gunfire almost continuous. On the bluffs across the river, a column of horse-soldiers rode. One of them rode out to a point of rock and sat his horse for a moment. Then he waved his hat in a signal, and disappeared.

Ripping the lodgepole free, Beau scrambled on the wagon again and whipped the ponies. They laid their ears back but plunged into the harness and dragged the heavily-laden wagon swiftly. Following the course of the Fat Grass, the wagon bounced and rocked through the camp, past the abandoned *tipis* of the Miniconjous, the Sans Arcs, past the fleeing women. Young girls clutched shawls around their heads, fat matrons perspired and puffed and watched Beau's wagon with wonder. Old men and old women, shriveled as mummies, hobbled on sticks and watched him go. A sad surprise was in their eyes, and a wrinkled grandfather called something after him, and waved a stick. Beau did not look at them. He could not. He was betraying them, the people who had taken him in and fed him. But he would not be trapped again, as he had been that day when he killed the white soldier.

He came to a shallow ford in the river, at the foot of a precipitous *coulee* which bisected the far hills. If he could cross there and skirt the bluffs which led northward, he might be able to outdistance the horse-soldiers he had-seen. But it would be a near thing. He stood up in the seat, cracking the whip over the flattened ears of his team.

*"Hopo!"* He put all the strength of his arm into the long strip of rawhide. "Go! Run! *Hopo!"*

The banks of the stream at that point were steep and muddy. The wagon almost overturned when the *pintos* dragged it over the edge. For a moment the wheels sank into the soft bottom and the horses plunged and reared, neighing with panic. But in that moment he saw the way ahead was blocked. The horse-soldiers were already coming down the *coulee* toward the ford. He did not stop to count them, but there were many of them; perhaps one or two hundred. Sawing on the reins, he whipped the pintos until they dragged the wagon free from the sucking bottom. He whipped them down the bed of the river for a hundred yards, and then wheeled up on a sandy bar and back toward the village again. Although his way to freedom was blocked, he felt a relief, a lightening of his heart. Now he was back with his people, standing between the old and the infirm against the charge of the horse-soldiers. They were no longer horse soldiers to him. They were enemies, and he would count *coup* on them. He pulled up the wagon, and took out his Springfield and ammunition.

A few Cheyennes, men of the warrior societies, guarded the weak and the infirm, urging them on toward safety, gentle as they could be, but striking some with their bows and their lances in an effort to hurry them. None had yet noticed the dark column of horse-soldiers coming swiftly down the *coulee.* Beau yelled at the Cheyennes, and pointed with the barrel of the Springfield.

"There!" he shouted. "Friends, there they come! Let us all go and fight them."

The Cheyennes looked startled. They gazed from their charges to the *coulee,* and back again.

"Friends!" Beau yelled. "There is not much time!"

There were no more than a half-dozen of the Cheyennes, but the Cheyennes were renowned warriors. They followed him to the slippery bank of the Fat Grass, plunging in thigh-deep, and running low and quick to the far bank where they knelt and aimed their rifles. The first volley produced a noticeable faltering in the progress of the horse-soldiers. They had picked their way out of the *coulee,* and were on flat ground which they could cover now in minutes, falling heavily on the undefended upper end of the camp. But at the very instant of their quickest movement, the lead company faltered, and then stopped. It was a gray-horse company, and the soldiers swung off their mounts and stopped on the flat shelf of land. Beau, squeezing off shot after shot till the rifle-barrel was hot in his hand, did not know why they stopped. Perhaps the stand of the handful of Cheyennes had made them suspect a trap. Perhaps it was all a part of the plan of the horse-soldiers; a flanking movement to pin down the Indians until the main body could come up and cut off any retreat. The battle still went on at the lower end of the camp, though, and a determined charge by the horse-soldiers at the ford would have carried all the way through the undefended upper camp to catch Gall and Crazy Horse between two hammers. But the gray horse company stopped; with military precision each fourth man took the reins of four mounts and led them back, while the dismounted soldiers knelt in the grass and fired at long range.

"Friends!" Beau cried. "They have stopped! We have stopped them!"

For a moment they had slowed the tide, but only seven of them were at the ford. At the other end of the village the rolling of the rifle-fire still sounded, and heavy dark smoke rolled upward from burning *tipis*. They did not know how things were going down there.

Low in the grass, the horse soldiers started to move forward as skirmishers, expertly, probing this obstacle in their path. Protected behind the bank, Beau and the Cheyennes kept up a withering fire, although in the deep grass it was not certain they were hitting anyone. On a ridge behind the horse soldiers waited a small group of men, obviously the officers in charge. Beau propped his rifle on a boulder and sent a long shot at a man in a white coat and a big hat, but the shot went high in the air over them.

"Many Fingers," a Cheyenne said, "this is a good way to die, I think."

"Any way is a good way, friend," Beau said. "It does not make any difference now."

Almost in front of them, a man with chevrons on his sleeve stood up out of the grass and fired point-blank. The shot buried itself in the bank with a gush of mud, but the man fell over backward and none of them had yet shot. Looking over his shoulder, Beau saw the warriors from the lower end of the village coming to their rescue. Crazy Horse was at their head, screaming and waving his bow.

Shaking the ground with the fury of their coming, the Sioux swept by the defenders of the ford, plunging across the Fat Grass in a shower of spray. Beau waved his rifle and cheered them on, and he and the Cheyennes ran after them, splashing through the water and yelling. In the first shock of their attack, Crazy Horse and his people rode down and through the gray horse company, breaking it into fragments that regrouped and knelt to fire with professional discipline. But the gray horse company had lost the unity that welded it together. Although they fought well from small pockets of resistance, it was not too hard for Crazy Horse to smash the pockets one at a time. This was made easier as it appeared the reserve ammunition of the gray soldiers, the sixty extra rounds for each man, were in the saddlebags of the mounts held by the horse-holders. In addition, it was obvious that something frequently went wrong with the ammunition the gray horse people did have. Beau saw one mustached soldier digging frantically with his thumbnail at a jammed metal cartridge which would not eject. Then the man dropped the gun and stood up, an arrow feather-deep in his chest. He looked down at the arrow and fell forward, the shaft twisting and breaking under him.

Leaving his empty Springfield, Beau whooped a war-cry and went after the horse-holders. Snatching a rolled blanket from a dead horse, he unrolled it and flapped it at the line of grays. A shot ripped through the toe of his moccasin and numbed his foot but he hobbled on, waving the blanket. It was enough. Many of the horses ran away, whinnying in terror. Others reared, and kicked at the horse-holders. In minutes the reserve ammunition was gone, carried down the valley in the saddlebags of the stampeding horses. Beau dodged a swung rifle-butt and went at a soldier with his bare hands, getting his brown fingers around the man's throat. The man took a long time dying, and if a Cheyenne named Yellow Nose had not stood over Beau and driven off the soldiers, Beau would have died, too, knees astride the man's laboring chest. When it was done, Beau rolled off the man and stood up, brushing the long black hair out of his eyes.

"Thanks, friend!" he yelled at Yellow Nose. But the Cheyenne had found a battle flag that belonged to the gray horse people, and was riding around the fight, waving it in the air and singing his victory song. It was a beautiful flag and Yellow Nose was proud of it, a swallowtailed flag with gilt stars.

Up the hill, the rest of the soldiers made one or two tentative moves that looked as though they were going to come to the aid of their comrades. The man in the white hat rode forward and stopped, as if lost in thought. More Sioux poured across the ford, yelling and whopping. They had gotten behind the soldiers now. Beau could see them spring up atop the bluffs like quickened flowers, and puffs of smoke spurted as the Sioux shot down into the soldiers. Growing bolder as their numbers increased, the Sioux came down the hill in short vicious rushes, driving the rest of the soldiers toward the onrushing hordes at the river. Bit by bit the soldiers lost the semblance of an organization. The attackers chewed off a little bit here and a little bit there. One luckless soldier, cut off from his comrades, ran away. When he saw there was no way out, he stopped and pulled a pistol from his belt and shot himself through the head. Another soldier—a captain, with bars—had been shot through the chest, and was believed dead. But he suddenly got to his feet and ran away. A Cheyenne rode after him and shot the captain in the back as he ran. This time the captain did not get up.

As the battle swirled, Beau found himself in a knot of struggling men, striving to throw back the Sioux who surrounded them, pressing hard. One of the soldiers was the man in the white hat. Someone hit Beau then, on the back of the head and he reeled forward, throwing out his arms. After that his head hurt and he did not remember things very well. But the soldiers did not last long. By the time the sun was overhead it was all done. No soldiers were left alive. Beau got up on one knee, feeling at the back of his head. No blood, but his head ached. The man in the white hat lay dead a few yards from him. His hair was short, and the dead face was white above the stubble of auburn beard. A scorched hole was in the breast of the man's dirty blue shirt, and another in the temple. This, then, was Pe-Ttin Hanska—Head Hair Long—the great boy general, Custer. He was dead, and with him hundreds of his men, broken on the rock of Sioux valor and stubbornness. Feeling strange and disturbed, Beau turned away from the dead bearded face.

The field of battle swarmed with exultant Sioux and Cheyennes. One warrior snared a dead soldier with his rope and dragged him around the field until the man's head came loose and rolled away, bouncing down the slope toward the ford where more Sioux were still coming. The women and children followed the horsemen up the slope, laughing and chattering to each other. Someone started a fire in the sun-parched grass. When it reached the saddlebags on the dead horses, the big cartridges banged and bullets whined in the air but no one was hit. They all thought it was funny. The children and the women went through the clothing of the dead soldiers and found money, a lot of money. They did not know what it was, but they threw it up into the air and watched the wind carry it away like fallen autumn leaves.

Red Knife found Beau and grabbed him by the arm.

"We have beat them!" His face was grimy, and stained with blood and smoke and the war-bonnet torn almost in two. *"Onhey,* Many Fingers!" Red Knife had a bundle of sticks in his hand. When he came to a dead soldier, he took a stick from the bundle and placed it in his belt, thus counting the dead soldiers. His belt was already full of sticks, and there were not room for many more. *"Onhey!"* Red Knife shouted, doing a little shuffle with his feet as he passed among the dead bodies.

This would be a great year in the Calendar. *When All The Soldiers Were Killed.* It would be The Great Year—the finest time of the Sioux nation, the one talked about until the end of time. In every *tipi* people would recount the story. Old men would brag about the *coups* they counted, the children would be grown men and would tell about the green papers they tossed into the air and danced among. Many men would lay claim to having killed Pe-Ttin Hanska, and no one would know for sure. They would know nothing that anyone could prove except that Pe-Ttin Hanska was dead, but they would all claim to have slain him. Beau felt the sun soak into his weary muscles, and he smelled the smoke and the blood on the warm wind. This was the great ending to the Winter Calendar. This, above all the others, was the one he must paint. This was the bloody smoky end of it, the one that brought the long series to a grand and tragic end. After this, there could be nothing. The Sioux could never again stand the way they had stood today. This was the finest time, and after this there would be nothing left but flight; a breaking up into little bands, a fleeing, escape from the thousands of soldiers who would swarm over this land to avenge the death of Pe-Ttin Hanska and his men.

He walked among the dead, looking down at the still faces. Some were twisted and filled with fear. Others were peaceful, and the bodies lay gracefully among the rocks, composed as if for sleep. Among them moved the women, intent and purposeful as other women shopping on Market Street in San Francisco. The women pulled the boots from the feet of the dead soldiers. They did not want the boots. The boots were uncomfortable, but they would cut off the bottoms and save the upper parts for leggings. Some of the older women cut off arms and hands and genital parts of the dead men. The children, as a game, dragged one bearded man upright and stuck lances into him to make a kind of prop for holding the dead body upright. Then they shot arrows into it.

Walking aimlessly about, exhausted with the terrible grandeur of the scene, he stumbled among the corpses, feeling soft bodies under his moccasins. He was drunk—drunk with fatigue and excitement. The smell of smoke seemed to sink deep within his bones, and make him tremble and shake. Blood was there, too; the smell of fresh blood, and horses, and black powder, and trampled grass, and the mingled sweat of men and animals. A powerful stimulus seemed to separate his mind and his body, and it was if he were in a dream. His head hurt, and tears came from his eyes so that he had to dig at them with his knuckles. But he still could not see very well. It was getting dark, perhaps; they had fought all day. Yes, that was it. That must be it. Dazed and spent, he wandered the field of battle.

"Chahumpi!" he called. "Come help me! Chahumpi!"

Someone helped him—he did not know who—and after a while he was lying in the wagon again, his own wagon. He could smell the paints, and the smell somehow infuriated him. Angrily he tried to rise, to destroy the paints, to destroy himself. But Chahumpi pushed him down among the robes, and talked to him like a child, soothingly.

"You are very sick. Lie still. I have put a good medicine on your eyes."

His fingers touched the plaster of mud and seeds and feathers she had bound across his eyes. "Am I blind?"

"You fought very well today," she said. "All the people are saying you fought well. Without you and those Cheyennes, the horse-soldiers would have come on our backs and killed us all. You stopped them. You and the Cheyennes. It was very brave."

"Am I blind?" he asked again.

"No." Her voice was gentle. "You are sick, and there is a devil in you that must be let out. Your eyes are sick, too, but the medicine I have put on them will make them well."

He tried to tear the stuff away from his eyes, but she pinioned him into the robes with her heavy body and lay across his arms till he tired.

"You will hurt yourself," she said. "Do not hurt yourself, Many Fingers. I will die if you do not get well. We will all die. We do not want you to die."

That night there was a big scalp dance. Although some of the soldiers still fought on the bluffs at the south end of the camp, where they were penned in and without water, most of the people danced and sang all night. It was a great victory. The people put on their best clothing, the shirts of deerskin and mountain sheep decorated with human hair, long fringes trailing from sleeve to legging. Tassels of scarlet-dyed horsehair and red flannel waved from every lance, and brown chests glistened in the firelight under necklaces of bearclaws. A virgin was chosen to cut down a sacred tree, and the tree was carried into the middle of the camp on a trestle of poles, the way the body of a great warrior is carried. After being dedicated, it was set up in a hole in the ground, and decorated. Dancers formed a big circle and danced all night around the tree, facing inward, wedged shoulder to shoulder. So that no one could quit till the dance was over, the dancers tied themselves together with leather lariats. They danced all night that way. Except in his mind's eye, Beau did not see them dance. He knew, though, what they were doing. He knew every movement, every flash of firelight on naked glistening body, every stamp and shuffle of the foot, every cock and angle of feather. He lay quietly in the wagon, seeing it all. Chahumpi had given him the old tattered deck of cards, and he lay still, running the cards through his fingers, his hands the only movement in the darkness.

In the morning, the few soldiers on the bluffs still held out. But it was not important. The Sioux had won; the Sioux and their Cheyenne allies. Then, too, there were rumors that more soldiers were coming. The chiefs decided it would be a good idea to go away from there, up Lodgepole Creek and into the White Rain Mountains. The warrior societies got the movement organized, which was a tremendous task with several thousand people. But finally the immense mass started to move toward the distant Big Horns; *travois* with families and belongings, pony herds, the long dark columns skirted by warriors on guard. Near the end of the column was a painted wagon pulled by two unruly pintos. The fat old woman who drove the wagon was very expert, and kept the wagon in its place in the column. Finally the end of the column came, and a small rear-guard of Cheyennes. When they were gone, looking occasionally over their shoulders for pursuers, the valley of the Fat Grass was quiet again. There was nothing but the white upturned faces of the dead, like pale flowers in the grass; nothing but those, and the broad wide trail, scarred by hoofs and *travois*-poles, that marked the westward course of the people.

**Item 17.** Canvas in oils, approximately 20 by 30 inches. Great grass fire burning on the plains; small animals fleeing before it. Poorly done—draftsmanship careless and colors wrong. Signed M/F but doubtful it is Mannix's work.

This was a queer summer season, a summer filled with heavy rains and lightning. Great balls of ice pelted the people, bouncing in and out among them, ripping *tipis* to shreds, and hurting some. For days the skies were filled with heavy clouds, and swords of lightning flashed across the heavens. The air grew unaccountably cold and the people shivered in its frosty breath, not being prepared for a winter at this time of the year. Yet the long column wound on toward the distant Big Horns, the hoofs of the ponies sucking in mud, the *travois* poles cutting furrows in the earth, the people wet and uncomfortable and forgetting already the joy of their big victory on the Fat Grass.

The Cheyenne allies became convinced that the bad weather was due to someone's having offended the gods, and there was much wrangling and disagreement about what to do. From having been so firmly united in battle against the horse-soldiers, fights and bickering broke out, and a Cheyenne named Yellow Shirt was killed. His slayer was banished from the camp, and the Cheyennes smoked a pipe with the Oglala Bad-Faces, but the trouble went on, and finally the Cheyennes left the column and went away.

Man-Who-Ate-The-Wolf knew what the trouble was. It was *Iktomi*, the trickster and fool, who was plaguing them. Man-Who-Ate-The-Wolf mixed ochre with buffalo-fat and painted his face and limbs. He put on his best deerskin shirt, dressed his hair, and went out into the cold rain, taking his buffalo-shield with him. For two days he stayed in the rain, exposed to the elements, singing his medicine song and asking for help from Rock, Earth, Buffalo, and Sun—telling them that these good people were being plagued by *Iktomi,* and that the time had now come for the greater gods to drive away this malevolent trickster.

"*Sha,*" said Red Knife. "*Sha,* all you people. This is very good. This is how it should be done. Rock will listen to this man, you will see."

The second day the wind changed. Bits of blue peeped through the leaden clouds, and a softness came into the air. The wind was from the south, and ordinarily a south wind was considered unlucky, the south being the Land of Death. But who were they to quarrel with Rock? Rock had driven away the bad weather, and if he choose to use the south wind to do it, was this not his business? They shook the rain from their garments, spread blankets and *tipi*-coverings out to dry, made fires and cooked meat for the first time in weeks. It was a time of rejoicing, and fun. The south wind warmed them and dried them, and the old men sat in the sun and smoked their pipes.

"I do not like this," Chahumpi said to Beau. She handed him a dried buffalo-rib, and took another for herself. "While the weather was bad, the horse-soldiers did not come after us. Now the sun shines. The horse-soldiers will remember all those people we killed, and they will come after us. You will see."

His eyes had healed somewhat. Chahumpi's poultices soothed them, and stopped the smarting. But now that the poultices had been removed, the world was blurred and indistinct to him. Colors swam and faded and then grew strong again, so that he could hardly tell red from green.

"I do not care," Beau said. He sat on the seat of the painted wagon, gnawing at the buffalo-rib. "It is all right with me if they come. This time I will fight them again, and maybe they will kill me, but that will be all right. I can not see very well any more. What good is a man that can not see?"

"Listen," said Chahumpi. She put her hand on his arm. "There is a devil in you. That is all. The medicine I gave you, that was not strong enough. The devil has taken it and eaten it up. But I know how to deal with this devil. Listen. There are medicine men in the Oglalas that can take hot coals in their fingers, right out of the fire. They can put their hands right in the cooking pot, and take out meat without being burned. They are great men, and they can help you."

He shrugged and threw the bone away.

"All right."

She went scurrying to talk to the Oglalas, taking as a present a fine decorated pipe that had belonged to her husband. Sitting in the sun, Beau watched her go, thinking how foolish was her errand. But was it foolish? He found himself of two opinions. The remnant of white man in him laughed at the fire-handlers, and suspected he was going blind. The Indian part of him, growing ever stronger, took reassurance. Anyway, what harm would it do? There were many unexplained things in the world.

The Oglala fire-handler was an impressive man. His name was Blue Horse, and he wore a band of black fur around his head, with a buffalo-horn attached to each ear. His face was painted blue, with a white moon on his forehead, and a star across the bridge of his nose. He wore the distinctive robe of the doctor, with the hair side out. His medicine was very strong, all people said, and they crowded around in the noonday sun to watch his treatment of Many Fingers.

"Nobody talk," said Blue Horse. "My medicine does not like for anyone to talk."

"Nobody talk," echoed Chahumpi. She ran around the circle, waving her hands. "Nobody talk. All people be quiet."

Blue Horse sat opposite Beau on the grass, and questioned him closely.

"Is this devil inside you, or out?"

"I do not know."

"I mean this," said Blue Horse. "If you have done something wrong at one time, then the sickness is inside you, and I have to do certain things. But maybe this devil is not inside you. Maybe you have not done wrong things. Maybe this devil is just outside, bothering your eyes, and I can get rid of him easy."

"I do not know. I have done wrong things. Maybe it is inside."

Blue Horse lit his new pipe, and blew smoke to the four corners of the world. He puffed hard, and then put his fingers in the bowl, drawing out the coal for all to see.

"Like this," he chanted. "Like this I will draw out the devil that is bothering Many Fingers."

The watchers groaned in awe, and many of them hid their faces in their hands.

"Start a fire," said Blue Horse. "Throw horse-dung on it, and gunpowder. Let it burn down well, so that I may have coals to treat this man."

As the fire burned, Blue Horse went into a trance. He closed his eyes and sang for a while, rocking back and forth. Then his whole body began to jerk and switch. So violent were his movements that he fell over, and lay for a long time, continuing to shake and tremble. After a while he got up and ran around the camp, baying like a wolf.

"It is working!" he called. "My medicine is working. I am having a dream!"

In a little while he came back and sat down within the ring of spectators, panting and exhausted, his face shining with sweat so that the paint ran and smeared. But his face was exalted, and he spoke with dignity and assurance.

"I know what the matter is. I saw the devil in a dream. He is a little devil, and he has hair on his chin. But do not be afraid, friends. I know how to drive out this devil, so that Many Fingers can see again. Watch me, friends. Watch what I do and listen to the sound of this devil as he leaves Many Fingers."

*Shadduck,* thought Beau. *The little devil with the hair on his chin!* No, it was too fantastic! He had from time to time mentioned Shadduck, but he did not know Blue Horse, and Blue Horse did not know him. Yet it was queer. *A little devil with hair on his chin.*

He was unprepared for Blue Horse's sudden movement. Scooping a handful of coals from the fire, the doctor picked out a large and glowing brand, and held it in the air for all to see. Stepping forward, he pressed it against Beau's forehead. "This is the way!" he called. "This is how to chase out the small devil! Listen! Hear him struggle, trying to break away!"

Beau rolled backward, trying to get away from the agonizing pain. He did not scream, but only writhed and groaned, smelling burning flesh and the stink of scorched hair. Blue Horse followed him relentlessly, grinding the coal into his forehead, chanting and victorious.

"Go out, small devil! Leave this man! Go away from his eyes!" He pinioned Beau with a knee against his chest, and kept up a high-pitched song. "Go away! Go away! My medicine is strong! My medicine is working! The devil is burning! He is going away! He is afraid!"

Beau bit his lip, and felt blood in his mouth. It was important not to scream, not to cry out. He felt weak, and faint; over his head the blue sky reeled and seemed to fall. He knew he was going to faint, and perhaps ruin Blue Horse's medicine, but he held on, gritting his teeth, and finally Blue Horse took away the dead coal and said, "Now. The devil is gone. I chased him away. He is afraid of fire."

Shakily Beau got to his feet. He thanked Blue Horse, and gave him tobacco in a deer-bladder pouch, and some red paint. Then Chahumpi took him by the hand and led him into the wagon, where he lay down while she covered him with a blanket.

"You will see better now," she said. Arranging the blanket around his chest, she looked closely at his forehead. "That is where the devil came out. It will be sore for a while. But you will see better now. I know it."

"I know it too," he said. "I know it."

After a great victory, such as on the Fat Grass, it was the custom to set the grass afire. But due to their hurry to reach the White Rain Mountains, and the unseasonable weather, they had not done so. Now, reaching a place of refuge in the mountains, there was time for celebration. The summer sun had dried the mountain grass, and already it grew brown in patches. The young men took torches and fired the grass, and the pall of smoke went up to *Wakan-Tanka* in the sky. Rabbits and deer and small game of all kinds ran before the great blaze, and the smoke hung in the sky like a warning to the horse-soldiers. It could be seen from a great distance, but no one cared. They had beaten them at the Fat Grass; they could beat them here, in the mountains. The people were invincible. At night they sat before their *tipis* eating fat buffalo meat, reminding each other of the *coups* they had counted on the Fat Grass. It had been a good time. Beau sat in his wagon, working on a canvas of the great victory fire. His eyes had improved considerably, he felt, yet there was no longer any sureness in his touch with the brush, and he could not mix colors that satisfied him. Nothing had life to it any longer; the vivid reds and greens and blues looked grayish and dead. The whole world seemed shrouded in a mist, and even the red coal of the morning sun was enveloped in a clinging haze. He rubbed the scar on his forehead, and stared at a canvas. Try as he would, there was something missing from his painting. He botched one precious canvas after another, and swore, while Chahumpi watched him uncomfortably.

"You try too hard," she said. "There is time. You ought to rest."

"There is *not* much time," he said. He provoked quarrels with her, and sent her from the wagon red-eyed and weeping. The children who used to come to him now avoided him, and the old men shook their heads, and made signs to each other. He took to wandering the camp, lost in thought, and often sat all day on a high rocky ledge. The grass fires still burned in the distance, and he turned his head this way and that, sniffing the smoke. "Time is running out," he said to himself.

The great fires had flushed much game, but it remained for two half-grown youths to bring in the queerest bag. Red Knife's boy and a stripling friend went out for a hunt one day and came back with a white man; a singed and blackened little man whom they drove before them with lances, singing and chanting as they pricked him.

"He was hiding behind a burned bush!" they told Red Knife and the elders. "We found him there! He had a mule which died, and a can of water, and a gun! *Onhey!*" They jabbed the man again, but he did not cry out; instead, he set his lips grimly over the scorched tuft of beard, and rolled his eyes heavenward, moving only his lips.

"You should have killed him," Red Knife said. "What good is this man to us?" He walked around the little man, poking and prodding with a finger. "He is not a horse soldier. I don't know why he has come here." Curious, he tried to talk to the prisoner, but the man did not understand the language of the people. Then Red Knife tried signs, but got no further. Finally, in disgust, he said, "Take him out there, away from the camp, and kill him."

The spectators nodded. *"Hau,"* they said. *"Hau.* Kill him."

They did not see Many Fingers push his way through the crowd, but as the two boys started to herd the prisoner away with their lances, Many Fingers stepped forward.

"Wait," he said.

There was a buzz of excitement, and some anger. Red Knife protested also, but Beau held up his hand, peering at the stranger, and said again, "Wait."

The noise quieted. The people shuffled their feet and craned their necks. All of them knew of the recent strange behavior of Many Fingers, and a man who acts like that is entitled to consideration, since he may be in the grip of a spirit. Red Knife fanned himself with his eagle-wing and awaited Many Fingers' pleasure.

"Speak," said Many Fingers to the prisoner. He spoke in the white man's tongue, and the people looked at each other, puzzled, and whispered. "Speak to me," Beau said again, peering at the white man, his head awkwardly forward like a crane.

"I will speak to thee," said Shadduck. His lips were dry and cracked, and the words were more a croak than human speech. "Understand, Mannix, I do not ask for anything for myself, though. I am not afraid to die, if that is what they want."

For a long moment Beau stood silent. Someone among the spectators coughed, and the sun shone down warmly. The smell of smoke was in the air, and the smell of death. The two boys looked at Red Knife, and one of them shifted his lance.

"What does he say?" Red Knife asked.

Beau did not speak. He did not trust his voice. Instead he signed to Red Knife. *I know this man. I knew this man a long time ago. This man came here looking for me. Now he has found me.*

Red Knife scowled. "What is that to us? We have killed many white men. One more does not make any difference!"

*"Hau,"* someone said, nodding to his neighbor.

"I do not want you to kill him," said Beau.

Angry, Red Knife held up ten fingers, and then ten fingers again, and again, and again. "We killed this many, and this many, and this many, and more than that on the Fat Grass! This man is a spy for the horse soldiers! He has come here to seek us out, and tell them how many we are!"

*Shadduck,* Beau thought! *Sam Shadduck!* After all that had happened—after all these months, and years—after all these times and seasons Sam Shadduck was still after him! Shadduck was like a natural force, like the wind and the rain and the stars, an immutable and unchanging influence. He was a devil. Yes, that was it. Shadduck was a devil. Beau raised his hand, stilling the hubbub.

"I will tell you why I do not want you to kill this man. This is not a man. This is a devil. This is a very great devil, and he can not be killed. He will put a spell on you all, as he has me. Friends, this is my own devil. This is the devil with hair on his chin that Blue Horse spoke about. You all remember Blue Horse. He tried to drive the devil out of me. But the devil is still with me. If you try to kill him, it will be unlucky for you all."

They drew back then, even Red Knife, and put their hands over their mouths.

"I will take this devil with me," Beau said. "I will take him into my own *tipi,* where I must struggle with him and overcome him. There is great magic in this devil, and it will be a hard fight, but I will win, friends. Anyone who harms this man harms me. I will never get away from his magic until I overcome him myself. You all know that. You know that it is true."

They drew back from the whiskered devil. Yes, it was true. They remembered the statements of Blue Horse, and whispered to each other. Many Fingers had been acting very queerly, and certainly this was his own business. If he wanted to deal with this devil himself, it was his privilege. Respectfully they drew still farther back, careful not to look the devil in the eye. It was well known that a devil's power is magnified if he can look you in the eye.

"Come," said Beau. "Follow me." He motioned the detective toward the wagon. "Pull yourself up straight, and walk after me. It's important."

Shadduck stared at him. "I do not want to owe thee anything."

"You don't owe me anything," Beau said, and walked away. Shadduck looked at the hostile faces, wondering why they shrank from him so. Then, hardly staggering at all, he followed Beau Mannix, looking neither to the right nor left.

Samuel Shadduck had been closer to death than Beau at first realized. Not from the lances of the people, although that had been close also, but from sheer physical exhaustion, exposure, and lack of food. Once in the painted wagon, Shadduck seemed to crumble. The iron resolved that stiffened his backbone left, and he fell in a faint. Beau, loosening the remnant of collar that still encircled the detective's thin neck, ordered Chahumpi to bring a cup of water, and to prepare some meat broth.

"For him?" She gestured obscenely. "I do not cook for him. I cook for you."

He was patient. "Whatever you do for him, you do for me. Go quickly."

Still she argued. "I do not like this man. Why do you bring him here? We will all be sorry. Why—"

"Do not ask me why this and why that!" he shouted. "Go, and do what I have told you!"

She sniffed and went grumbling away, calling on people to witness that Many Fingers was crazy. But she cooked the broth, and brought also a piece of dried hump-fat. "There is strength in hump-fat," she said grudgingly. "He is not much to start with, but the hump-fat will do to begin."

For days Shadduck lay in a stupor. A high fever came on him, and the flesh around the lance-wounds became green and offensive to smell. He was completely helpless, and irrational as well. Chahumpi, seeing Beau blundering about the wagon, trying to help Shadduck, wanted at last to help, but Beau refused her, not unkindly. "This is my work," he said. "This is something I have to do myself."

He washed and bathed the detective, and fed him a potion of boiled sage and chokecherries, in which was mixed powdered deerhorn. Blue Horse, consulted by Beau, prescribed it as efficacious. Shadduck gagged and fought against Beau's restraining arm, but most of the mixture went down his thin gullet. Finally, one day late in the summer, he lay spent and glassy-eyed in the wagon, but for the first time rational. The long fever had abated, and though he was little but sagging skin and sharp-angled bones, he knew Beau, knew where he was.

"Mannix," he said.

Beau turned from the paints he had been mixing.

"Eh?"

"I have to thank thee, it seems," Shadduck whispered. He blinked, and swallowed, and his fingers worked at the blanket pulled around his chest. "I remember all that happened, now. I wonder I live."

Beau put down the paint-pot and squatted beside him.

"Don't bother yourself to talk," he said.

"But I must!" Shadduck protested. He struggled to prop himself up on his elbows. "It must be explained, and justified somehow!" He was a man with a great problem on him, and he started to babble and ended weeping and distraught. After a while, he turned his face away and lay for a long time staring at the sideboards of the wagon, and Beau was wise enough to leave him so.

Gradually the detective's strength returned. He sat for short periods on the wagon-seat, taking the sun, wrapped in an old blanket and staring about him like a scarecrow. He watched the activity of the camp with unbelieving eyes—not frightened, but somehow unconvinced that it was real. No one harmed him; he was understood to be Many Fingers' problem, and was left strictly alone. But his eyes followed Beau as he went about the camp, greeting friends and pausing to talk with them, chaffing the old men, telling stories to the children. Many Fingers himself seemed to the people to be improved. His eyes were no better, and from time to time he blundered into the protruding ends of lodgepoles and knocked down things, but he was more the Many Fingers of old. Perhaps, the people thought, he had conquered his devil. They were not sure, but they hoped so, and wished well for him. Samuel Shadduck listened to the harsh sibilant Siouan tongue, and watched Beau, and kept his thoughts to himself. He had a devil of his own to conquer. One day, almost recovered, he decided the time had come to talk about it.

"These are very good," he said to Beau, looking at the Winter Calendar paintings. "I am not a cultivated man, but I can see thee has done a good job—a remarkable job."

"There are more to do," Beau said. Sitting cross-legged in the gloom of the wagon, be held a brush in his fingers and turned it carefully about, end for end. "God, there are a lot more! I've only just begun."

Shadduck looked away. There was a strange look on his face. "Thee is very taken by this task thee has set for thyself."

"It's all I've lived for." He pointed the brush at Shadduck like a weapon, and his voice rose. "Do you know what it means to find something that's good to do, something that has meaning to it, something that causes your life to make sense and take on—I don't know what to call it. Stature, maybe. Identity. Do you know what I mean?"

The detective's face was without emotion. Only his eyes seemed to have life to them. "Yes," he said. "I did."

"I wasn't worth much," Beau said. "You know that. I didn't have much to look forward to. Only now it's different. I've done something. It makes no difference what people will think of it. Maybe it's good to them, or bad. I don't care. It's the meaning to me that's important. Do you understand that?"

"Yes," said Shadduck. "I do. I understand many things now."

The detective looked down at the quilled shirt he was wearing. Gaudy, barbaric—and it belonged to Beau Mannix. "I have meant to speak to thee about this," he said. Two bright spots of color came into his pale cheeks, and the regrowth of his beard stuck out at a defiant angle. "Thee does not have to protect me any more." He nodded, toward the hubbub and clamor of the camp outside. "I am recovered. I thank thee. I will take my chances with them, now, whatever they want of me."

Beau peered at him. "What do you mean?"

"I do not ask anything of any man. I am ready to die, if that is what they want."

Beau grinned, a hint of maliciousness in it. "They are very fierce."

"Nevertheless—"

Beau laughed. It was the first time in a long time that he had laughed so, full-throatedly and heartily. He laughed so loud that Chahumpi came running in alarm, and the old women stopped their endless scraping of skins and stared at the wagon.

"No one will harm you," he said. "When you are ready to go, I will get you a horse and a pack mule and an outfit for the trail."

"No!" Shadduck protested. "Damn thee, I am thy prisoner! Thee can not let me off so easy! I came here to catch thee, Mannix, and thee knows it! I had violence to thee in my mind! It was right, and fitting, but I would have taken thee back if I could have!"

"Fair enough." Beau sat impassively in the darkness. "That was your job, and you worked hard at it. It wasn't your fault you didn't bring it off."

"It was my fault." Shadduck's voice was a whisper. "I could have done it. I let thee fool me, though. I did not give thee enough credit. Thee is a very remarkable man. I underestimated thee, and it was my fault." He was angry, and Beau's kindness hurt him worse than the lances of the Sioux. "I do not care what happens to me, anyway. Let them kill me. A fair end for an incompetent. And thee!" He lashed out at Beau with animal fury. "Talking of painting, of making more pictures! Thee is going blind! A fine end to both of us!"

Beau's face drained of all color. He raised his hand, and would have struck Shadduck. But something restrained him. His face was livid, and his knotted fist trembled. Then, suddenly, all the anger went out of him. He tossed the brush aside and jumped down from the wagon. Shadduck watched him stride away through the camp, watched him until his tall figure was lost among the smoke of cooking fires and the many busy people.

Beau did not come back. No one went after him; all understood that he was in the midst of a difficult time, and with delicacy they ignored his absence. Chahumpi was worried, but she too understood why he must be alone, and she looked very serious but said nothing. Shadduck stayed apprehensively in the wagon, not knowing when the painted savages might take it into their minds to drag him forth and lash him to a post for burning. But nothing happened. The days wore on, a chill came into the air, the leaves of the trees dried and colored. In the mornings the small stream that ran through the camp formed a narrow crust of ice along its borders, and the boulders through which it tumbled wore a glassy coat. Autumn was on them, come early in these high places; winter was not far away, and The Moon When The Wolves Run Together. The camp was busy all day. The men hunted, the women dried and smoked meat, making a winter supply of brown pemmican, larded with buffalo tallow and chokecherries. Shadduck watched suspiciously, and felt the chill in the air, and shivered.

The battle on the Fat Grass had been the glue that stuck the allies together. Now, with winter coming on, reports of fresh detachments of horse soldiers in the field against them, they decided to separate. Some were for going northward, into the land of the Red River half-breeds, the Slota, the Grease People. They were called that because they greased the wheels of their big carts with buffalo-tallow. Others were for wintering in the mountains, which would be hard for them, and uncomfortable, but would make it doubly hard for the horse soldiers to get at them. They wrangled, and consulted Rock, the god of war, and smoked many pipes. Bit by bit they broke up into small bands, taking leave of each other, going their separate ways. Finally, out of the thousands who had stirred the gravy on the banks of the

Fat Grass, there were in that place in the White Rain mountains only Red Knife, now *wakicunza* of the small band, Man-Who-Ate-The-Wolf, and their immediate people, numbering only a hundred or so. Finally they also decided to go north, making a belated trip after Sitting Bull and the rest who had gone that way months before.

Watching the activity of the camp, Shadduck asked Chahumpi, "What are they doing? What is happening?" She understood no English, and only gave him a brief stare and went on with her packing, stuffing *parfleche* panniers with food, wrapping Beau's *pishers* in strips of hide.

"What is going to happen?" Shadduck demanded, and tugged at her skirt. But she paid him no attention, and he went back to watching the activity through a slit in the wagon-cover, scratching thoughtfully at his beard. Things were coming to a head, that much was plain. Closing his eyes, he said a small prayer and gave his custody into the hands of the Lord. He wished Beau would come back.

On the day of the first snow, Beau Mannix returned. He was thin and gaunt, but in good spirits. He made the rounds of the camp, carrying a staff, and occasionally probed before him with it. He joked with the old men, told stories to the children, and finally went into the *tipi* of Red Knife, where he stayed for a long time. He did not come near his own wagon. Shadduck peered through the flap at the dusting of white that covered the ground. It was cold in the wagon, but he did not avail himself of the robes that were there. Instead, he knelt at the flap, and watched, and shivered. He was afraid, very much afraid.

After a long time, Beau came out of the *tipi* and stood for a moment, looking around him. Shadduck stiffened. Slowly, very slowly, Beau walked across the snow toward the wagon, feeling his way with the staff. Shadduck put out his hand and helped him into the wagon. He did not ask Beau where he had been. It was as if he had been away for only a minute.

They sat cross-legged in the dying day, and somewhere in the wagon-bed a board creaked from the cold. The small stream ran thinly, and tinkled with occasional ice.

"It's winter," Shadduck said. "Winter's come."

Beau nodded. His gaunt face was serene, and there was a peace in it that Shadduck marked. It was the peace of God, he might almost have said, except that the Lord was certainly not here, in this den of painted savages.

"What will happen now?" Shadduck asked.

"You had better go," said Beau. "I have had a long talk with Red Knife, and he is willing to give you a horse and pack mule and everything you need to go back to Deadwood, or Cheyenne, or wherever you want. Can you find your way?"

Shadduck chewed at a corner of his whiskers. "Yes," he said. "I have been around a great deal since—since I was last in Cheyenne. Yes, I can manage."

Beau was silent for a long time, hands gripping the staff that lay across his knees. Finally he said, "There is one thing I would like to ask you. I have some pictures I would like you to take back with you. See that they get to Mrs. Corotis, in Deadwood."

The detective fingered his beard. "Any message to her?"

Beau shook his head. "She'll know."

"I'll see that she gets them." Shadduck stared down at his broken boots. "Before I go, I have something to say to thee, also."

"Say it, then."

Awkwardly Shadduck said, "I never owed any man, nor thought to. Now all that is changed. It will be hard for me to live in a new way, when even living is a gift from a man I once hunted. Does thee understand that?"

"I understand," Beau said.

"But I will try."

"We all have to try," Beau said. "Things happen to all of us. We have to try, because that's all that's left to do." He put out his hand, and since he did not know exactly where the detective sat in the gloom, Shadduck had to reach out for it, and pull it to him.

"God bless thee," the detective said, "and keep thee too, wherever thee goes."

In the morning the detective left, riding a paint pony with a captured cavalry saddle, a saddle that had a numeral 7 on it. He led a pack-mule, with generous provisions. There was room also for many of Beau's paintings. Shadduck packed them himself, taking great pains. On a rise above the dwindling camp, he paused and looked back. A great many people watched him go, standing silently in a soft rain of new snow. He knew Beau was among them, and thought he could still make out the tall figure, but he was not sure. They were Indians, all of them, and from that distance they looked alike. Shadduck took off his fur cap and waved. Then he leaned into the saddle and the pony moved forward, the mule plodding patiently behind. For a long time he could see them in his mind, the silent people standing in the snow against the dark background of the pines and the spruce.

# EPILOGUE

When the Mannix paintings went on exhibition, the gallery was crowded; for many hours of each day, and for many days and weeks and months. Among the visitors were old people who claimed to remember Beau Mannix quite well, when these old people were young and lived in places like Cheyenne and Miles City and Bismark. Since there were so many of them who had known Mannix, after a while nobody believed any of them.

"And so," the lecturer said, "we really don't know what ever happened to this great master of the American scene. It's pretty certain he went to Canada with Sitting Bull in 1877, but that's the last anyone ever heard of him. He may have been killed in the Ghost Dance uprising in 1890, or he may have just lived out his days peacefully, unknown. No one knows."

"Who was this Mrs. Hanratty?" a spectacled girl asked, poising her notebook.

"She was just an admirer of Mannix," the lecturer said. "I don't know that she ever met him, or even knew him. But she recognized his work, and prized it. She was a wealthy woman, one of the wealthiest in South Dakota. Made a great deal of money in shrewd mining operations. She spent most of it running down Mannix paintings, and buying them. Her home was full of them when she died—bales and boxes. We owe her a great deal. It's that kind of public spirit that makes art live, and keep on living."

On the last day of the exhibition, after most of the paintings had been sold to private collectors, after the critics had written their reviews, after an international expert had decided to make a place for Beau Mannix in his new book of Nineteenth-Century art, a man asked a question.

"What about the Little Big Horn?" he asked. "Seems funny to me. Everyone else had a fling at painting it. Mannix must have been near there. Maybe he was actually there. Why didn't he paint the Little Big Horn?"

"I don't know," the lecturer said.

It was five o'clock, and time for the galleries to close. When all the people were gone, the guards left too, after setting the automatic burglar alarm. When they were gone, there was nothing left but the ancient glow of the Mannix paintings, lighting the dim corridors with remembered richness.

www.ingramcontent.com/pod-product-compliance
Lightning Source LLC
Chambersburg PA
CBHW020358030726
47496CB00007B/2203